MOVERS

MOVERS

MEAGHAN MCISAAC

TUNDRA BOOKS

Library and Archives Canada Cataloguing in Publication

McIsaac, Meaghan, author
Movers / Meaghan McIsaac.

Issued in print and electronic formats.
ISBN 978-1-77049-818-1 (bound). —ISBN 978-1-77049-820-4 (epub)

I. Title.

PS8625.I84M68 2016   jC813'.6   C2015-901066-7
                                               C2015-901067-5

Cover designed by CS Richardson
Cover image: © David et Myrtille / Trevillion Images;
(birds) © Zorana Matijasevic / Shutterstock.com

The text was set in DIN
Printed and bound in USA
www.penguinrandomhouse.ca

1 2 3 4 5   20 19 18 17 16

Penguin
Random
House

TUNDRA BOOKS

For Ian
You earned it.

MOVEMENT IN OAKLAND HILLS

11 APRIL 2077

VIEWS: 234, 789, 056
UPDATED: 1.2 SEC AGO

Another Movement incident has rocked the sleepy suburb of Oakland Hills in the city of Avin. Police were called to the apartment of Michael Mermick, a 39-year-old insurance salesman and father of two, early Sunday evening. Mermick, a registered Phase 2 Mover, was found by Bureau of Movement Activity Control (BMAC) officers in his apartment after Movement activity was reported by neighbours. Suspicions were confirmed when officers discovered the body of Mermick's unidentified Shadow at the front door of his fourteenth-storey apartment. The Shadow, BMAC reports, died at the scene, having suffered what appeared to be severe burns to the head. Mermick was promptly taken into the custody of Avin area BMAC. The Move itself has baffled experts, with wind speeds reaching 174km/h, the highest in recorded Movement history. Significant damage, not typical of Movement activity, was reported by residents within a 3km radius of the Move. Current BMAC status classification holds that only Movers with a Phase 3 status are capable of successfully Moving a Shadow from the future. How then, was Mr Mermick, who holds a Phase 2 status, capable of causing the Move in Oakland Hills? And so powerful a Move? BMAC has yet to comment. Mermick's wife, Isabelle Randle-Mermick insists that BMAC's monitoring of Mover status is flawed at best. And there are Movement activity experts who have voiced similar criticism. 'While the signs and symptoms of Movement are well known to us,' commented Professor Jacobs of Avin University, 'the cause of the disorder is not yet understood. There is no measurable qualifier for Movement.'

GOVERNMENT TO CHANGE PHASE RENEWAL POLICY IN WAKE OF MERMICK SHELVING

23 APRIL 2077

VIEWS: 344, 035, 928
UPDATED: 0.3 SEC AGO

Michael Mermick, a 39-year-old family man from Oakland Hills, was sentenced to the Shelves after being charged with Moving and murdering his Shadow, who has since been identified by Mermick as Oscar Joji (time unknown). But the question that has captured the interest of the country is now the subject of parliamentary debate. How was Michael Mermick able to Move his Shadow if he was only classified as a Phase 2 Mover? Mermick's last phase renewal occurred last year, according to his wife, in compliance with BMAC and government regulations. But what if he had been up for renewal last month? 'Annual phase renewal is simply not enough,' prosecutor Sheila McCain told press on Wednesday. 'If Michael Mermick had been monitored with the vigilance we expect of our government, his Shadow would not only be alive, but still in the year he belonged.' BMAC has announced that status renewal for citizens with Movement capabilities is to be increased from annually to monthly with immediate effect. We Are Now, a group known for their anti-Mover sentiment, welcomed the change.

PROLOGUE

All the windows were busted. The wind from the Movement activity shattered them all. The cool storm air rushed around me, pulling at my T-shirt and tickling my baby sister's nose as I held her in my arms. I sat there, under the table in our kitchen, away from the broken glass, while my parents whispered furiously in the bedroom. When I say bedroom, I mean living room/dining room/my room/Mom and Dad's room/the baby's room. It's the only other room in our tiny apartment besides the bathroom. Which meant, even over the rush of the wind, I could hear every word they said.

'BMAC will trace the Move here,' Dad told Mom. 'You know that, Izzy.'

BMAC – the Bureau of Movement Activity Control. They didn't like Moves. Their whole job was to stop Moves. But they hadn't stopped this one.

'They can't prove you're the one who did it!' Mom said.

And then the wind caught my sister's little purple hat, ripping it from her baby-soft head and carrying it away.

She screamed as the breeze tugged her fuzzy black hair. I rocked her gently in my arms, wanting her to shut up so I could hear.

'BMAC doesn't have to prove it. Look around you, Izzy.' Around us was disaster. The splintered pieces of our apartment, our lives, scattered across the floor or half out the window. 'They'll take one look at this place,' Dad said, 'and then it's the Shelves.'

My stomach leaped into my throat. I might've been eight, but I knew what Shelving was. Every Mover knew what Shelving was. Still is. An endless sleep. A living kind of deadness.

Mom didn't say anything for the longest time. Neither did Dad. Even my sister stopped crying. The only sound was the roar of the wind outside. How did this happen? One minute we were watching my favourite show, about a ninja who lived in a kid's pocket, and the next my parents were making me climb beneath the kitchen table while the world exploded around me.

And then a bang made me jump.

It was coming from the door.

'Is it BMAC?' Mom whispered.

Dad stepped into the kitchen, his brown curls a frizzy windblown mess.

Another bang.

'Daddy?'

Dad held out his hand. 'Pat, take your sister to the bathroom.'

But I didn't have to. Mom was already grabbing Maggie out of my arms.

I stayed there on the kitchen floor, my hot hands sweaty on the cold tile as my dad peeked through the hole in the door.

Bang!

'Breezes!' Dad shouted. 'Izzy, help me!'

And he opened the door.

All I saw was red.

Blood red.

A guy tumbled in, falling into Dad's arms and bleeding from his mouth, choking out our last name: 'Mermick.' And another name I'd never heard before. 'Oscar Joji.' He clutched his head with one hand, blood caked to his hair and seeping through his fingers, the skin blistered, red and peeling. 'Oscar Joji.'

I can remember that I screamed.

And then the guy collapsed.

None of us said anything – Dad, Mom, me. We just stared at the fallen guy's body, seeping blood into our rug. He wasn't gasping any more. He was dead. It's the quiet that tells you that kind of thing. The quiet just lets you know. Even at eight, I knew it.

Mom's voice broke the silence. 'Shadow?'

Dad stared at his red, stained hands and nodded.

I felt cold. Freezing cold. Like everything that had been warm and safe and good about our home had been sucked out the shattered windows. A Shadow. I looked at the bloody lump on the floor – he was from the future. And he was here, in our apartment. He wasn't allowed to be here.

'Mike,' said Mom. She walked up to Dad as if the dead

guy wasn't even there – wasn't there dead – and held Dad's face in her hand. 'Mike, we have to run. We have to go. BMAC is coming.'

An entire flock of feathery, angry wings flapped in my gut and I pulled my knees up to my chest. BMAC is coming? Coming for who?

'We can run, Mike,' she told him. 'We can still run.'

Dad shook his head and kissed Mom's hand. 'They'll find us.'

And then Mom cried. So did the baby in her arms. And Dad hugged them both.

The wings in my stomach pushed up against my throat and my eyes began to sting. BMAC was coming. What would they do when they found the Shadow? He couldn't be here. How did he get here?

Mom wiped away her tears and took the baby over to the bed. I didn't move. Couldn't remember how. There was a Shadow in our home. A real dead Shadow. And BMAC was coming.

'Pat?' Dad crawled under the table and we stared at each other for the longest time. He had brown eyes. I'll never forget them. And when they caught the light, I could see flecks of green. 'Pat, son, I need you to listen to me. BMAC is going to be here any minute and I need you to be ready for it.'

My heart hammered in my chest so hard I could feel the beat of it vibrating down into my feet. 'What will they do?' I barely managed to whisper.

Dad closed his eyes and took a deep breath. When he opened them again, they were wet. 'They're going to take me.'

I knew it. Even though I didn't really know it, some part of me had been waiting for him to tell me that. I leaped at him, wrapping my arms around his neck, and cried. BMAC was coming for my dad.

'Listen to me, Pat,' he said. 'I need you to look out for your sister for me, all right? You need to take care of her because she won't have me here.'

'I don't want you to go,' I told him, and squeezed him tight, as if my arms could somehow glue him to me and then no one could take him away. Not even BMAC.

'You're gonna be good for me, all right?' His voice broke then. And a new bolt of fear shot through me, one that still makes the muscles in my stomach constrict when I think about it. He was scared. 'You're gonna be good and you're gonna help your mother, because she's going to need you, right?'

I wanted to tell him yes, but my voice was caught, strangled in my throat. I remember the feel of his big hand on my back, warm and strong as he rocked me. He sniffed three times. Big runny sniffs that told me he was crying. My dad never cried. But he did then. The last time I saw him.

I don't remember how long we stayed that way, clinging to each other. Don't remember the pounding on the door before BMAC finally broke it down. Don't remember how many BMAC agents it took to prise me loose from my dad's neck.

I just remember the grey of their uniforms, swarming our tiny home like phantoms. I remember the current bindings they brought with them. The way they hissed and crackled a menacing electric blue around my dad's wrists.

I remember Mom screaming and cursing as they dragged Dad off.

I remember, they walked right through the Shadow guy's blood. Dad left twenty-eight red footprints from our door to the elevator. I counted them later.

They took Dad. They left the Shadow.

They took Dad to the Movers' Prison and Shelved him till his trial.

A living kind of deadness.

Said it was procedure in a Mover's case. That was six years ago. His trial didn't help him much, cos he hasn't been awake since.

ONE

It's busted again. I'm sitting on our fire escape, fiddling with the hoses on our water tank. The warm rush of the Eventualies winds wrap around my arms and through my T-shirt. They say in the time before Movers, the Eventualies didn't blow.

I've got about twenty minutes before I have to leave for school and I still haven't had my shower. This is the fourth time the tank has broken down this week. In the time before Movers, people didn't have to deal with tanks either. Back then, water wasn't as scarce. People just turned on their tap and didn't even know where the clean, fresh water came from. At least, that's what my teacher, Mrs Dibbs, says. Then again, if you ask Mrs Dibbs, everything was better before Movers.

I boot the rusted metal barrel and there's a loud clank.

'You'll break it that way.' My sister's sitting just inside the window, her cheeks resting in her fists, a black crow perched happily on top of her head. 'You even know what you're doing?'

No. I don't know much about water tanks at all. We've had the same one since before I was born. All I know is, when we need water, it comes out of there. Two steel drums bolted to the wall of our tiny apartment. The government fills up the big one each month, and if we get rain, it fills up the smaller one. There's gauges and filters and when it's working right, blinking green lights, but that's about all I know. My eyes wander over the side of our building, dozens more windows with dozens of their own tanks. *Their* green lights are blinking.

I look back at Maggie. 'You got a better idea?'

She grins smugly, big dimples dipping into her cheeks. 'I do actually.' She climbs out the window and the bird hops off her head and onto the railing, from where it squawks angrily at me and flaps its wings.

I frown. 'Grumpy today, isn't it?'

'Maybe that's because you keep calling *her* an "it",' says Maggie.

I don't care what it is. I wrinkle my nose at Beauty – that's the awful name Maggie gave it. The bird and I have never cared much for each other. In fact I keep leaving the window open, hoping the stupid thing will leave. And it does. But then it always comes back. The dumb bird comes and goes as it pleases. Has for years now. And every year it seems to hate me just a bit more.

Maggie stands in front of the tools I've splayed out on the metal grate of the fire escape. I don't know if you could really call them tools – a wrench that's gotten rusty over the years, a butter knife and a shiny new screwdriver Mom bought the last time the tank broke. I still haven't figured out what part of the tank requires the use of a screwdriver.

Maggie stares down at the tools, the right corner of her mouth twitching.

'Well?'

'I'm thinking,' she says, and Beauty snaps its ugly beak at me.

I don't know what she's thinking about. Maggie knows less about tanks than I do.

Her eyes flick to the tank, and she cocks an eyebrow.

'What?'

'Do you know what this does?' She points at a thin, cloudy hose poking out the top.

'No.'

She reaches for it anyway, unhooking it and blowing hard into the loosened end. As soon as she does, she starts coughing and Beauty takes to the air, flapping around and squawking in a panic. Maggie pulls the hose out of her mouth and a green, goopy sludge plops out onto the grating.

'Oh, gross, Mags!'

I grab the hose from her and she continues to sputter, clawing at her tongue to get rid of the taste.

'It tastes like—' She gags.

I swat the bird out of my face, but the dumb thing won't get out of the way. 'Yeah, that's why you're not supposed to stick your mouth on it.'

'I'll bet it helped though.'

Maybe. Beauty's come to a rest on top of the tank, its feathers ruffled from the commotion. 'Move,' I order.

The bird just looks at me with its beady black eyes.

'Beauty,' says Maggie, and nods to the railing. The bird takes off, flapping its way over to Maggie, perching on the cool metal of the fire escape.

With a roll of my eyes, I fasten the hose back to the top of the tank and stare at the gauge. 'Nothing.'

Maggie scoffs and pushes me out of the way, fiddling with one of the knobs. I'm happy to let her try. I'm out of ideas and I'm not gonna get my shower before school at this point anyway.

'Pat,' she says, wiping her sludge-soaked hand on the front of her shirt, 'where did Oscar Joji come from?'

The name makes my skin prickle against the rush of the Eventualies. Oscar Joji, we figured out later, was the name of Dad's Shadow. My eyes narrow. 'You know where he came from, Mags.'

She keeps her focus on whatever she's doing to the knob. 'Yeah, but what year exactly?'

'They don't know what year, Maggie. You know that.' I crane my neck around, worried I'm gonna catch someone listening. But there's no one out here. Just us and the water tanks. 'We're not supposed to talk about it.'

'But BMAC knew where that East Grove lady's Shadow came from.'

A sigh rushes up from my lungs. Last month, some woman in East Grove was caught by the Bureau of Movement Activity Control for Moving her Shadow. They caught the woman's Shadow too, and the Shadow confessed she was from the year 2242. Oscar Joji couldn't confess anything. He was too dead. I grind my teeth, trying not to call up the memory of him lying in his own blood by the front door.

'Breezes, Mags. Why do you care so much about the East Grove lady?'

Maggie shrugs, blank eyes staring at the tank, her finger tracing the rim of the main gauge. 'Do you think BMAC Shelved her?'

Yes. That's BMAC's job. Ever since Movers started bringing people like Oscar Joji from the future back here to the present, the population has exploded. Some places in the future aren't all that great – wars, famine, disease and stuff – so a lot of people want to get back to now, where it's safer. The government says there's just not enough room, not enough resources, to go around. That's why they created the Bureau of Movement Activity Control. To hunt down any Mover who breaks the law and lets a Shadow in.

Movers like Dad.

And the East Grove lady.

Maggie knows what my silence means. 'Do you think Mom can make them stop Shelving people?'

No. Ever since Dad was Shelved, my mom's been on a crusade to ban Shelving. Putting a Mover to sleep for the rest of his life doesn't sit well with her. Mom's not a Mover, but she loves enough of them to make it her business to put an end to the whole process. She meets with Movement experts and scientists and Movers' rights people. None of it gets her any closer to banning Shelving.

'Do you think Mom could've – you know – I mean if the East Grove lady came to her . . .'

'Maggie,' my voice carries more warning than I mean it to, but she needs to stop before she says something that could get Mom in serious trouble.

'But could she have? Gotten her FIILES?'

As soon as it's out of her mouth I lunge, grabbing her tightly by the arm. She cries out, and Beauty's screeching at me, but I don't care. 'Are you crazy? You want someone to hear you?'

The thing about Mom is, she has a reputation – a Mover sympathiser. Not a lot of Non-Movers (including Mrs Dibbs) like that much about her. But there's plenty of Movers who do. Movers who need help. Movers who broke the law. And their Shadows. So they seek Mom out.

And she helps them.

And it's *way* not legal. FIILES – Federal Information and Identification Licensing Electronic System – are a digital account of your entire life. That's how Mom helps. She's never said so, but I live in the same apartment. Whispered phone calls and late-night 'meetings'. She's even got a secret second closet that I'm supposed to pretend doesn't exist – a hidden panel at the back of our bedroom closet that stores some of the things she needs to help people evade BMAC. Over the years I've overheard her plenty, talking about phoney FIILES – birth certificate, driver's licence. It takes a lot of work to falsify digital licences like that, and Mom can barely work her smartdesk. I don't know who programs these phony FIILES for Mom or how she even knows someone who can do that stuff, and I'm not supposed to know. But I do know BMAC would arrest her for it if they ever found out.

'You *cannot* talk about that stuff, Maggie.'

'Ow,' she whines, pulling her arm back from me as Beauty perches protectively on her shoulder. She pouts, rubbing where my fingers pinched the skin.

'You don't know what Mom does,' I say, 'and talking like that could get us all in real trouble, so just shut up about it.'

Maggie doesn't say anything, just keeps pouting.

'Since when do you care so much anyway?'

She turns back to the tank, fiddling with the knobs so that she doesn't have to answer. Maybe it's better if she doesn't. The conversation shouldn't have started. Still, she didn't used to ask about these things. Never seemed to think about it much at all. So why start now?

My eyes drift out over the city, sky scrapers and towering apartment buildings, a jumbled mass of concrete and glass. I can see giant cranes and scaffolding too, lots more buildings going up.

'I fixed it,' she says, and steps back from the tank.

I doubt that. But now there's a mechanical ticking sound coming from inside the tank and I'm surprised to see the green light at the top has started to blink. The gauge springs back to life, waffling between empty and full.

'Ha!' I tap the glass and the needle settles somewhere around half. 'Mags, you're a genius! How'd you do it?'

She shrugs and Beauty clucks proudly.

'Success?' Mom's leaning out the window, wearing her work clothes, her hair in a frazzled greasy ponytail.

'Yeah!' I say. 'Thanks to Maggie!'

'Maggie?' smiles Mom. 'Mr Sibichendosh teaching you about water tanks in school these days?'

Maggie tries not to grin. 'I just turned some knobs.'

Mom watches her for a moment, and something in her smile fades. Mom shakes her head. 'Well, whatever you did, I wish you'd done it faster!' She looks down at her watch.

'I'm not going to have time to wash my hair before my seminar, and you two are already late.' Her eyes narrow on Beauty. 'Maggie, send Beauty off, please. You shouldn't encourage her.' Mom's not a fan of the bird either.

Maggie strokes Beauty's feathers and the bird lifts into the air, flapping away to wherever it goes when it's not annoying me.

'What are you talking about at your seminar?' asks Maggie, letting Mom help her through the window.

'Same old stuff.' She smiles before snapping her fingers at me. 'Come on, Pat. Let's go.'

'I'm coming.' I gather up the wrench, the screwdriver and the butter knife. I check the gauge again, just to be sure. The needle's still alive, the light still blinking.

Same old stuff. I wonder how long Maggie's going to let Mom get away with answers like that. How long either of us should.

TWO

By last period, I still haven't stopped thinking about what Maggie said, about Oscar Joji. I lean my elbows on my desk and stare out my classroom window. We're fifty-two floors up, so there's nothing to see except the office tower across the street. I've counted the windows on that building more times than I can remember, and I'm sure I'll do it a dozen more before the end of the year. They look silver and black, the stormy sky perfectly reflected in the glass. The clouds churn slowly, and as I watch them I can't help but think about Dad. What's it matter to Maggie where Oscar Joji came from? He's dead.

I grab my droidlet – a little red sphere that stores all my FIILES, and pretty much my entire life. I swipe the surface and the holographic screen blooms to life around it. *2.48 p.m.* dances across the little ball's centre. I have to pick up Maggie at three fifteen.

A low sound calls my attention from the time. 'Gooooooooo-ooooba,' moos Ollie Larkin, sitting in the desk in front of me.

The whole class is laughing outright and I try to hide my smirk. Gabby 'Gooba' Vargas stands at the front of the room, nose pressed to her droidlet notes as she presents her physics project – tubes and batteries and light bulbs all connected by a nest of wires. She's fat and I don't just mean chubby; she's the biggest in our grade, has been since kindergarten. She's also the only Mover in our school higher than Phase 1. With those two things alone, Gabby never stood a chance at the Romsey Institute for Academics. Not even her brainiac-ness helps her. Whenever she's called on to answer a question, she not only knows the answer, but she usually mumbles a whole bunch of additional stuff that our teachers never end up covering.

And none of it gets her good grades. Mostly because every project I've ever seen Gabby do has something to do with the mechanics of Movement. And that means talking about Movers. And in my experience, talking about Movers makes teachers uncomfortable.

Teachers like Mrs Dibbs.

'Goooooooooooba,' Ollie says again, causing more giggling.

Mrs Dibbs doesn't even look up from whatever she's watching on her droidlet. She hasn't been listening to a word Gabby's said. Gabby's been mumbling barely above a whisper about gravity and black holes and electromagnetic radiation for twenty minutes now, trying to explain her machine. Even if any of us could hear what she's saying, I doubt we'd understand it anyway.

A bored Kevin Prenders joins Ollie. 'Goooooooooooba.'

The 'Gooba' thing started last year and I don't think it's clever or anything. I don't think it even means anything.

It's just a made-up word. But Kevin manages to make the most perfect cow sound when he says it and I can't help but smile.

Gabby's not smiling.

Her skin's gone all blotchy and her hands are shaking. She glances up from her droidlet, right over at me, and she sees my grin. Her eyes are extra shiny and I know she's doing her best not to cry. She looks back down at her notes and clears her throat, placing a hand on the big glass tube in front of her. 'The idea is kind of like an X-ray,' she says. 'Only X-rays don't really pick them up. Neither do normal light rays. So, by finding the right frequency, hopefully I can expose the pungits so they can be measured and better understood.'

Mrs Dibbs stands. 'The what?' she says with a bored sigh.

'P-pungits,' says Gabby, raising her voice slightly. 'The particles that I believe are connected to Movers, the particles that make a Mover Move. I have a theory that the Mover manipulates these particles, which is why they have the ability to pull their Shadow from the future here to the present. If I can figure out how to see these particles, or even measure them, then we would better be able to understand Movement phases. For example, a Mover who is Phase 1 would have a low pungit count, while a Mover who is Phase 3 would have a high—'

Mrs Dibbs suddenly claps her hands together. 'All right, Miss Vargas, thank you for that.'

'I, uh, I wasn't finished.'

'That's all the time we have, Gabby. Please take your seat.'

Awkwardly Gabby scoops her contraption into her arms

17

and waddles her way to her desk. She's wedged into the very back, right between the vents and me.

'And, Miss Vargas?' Mrs Dibbs's eyes narrow, carving crow's feet deeper into her wrinkled face. 'Tomorrow is the first of the month. I trust you have your Phase Licence Renewal Forms ready for Officer Dan?'

Gabby nods, greasy strands of dark hair falling over her moping face.

Mrs Dibbs makes a note on the smartboard behind her and turns back to the class. 'Mr Doig?'

Matthew Doig raises his hand so Mrs Dibbs can see him, as if she doesn't know this classroom and her own specially designed seating arrangement like the hairs on her chin. His desk is on my left. Because this is where we belong, me, Gabby and Matt. In Mrs Dibbs's class, Movers sit at the back.

'You'll remember to complete your forms for tomorrow?'

'Yes, ma'am,' says Matt with a forced smile. He's always trying to smile for Mrs Dibbs. He rummages through his bag for a second and pulls out his droidlet. He holds the little green ball high above his head. I sigh. Every month, Matt Doig makes sure he has his phase forms a day early. He's only a Phase 1 Mover, like me. Phase 1 doesn't mean much of anything. But for whatever reason Matt feels he's got to make up for it and sucks up to Mrs Dibbs like it's his job. It's a wasted effort. For Mrs Dibbs, Phase 1 is one phase too many.

'I finished them today for you,' he tells her, 'in case you wanted to look them over.'

Mrs Dibbs snaps open her hand and Matt barrels to the front of the room. She's not even looking at him when he eagerly places the little ball in her palm. Her eyes are on me.

'Mr Mermick?' she says, as she swipes the surface of Matt's droidlet and signs with her fingerprint. 'I hope I'm not expected to place *another* phone call to your mother about your phase forms after last month's fiasco.'

I watch as Kevin Prenders nudges Leelee Esposito with a grin and they laugh. The fiasco was real amusing for everyone, except for me. I forgot to complete the forms last month. Well, actually Mom forgot. I answered all the questions, as usual. Kind of like a psych evaluation. But at the end you have to get a statement and signature from your parent and teacher. I asked Mom to sign them when she was elbow deep in articles and phone calls that were supposed to help some Mover lady, and she told me she would deal with them later. She didn't deal with them later, and I showed up without my forms completed.

'No, ma'am, she knows.' But I'm really not sure. This month could just as easily be as bad as the last.

'Good. Because her slippery memory when it comes to your phase status, I don't need to remind you, Patrick, could land us all in jail.'

She doesn't need to remind me. Officer Dan gave me a pretty hard time when I didn't have Mom's statement for him last month. He escorted me home and demanded Mom complete the forms, before he looked over the whole thing himself. It was awful.

'Remind her when you get home, please.'

More snickering.

'Yup,' I sigh, watching the clouds spiral into what looks like the rusted knob on our useless old water tank.

'I beg your pardon?'

'Yeah! I'll remind her!' My cheeks burn and I know they're red.

Mrs Dibbs glares at me. 'I. Beg. Your. Pardon?'

'Yes, Mrs Dibbs,' I grumble.

The whole class breaks into giggles and Mrs Dibbs raises her saggy chin into the air – her *Do you want extra homework?* face – and the class shuts up.

When they do, Mrs Dibbs moves on with business as usual, telling everyone to load tonight's mathwork into our FIILES before the bell.

I point my droidlet at the smartboard to capture tonight's algebra activity and check the time again – 3.02 p.m. Thirteen minutes to get to Maggie. She's around the block at Wynchwood Elementary. I'm gonna have to sprint to make it . . . if Mrs Dibbs ever lets me leave.

'All right, see you tomorrow.'

Finally.

I slam on my hat – Romsey Raiders, the school's team – and make a break for the door.

'Pat!' It's Ollie Larkin. 'Wait!'

I look back and see the little squirt pointing to his droidlet, the blue flames of SpaceDraccus5 blazing across its surface. 'Mission 72, man!' Yesterday it was BlastForce, last week he wanted to try Blood Night. And every time I have to tell him the same thing.

'Can't! Maggie!' and I fly out the door.

The halls are a mess of students and as I run through them I see the elevator bank, a sea of seventh graders all waiting for their ride down to street level.

'That's a solid ten-minute wait.' Ollie's at my side

already, his shoulder bumping into my elbow as people try and squish their way closer to the elevators.

'I'm so late for my sister.'

Ollie doesn't say anything, sulking while he plays SpaceDraccus5. He's mad because I won't play him. But I can't. Maggie is going to be waiting for me. I watch the waves of kids, the shifting bodies piling up in front of me, and then I have an idea.

'What?' asks Ollie, when he sees me looking at him.

'Vator bomb?'

His eyes go wide before he frowns. 'There's only two of us!'

A vator bomb is a three-man job.

I roll my eyes and grab the closest backpack to me, pulling some scrawny zit-faced ginger I don't know into our pocket of space. He looks surprised but I'm in a rush so I get right to the point: 'Dude, vator bomb?'

Zit-Face shrugs. 'For what?'

'Pat, this is a bad idea,' says Ollie, and I notice the blue flames of SpaceDraccus drifting up from his droidlet. 'Two hundred SpaceDraccus points?' I ask Zit-Face.

'Whose points?' says Ollie. 'Not my points!'

The guy nods, holding his droidlet up to Ollie's so he can take the agreed sum.

'I'll pay you back,' I promise, even though we both know I probably won't ever have two hundred extra points to give up.

Before Ollie can argue about it more, I grab his wrist to make him hold up his droidlet and the transaction is complete.

'Ollie, you get on the left.' I move him to the other side of me so I stand between him and Zit-Face. The three of us shift through the crowd, shoulder to shoulder, so we are in line with one of the elevator doors. There's at least twenty kids between us and the only way out of here. I haven't pulled a vator bomb in a long time, probably not since fourth grade when we first learned how, and I'm not sure how well this is going to go. The red number above the elevator door reads '58', and it's coming down fast.

'Go, go!' I shout at Ollie, as he bends over and makes a cradle with his hands. Zit-Face does the same and I use their shoulders to steady myself as I place my feet in their hands.

'What do you think you're doing?!' yells some girl behind me, but she's too late. The floor counter switches to '52', and at the sound of the *bing!* Ollie and Zit-Face let out a yell, lift with all their might and I'm airborne.

I scream, 'VAAAATOR BOMB!' – as per etiquette – and sail over the terrified kids ducking for cover. The elevator door opens to reveal a jam-packed chamber of older Grade 9s with nowhere to go. A couple of them put up their arms to stop me, but it's no use. Like a bowling ball, I crash down on top of them, setting off a string of loud profanities and angry grumbles.

'What's your problem, kid?'

'Who does that?!'

My hands fly to my head; I lost my cap in the flight. When I look down at my chest and see the grubby old thing sitting on top of me, I let out a laugh. *Successful vator bomb.*

'Get the hell off of me!' screams the owner of a pair of legs pinned beneath me, some girl with blue hair and sunglasses. There hasn't been a sunny day since before I was born.

I get to my feet and pull the cap down over my eyes, 'Sorry, sorry! My fault.'

A big guy behind me gives me a shove and I try not to laugh. I know vator bombs are annoying for everybody besides the bomber, but in a rush they sure are effective.

'He's a Mover!' growls sunglasses.

Oh no.

'Figures! He's a Mover!'

'For real?'

'It's on his droidlet,' she announces, holding up the little red sphere that must have fallen out of my pocket when I landed. An alert pulses from its centre for everyone to read – *phase forms, Mom!* Officer Dan made me program the alarm last month so I wouldn't forget. '"Phase forms". He's a Mover.'

And then it starts. The whole ride down is an angry discussion about Movers and all the ways they're destroying the world: letting in the Shadows, letting future people over-populate the present. I've heard it all a thousand times. Since the first Movers were discovered only fifty years ago, the world population has exploded. People from the future invade the present, use up our resources, have children, and their children have children, and the more they keep coming to our time the less there is for everyone. I don't know what they're so mad at me for though. It's not like *I've* ever Moved my Shadow.

I try my best to ignore them and watch the monitor above the door. An advert for Junior Formal is followed by a picture of Officer Dan and a phase-forms reminder. The phase-forms reminder is the same every day, and it cycles through the different phases. *Phase 1 – minimum potential hazard to state and environment.* That's me. Minimum hazard. More like no hazard. If you gotta be a Mover, that's where you want to be. Sure, I have a Shadow, I can feel him somewhere ahead of me. But I'm too weak to Move him. That's what BMAC means by minimum risk. I'm practically a Nowbie – er, regular person. Most Movers are Phase 1, like me and my sister Maggie.

The video of Officer Dan drones on. *Phase 2 – moderate potential hazard to state and environment. While those classified as Phase 2 are unable to Move their Shadow to the present, their connection to the future is strong enough to allow for clear communication between Mover and Shadow.* BMAC sure hates that. Phase 2s can cause them all sorts of headaches. They basically have a window to the future. Their Shadow can communicate clearly enough with them to tell them stuff Nowbies can't know. From things as small as who's going to win the big game, to things as big as stockmarket crashes. I think BMAC sees Phase 2s as cheaters. They've got an advantage over Nowbies. And Nowbies don't like that.

The screen goes dark, filled with a swell of black churning clouds. There's music too. Always the same music. Heavy drums and whiny violins. *Phase 3*, Officer Dan's voice is super-serious now. *Highest threat level to state and environment. The Phase 3 Mover poses the risk of Movement activity, allowing for a traveller from the future to infiltrate the present.* And that's the whole reason BMAC has to exist. Phase 3. BMAC doesn't stress too hard about the 1s like me, so long as I get my forms in and nothing changes. They keep an eye on the 2s, scrutinising their forms a little more closely to make sure they aren't getting stronger. But the 3s – well, I've never met one, but I do know that once your status changes to Phase 3, you get your own BMAC officer, checking in with you weekly like you're on parole. It's not illegal to be a Mover. It's illegal to Move. But for the Phase 3s, they live their lives just a thread away from the Shelves.

My eyes flick to the floor counter.

Being in a school with sixty-four floors, 27,000 students – 4,000 of those in my grade alone – makes for a long elevator ride. Six minutes from my floor to ground level. I usually get through the phase status video one and a half times before I finally make it to the bottom.

The bell *dings* and the giant G in the centre of the floor buttons lights up – ground level.

The doors open and I shove my way out.

'We're reporting you!' Sunglasses.

I turn back and tip my hat at her. Let her report me, like she even knows who I am. And if she does, the school's too big and a vator-bomb incident is too small a deal for anyone to waste their time looking for me. At most they'll make an announcement in the morning, *A reminder to all students that vator-bombing is strictly prohibited.* Big deal.

The revolving doors are jammed with students, no surprise. When I finally make my way through and out onto the street I break into a full sprint.

It's stormy out. It's always stormy out, thanks to the Eventualies: the warm winds that blow in clouds of varying shades of grey, brown and black. They blow in from the future, attracted to the Movers. Something to do with gravity. I don't really understand it. But to be honest, I'm not sure anyone really understands it. Lots of theories. But that's all they are. Theories. And that's what frustrates BMAC and Nowbies so much. Movement is an inexact science. One thing is for sure though, the Eventualies blow for Movers. And that, I kinda like to think, means they blow for me. The winds surround me as I run, whipping against my face and weaving through my arms. I know I'd miss them if they ever went away.

The streets are crawling with people – jam-packed, shoulder to shoulder – but I'm good at finding my way through. The thing about a crowd is, you gotta think of 'em like pigeons. Everyone's just sort of bobbing around not paying attention to anything, but if you just barrel through like a rabid dog on a mission, they scatter and make way. I run down the street and nearly trip over a group of guys in suits as they shuffle out of the way of a BMAC vehicle. My mom says that when she was little, her family was still allowed to drive a car. By the time she was in high school, there were too many cars on the road and the government banned them. Now only BMAC is allowed to drive – unless you're a celebrity or famous person or something. Then you can hire a private car service for some crazy amount of money. But the rest of us walk or take the underground. And no one likes to take the underground – not unless you're OK with hugging a bunch of smelly strangers while the transit assistants shove you into overcrowded cars.

Maggie's school is just around the corner from Romsey, which is good cos my lungs are about ready to burst. Her school's a lot smaller than mine, fourteen floors, and it's only kindergarten to grade 3. It's yellow with blue shutters on all the windows, like something out of a nursery rhyme. I guess that's the idea.

The front's pretty quiet when I get there, just a bunch of moms and dads and nannies. I look at my droidlet: 3.13. I made it just before the bell.

I throw my bag against a big cement planter with grubby plastic sunflowers in it and sit on the edge to wait for Maggie. I do my best to catch my breath. A pair of moms stand to my left, looking at me like I just took a dump here. I stare back – *Got a problem?* – and they turn away, getting on with their conversation.

'Have you felt the Eventualies today? The Movement in this area is getting out of control.' She's got a baby in her arms and she's wearing a skirt that's angel white. Her hair is perfectly done, complete with a polka-dot headband, but the snarl on her face makes her look like an absolute witch.

The other mom's lotioning her hands with some ether-smelling junk that's burning my nose. 'Well, I heard from Cathy – Cathy Fraser, her husband works for BMAC – and she was saying that this year's phase updates have seen more upgrades than any other year! So instead of a bunch of harmless Phase 1 kids running around the schools, they're developing into Phase 2s!'

'Well, exactly!' agrees Witch Mom. 'How long before they all become Phase 3s and we've got doors opening up all over the neighbourhood?'

I pluck a synthetic leaf off a sunflower and start twisting it in my hand. I'm glad Mom isn't here for this. She gets crazy when she hears people talking about Movers when they don't know anything about it.

'How dare you?!' she'd say. That's the standard intro to her *Movers are people too* speech. 'Are you aware that ninety-two per cent of all Movers are only Phase 1 or 2?' No one ever is. 'You can't open a door unless you're Phase 3, and yet Phase 1s and 2s get treated like criminals!' They don't really, at least not Phase 1s like me. Sure, Mrs Dibbs makes me sit at the back of the class, but I don't mind the back anyway. And a lot of parents didn't want me at their kids' birthday parties when I was younger, but I think that had more to do with Dad than my Mover status. Everyone knows Dad opened a door to the future. And because of it no one likes him. No one but Mom and me.

I chew on the inside of my cheek and try not to say anything.

The bell rings and kids start pouring out the doors, but the ladies drone on.

'Well, even Phase 1 and 2 make me nervous,' says the hand-lotioner. 'That woman from East Grove, they only changed her status up to Phase 3 a week before she caused her Move. And the Shimoda family? Their oldest—'

'She was Phase 3.'

The hand-lotioner frowns. 'Are the rest of the Shimoda kids still at this school?'

'No, they left the city after that. I mean, wouldn't you? How embarrassing.'

Embarrassing? I don't think anyone who loses a family member to BMAC would call it *embarrassing*.

'Good,' says Hand-Lotioner. 'I don't think any of these Mover children should be going to school publically. It's dangerous, don't you think? I mean, there're so many these days. The Shimodas, the Minkens' son, and there's that Mermick girl . . .'

My teeth grind. She means Maggie.

'You remember the Mermick case, don't you?' says Hand-Lotioner. 'Caused all that phase-form restructuring? He was supposed to be Phase 2! But that didn't stop him from Moving his Shadow.'

That's Dad's legacy. He was identified as Phase 2, but still he managed to Move Oscar Joji from the future. That freaked BMAC out because it meant Dad's phase status was wrong. He'd developed into a Phase 3 Mover without them knowing. That was back in the days when Movers only had to submit their Phase forms once a year. And now we have to submit once a month. Thanks to Dad.

I spot Maggie, alone in the sea of running, laughing, shouting kids. She waves. Her brown hair is wild and tangled – she must have taken out the braid Mom spent all morning on.

'Marigold Mermick!' I say, just loud enough for Witch Mom and Hand-Lotioner to hear. I steal a sideways glance and they do their best not to react, smoothing out their clothes and clearing their throats.

Maggie walks quickly through the swarm and I know something's wrong. Usually, she shouts 'PAT!', like she's surprised to see me. Usually, she runs, her purple star backpack bouncing around behind her.

Not today.

'I think I got in trouble,' she tells me and swings her backpack around to root through the pockets.

'Think?'

'Mr Sibichendosh gave me a letter to take home.' She hands me an envelope – a real paper envelope – a plastic smiley-face sticker sealing it shut. I can't remember the last time I held a piece of paper; everything's digital and carried around in droidlets. This is serious, whatever it is.

'You better read it.'

'It's sealed,' I say, pointing out the smiley. 'It's for Mom.'

She snatches it from me, tears off the sticker and hands it back. 'There. Now it's not sealed.'

'I'll tell her you did that.'

'Read!' she orders, pointing at the envelope.

With a sigh, and I'll admit a piqued curiosity, I take out and unfold the piece of paper. It's typed in small font. I have to stop walking and squint to read it. When I can see it clear enough, the first line sends ice through my veins.

This letter is to express my concerns surrounding Marigold's current phase status.

'Shit.'

'What?' She's pulling at my arm. 'What's shit? What's it say?'

I shrug her off and turn away, trying to focus on the rest.

As you are aware, Marigold is currently registered as a Phase 1 Mover by the Bureau of Movement Activity Control. The BMAC officer collects Phase Licence Renewal Forms tomorrow, Friday 5 March 2083. Marigold has shown a variety of behaviours in recent months that I am required by law to bring to the attention of her BMAC officer. This may affect BMAC's evaluation of her current phase status.

This is bad.

'Mags, what did you do?' I breathe.

'*You're* supposed to tell *me*!'

'Sibichendosh is reporting you to your BMAC officer!'

'So?'

'So he could upgrade your phase status, Maggie!'

'*She*,' Maggie corrects me. 'Officer Kelley is a girl.'

'Whatever! This is a big deal. Phase 1's bad enough, but Phase 2 and life starts getting really difficult, Mags! Why does Sibichendosh think you need an upgrade?'

She just kicks the ground and shrugs.

Phase status is never set in stone. If one or both parents are Movers, a baby is automatically identified as Phase 1. As a Mover gets older, that status can change. BMAC updates the list of 'flag symptoms' every year – frequently distracted, withdrawal, talking to yourself, expanded vocabulary or changes in speech patterns. If a Mover kid starts doing any of those things and someone tells BMAC, the kid's phase status always goes up.

'Mom's gonna flip,' I say, more to myself than anyone. I can only imagine the stats she'll throw out on Phase 2 Movers.

My thoughts are interrupted as someone ploughs through me and Maggie, slamming into my shoulder and nearly knocking Maggie off the sidewalk.

'Watch it!' I say, only to see the giant backside of Gabby Vargas hurrying on ahead.

'Gooooooooooooooooooooba!' About a hundred feet back are Zit-Face and Matt Doig with little Ollie Larkin, whose hands are cupped around his mouth. 'Gooba!'

I look ahead to Gabby and she's swiping at her face.

'Shut the hell up, Ollie!' I scream. I don't know why. I'm not mad at him. I'm mad at Sibichendosh – and Gabby Vargas. As she waddles on ahead I can hear her mumbling to herself. She's always mumbling to herself, and I hate her for showing me what a phase status change could mean for Maggie: too low to be feared, high enough to be noticed.

'What gives, Mermick?' calls Ollie.

I ignore him and grab Maggie's hand. 'Let's go.'

'Who's that girl?' she asks me.

'No one.'

'Why's Ollie being mean to her?'

Besides the obvious?

She's Phase 2.

THREE

I eat my morning cereal sitting on the end of the bed I share with Maggie. A screen glows above Mom's smartdesk, projected on the wall with the Avin news station. My phase forms are still unsigned, sitting in my droidlet on the top of my bag. I haven't showered. The tank's busted again. But Mom didn't wake me up in time to do anything about it. The letter from Sibichendosh is sitting on the end of Mom's bed beside me.

I expected a lot of yelling after Mom saw it, expected her to throw a lot of numbers, stats and examples at us. She didn't. It was weird. She just nodded a lot while she read, pressing her lips together like she was blotting her lipstick, even though she never wears any.

She spent the rest of the night sitting at the kitchen table, banging her wedding ring against the edge over and over, making a noise like a muffled jackhammer.

Movers Update – Phase Upgrades at All-Time High, Says BMAC flashes along the bottom of the screen. I guess Maggie's not the only Mover who got a letter home.

I can hear her screaming from the bathroom. Mom's attempting to do her hair again and it sounds like a more savage battle than usual.

At this rate she's not going to have time to fill out my forms. I grab my droidlet and sit at Mom's smartdesk to fill them out myself. I swipe open the screen on my droidlet and pull up the forms, projecting them onto the desk.

I did the phase test last night. A bunch of random brain-teasers that change all the time, test to test. I'm not sure how it works exactly. I just know that BMAC can tell if your thinking changes, based on your answers. Movers who spend a lot of time communicating with their Shadows in the future pick up new habits in their ways of thinking. Because future people think a bit differently than we do. They use some different words, have different ideas. And if a Mover's thinking changes, then that means they're communicating a lot. And if they're communicating a lot, then that means they're getting stronger. And if they're getting stronger, then that means they need a phase upgrade. Anyway, I did mine last night and I'm not worried. My Shadow and I have never had anything to say to each other.

I grab one of the litepens sitting in a coffee mug on the corner of the desk to fill in the rest, and the corner of my mouth twitches. I stop. Maggie's been asking lots of questions about Movers lately. Did she say something to Sibichendosh? Something that made him think she was getting stronger?

I stare at the form, at the Sworn Testimony box. I've filled out that box the same way my whole life. Basically, since the Nowbies don't like that Movers might know things about the future that they don't, the government passed a bill that makes Movers report any information they receive about the future from their Shadow. ANY information. Seems silly to me. What's to stop Movers from lying? Sure, if BMAC finds out you lied it's the Shelves. But how are they going to find out? It's like that oath they make you say in court. 'I swear to tell the whole truth, and nothing but the truth, yadda yadda.' But it makes the Nowbies feel better. So I write as legibly as I can, my droidlet recording the movement of the litepen, *I have had no communication with my Shadow.* Which is the truth, but, even if it wasn't, I'm not sure I'd write anything different.

What will Maggie write in the Sworn Testimony box this month?

There's a buzzing to my left, and I see Mom's white droidlet, sitting beside the litepens, rattle on the desk.

'Phone!' I yell, but all I hear back is Maggie screaming about hating braids.

I snatch it and swipe the surface.

'Yeah?'

A deep raspy voice croaks out of the tiny ball's centre. 'Izzy?'

The caller's breathing is heavy on the other end.

'Is Izzy there?'

'She's busy,' I say. 'Who's this?'

'Can you get Izzy?' There's a smacking sound, like he's chewing a wad of gum.

'I said she's busy.'

He sighs.

'Pat?' Mom shouts from the bathroom. 'What did you say?'

'Can you tell her something for me, son?'

I nod.

Even though he can't see me, he's giving me the message anyhow. 'Hexall Hall,' he tells me. 'The match. Rani'll wait.'

I swallow. Hexall Hall? I know it from what I've seen on the news sometimes and hear when people talk. It's a place hidden somewhere in the old part of the city – the part that the city dump has started encroaching on. The people who lived there abandoned it when the smell got too bad. But a lot of people who didn't mind the smell started moving in.

People like criminal Movers.

Immigrant Shadows.

Hiding from BMAC.

'Hello?' he says. 'Kid?'

This guy. This person on the phone is from Hexall Hall? I know she's been doing stuff that BMAC wouldn't like, but I always assumed she was doing it with other people like her – Mover Moms and Dads and anti-Shelving activists. People with day jobs and kids and phase forms to sign just like Mom. Not people from Hexall Hall. What is she getting herself into?

Before I can ask, the droidlet is yanked out of my hand.

'Yeah, yeah!' says Mom. 'Hi, it's me! Give me a sec.'

She shoves a bud in her ear and the droidlet goes mute. Whatever's being said by the man, Mom's the only one who can hear it now. She's all decked out in a fancy white dress that makes her look like some big-time business lady.

She says *yep* a bunch, before she taps off without even saying goodbye.

'Who was that?' I ask.

'Just a friend.' She flings open the closet and I can hear her digging through the clutter to get to her secret second closet that I'm supposed to pretend doesn't exist. Hard to pretend when she rifles through it right in front of me.

'Just your friend from Hexall Hall?'

Mom freezes.

'Why are you talking to people from Hexall Hall?' I ask.

She cracks open the panel at the back of the closet and starts counting the number of droidlets she needs. 'One, two, three . . .'

'Mom!'

She slams the panel closed, clicks the closet door shut and turns to face me with a sigh. 'I've asked you not to worry about this stuff, Pat.'

'Yeah, but Mom—'

'Pat,' she says, closing her eyes with a sigh, 'the people in Hexall Hall are not like what you see on the news, all right? Leonard is my friend and he uses the skill set he has to help a lot of people.'

'What kind of—'

'Pat,' she says, almost pleading. She doesn't want to have to lie to me. *Same old stuff*. She doesn't need to anyway. I've got a pretty good guess who this Leonard is. He must be the person who's been programming for her all these years. Mom's FIILES guy.

I want to ask her more, but she's already moved on from the conversation, smoothing out her freshly straight-ened hair. Her eyes are painted and she's tossing the little spheres into her bag. She usually just takes one, two max.

'Why do you need three—'

'I'll walk with you today,' she says, cutting me off. 'I'm going in with Maggie anyway, to speak with her teacher.'

Sibichendosh.

Then she's just standing there, staring. Her eyes are dead, like she can't see anything but whatever's happening in her brain.

'Mom?' I say, pointing at the virtual forms glowing on the desk.

'Hmm?' She's back briefly, nervously spinning her wedding ring on her finger.

'My phase forms. You need to sign them.'

Her hands fly into the air, 'Right, right!' and she waves me out of the desk chair. She sits down and starts reviewing what I've done. She gets past the name and birthday and then her pen stops. She starts spinning the ring again.

'Mom?' I sit down on the bed just behind her. 'Maggie'll be OK . . .'

She says nothing.

'Really, Mom,' I try. 'My friend at school's Phase 2, and she's . . . cool.' I feel sick lying to her – Gabby's not exactly cool, and she's not exactly my friend – but I've never seen Mom like this. Well, maybe once.

Mom can't help herself and laughs, grabbing my nose like she's done since I was a baby. 'Of course it's OK. Her teacher's just an idiot.' That sounds more like her. 'Your sister does not need an upgrade, bottom line. Now hop to it. Don't want to be late.'

I nod, and take my empty bowl to the sink as Mom keeps working on my forms.

'Marigold!' Mom shouts. Her voice is pretty deep for

a mom's, and whenever she yells like that I can feel my brain reverberating against my skull. 'Pat, will you go get her, please?'

It's not really a question.

Reluctantly I head to the bathroom. The door's closed and I knock. 'Mags?'

When there's no answer, I open it up. The bathroom's empty.

But I can hear her whispering.

'I told you, I'm not allowed.'

I take a step inside and there she is, hidden behind the shower curtain, huddled over the drain. 'My mom wouldn't like it. It gets people in lots of trouble.'

'Mags?'

She jumps, noticing me for the first time. She looks as if I've caught her snooping on my droidlet.

'Who are you talking to?'

She looks tired, like she hasn't slept or has a fever. She's clammy and pale.

'What's the hold-up, you two?' calls Mom.

'We'd better go,' she says, climbing out of the tub. She hurries by me and runs to the front door where Mom's waiting, but I don't follow. My eyes are on the tub. It's empty, just empty. I don't know what I hope I'm gonna see there – a kitten maybe, or some other secret pet she's been hiding. Anything would be better than what's actually there. Nothing. Just our empty salmon-pink bathtub and a green bottle of 2-in-1 shampoo.

Variety of behaviours.

'Pat! Let's go!'

'Uh, yeah,' I say, and shut the bathroom door quietly.

I want to believe it's cos she's just a kid. Imaginary friends – kids have them. Like a purple unicorn or something lame. But all I can hear are the questions she asked me yesterday. About Oscar Joji, about the East Grove lady. And part of me worries Sibichendosh is right. Maybe Maggie will have to write something different in the Sworn Testimony box.

FOUR

I can't take my eyes off Gooba. I've been watching her all day, studying her. That's what Phase 2 looks like. She's sitting in her usual spot, against the north-east corner of the roof. She's never had a problem being so close to the fence. I have. I won't even retrieve a ball if it rolls too close. Really. I know I'm just being a baby. Sixty-four floors is nothing, next to the Avin Turbine looming a couple of blocks away. My dad told me that when people finally started to accept that the Eventualies weren't going anywhere, the government figured they might as well use the winds to help power cities and stuff. The Avin Turbine was the first-ever city turbine erected for the Eventualies. The giant landmark is 1,814 feet high. I watch its mighty blades slice through the grey sky. Mom took me up to the observation deck once. I was eight. She didn't have any Hexall Hall friends in those days.

'Am I on my own here?' says Ollie. 'Pat, hello?'

He's sitting beside me, his droidlet on fire with the holographic flames of SpaceDraccus5.

I shake my head. I'm not really in the mood for SpaceDraccus.

'Fine,' he grumbles. 'Some fun you are.'

'What's your problem?' He's been in a sour mood all morning and it's starting to grate on my nerves. 'I said I'll pay you back for the points! Breezes!'

Ollie just sits there, pouting and looking down at his dragons.

'He did it again today,' he says finally.

'Kevin Prenders?' But I don't need to ask. I already know what Ollie's going to say.

Ollie nods. 'He asked me if my *mommy* remembered my phase forms.'

Ollie doesn't need phase forms. He's not a Mover. But he's short and his parents are from somewhere in Europe and when we were younger they used to send him to school with this weird-looking purple soup. That was enough for Kevin Prenders to decide Ollie was a freak, and the rest of our grade usually agrees with Kevin Prenders.

So, Ollie and I sort of had no choice but to stick together. It was either that, or end up loners like Gabby Vargas. But since Ollie spends all his time around me, kids have started to think he's a Mover too.

'Could be worse,' I say. 'You could *actually* be a Mover.'

'Oh, please. You're barely a Mover.'

I roll my eyes. 'Tell that to BMAC.'

'No, but really,' says Ollie, 'you never even talk about your Shadow.'

'That's because I'm barely aware of my Shadow.' My Shadow is nothing for me. For some Movers, like the 2s and

42

especially the 3s, their Shadows are a constant issue. They say the 3s know everything about their Shadow – age, gender, how far ahead they are. The Shadows are there, in their heads, all the time. I saw a documentary once on this Phase 2 whose Shadow gave him a list of recipes of his favourite foods that no one in our time had ever eaten before, and the dude opened up a restaurant and made himself filthy rich. At least until BMAC shut him down and took his money. Like I said, Nowbies don't like that Movers get an unfair advantage.

'See? Cos you're barely a Mover.' Ollie scrolls through his droidlet. 'Still though. At least you have a Shadow. Everyone thinks I'm a Mover and I don't even get the bonus of having someone in my head telling me secrets about the future.'

'My Shadow can't tell me anything about the future,' I say.

'You must know more about it than I do. What time is your Shadow in?'

My attention's on Gooba. She has her head in her hands and she's shaking it, as if she's trying to get a bug out of her ear. No wonder she's a loner. Her lips are moving too, and her face looks like she's either concentrating or having a real bad migraine.

She's talking to herself – like Maggie did this morning.

Her eyes flick to me – and she jumps when she realises I'm watching her. She blushes and looks away.

'Pat!' Ollie.

'What?' I snap, startled by the sound of my name.

'Your Shadow, asshole. Tell me what you know.'

I don't like it when Ollie tries to understand Movers. As

much as everyone thinks he's one of us, he just isn't. He's my friend, sort of, but the Movement thing, that's not something he'll ever understand. 'I told you, nothing! It's not anything.'

'Boy? Girl? Old? Our age?'

'I'm Phase 1!' And I'm annoyed. 'I can't tell anything about my Shadow. It's just . . .' I stop. Explaining a Shadow to someone who's not a Mover is like explaining sadness to a droidlet. It's not concrete enough; you have to feel it. It's like . . . 'Fog,' I say finally.

'Fog?'

'Yeah,' I say, 'a fog. But like a small ball of it. I know it's there and that it's . . .' I wave my hand in front of myself, 'I dunno, ahead of me. But I can't tell how far. Or who's inside the fog, but I know they know I'm here.'

Ollie stares at me blankly. I'm out of ideas. That's the best way I could put it. Without thinking, I find my brain wandering to that part that's connected to it – my Shadow. I can feel him, like cold seeping through a cracked window. I don't even know it's a *him*, not really. I've just sort of always imagined my Shadow was male. I'm Phase 1, so the connection's too weak to know for sure. There's a faint surge in my temples as he becomes aware of me and I force myself to block him out again.

'That's creepy,' Ollie says finally, back to focusing on his droidlet. 'Talkin' like that around Officer Dan'll get you Shelved, for serious.'

I know he's kidding, but that's no joke. Shelving to a Mover, even Phase 1, is never a joke.

'At least you're not as weird as the Gooba.' And then Ollie shouts out to her. 'Isn't that right, Gooba?'

44

Gabby looks up again, right over at me.

'Goooooooooooba,' moos Ollie.

The red in Gabby's cheeks gets darker – from anger or embarrassment I can't tell. Both probably.

'Leave her alone, Ollie.'

He frowns. 'Like you've never called her that.'

I watch Gabby's eyes go blank again, and I feel like she's escaping. Escaping into her own head. Escaping the sudden attention. Escaping us – and I'm afraid for Maggie.

'I just don't see why you have to pick on her all the time.'

Ollie frowns. 'Me?! You say it plenty, Mermick.'

That might be true. 'But not in front of her. You're as bad as Kevin Prenders.'

'Watch it,' warns Ollie, '*Shelf-Meat*.'

'What are you gonna do about it, *Real-Time*?'

His eyes narrow at the dig. There's plenty worse names for Movers, but for some reason Nowbies don't like to be reminded they're isolated in the present.

Ollie stands up, his mouth tight as he glowers at me and I rise to meet him. I'm a solid head taller, but still the little squeak stares me down.

Until the thunderclap.

A fierce crack explodes above us, the flash of lightning illuminating everything on the roof yard.

Ollie and I both look up. The clouds just above us are churning in a spiral, black and circling, dulling the light from the flickers of lightning. The thunder deafens our ears. That spiral – the way the clouds are turning – leaves no doubt: this is Movement activity. A door to the future is opening.

I've only been this close to a Move once. Dad's Move. But this is more violent than I remember. All the Moves I've seen since Dad's just looked like really bad thunderstorms, but as the swirling mass above us roars so loud that my body starts to tremble, it's clear this is very different. With a crack that nearly blows open my skull, the storm lets loose a bolt of lightning so bright I'm seeing spots. Everyone on the roof yard hits the deck and the ground beneath us begins to shake.

As suddenly as they came, the vibrations disappear, like ripples on water, and the stunned roofyard can't do anything but listen to the deep purr overhead.

'W-w-was that normal?' asks Ollie.

I don't think so.

'Gooba!' Leelee Esposito is on her feet with wild, panicked eyes zeroed in on Gabby. 'What the hell do you think you are doing?!'

Oh no.

Everyone turns to look at Gabby, who's hugging the ground. Her mouth hangs open, like she doesn't know whether or not she should answer Leelee. I glance back up at the spiralling clouds, their coil getting tighter and tighter. How long before the lightning strikes again?

Our recess supervisor, Miss Farley, slowly rises to her feet. Her silver bun is in shambles. 'Miss Vargas,' she says to Gabby, approaching her like she's got a gun.

They think Gabby is doing this? I look at all the faces watching Gabby, some crying, some dumbfounded, most frowning. Gabby's the only Mover at Romsey higher than Phase 1. The whole yard thinks it's her.

46

'I need you to take a deep breath,' continues Miss Farley.
'Movement is a choice. You don't have to do this.'

'Make her stop it!' someone shrieks.

'Gabby, please don't,' cries someone else.

I feel my pulse throbbing in my neck. She's still only
Phase 2.

'Maybe we could knock her out?' says Ollie, looking
at me.

'What?'

'Well, she can't Move if she's unconscious, right?'

'She's Phase 2!' I tell him, furious that I seem to be the
only one to remember that. 'She's only Phase 2!'

Just like Dad.

Ollie looks at me like I'm speaking gibberish, and Miss
Farley keeps coming at Gabby. Gabby's frozen on the ground,
terrified eyes scanning the angry faces surrounding her.

They're all shouting now, pleading and jeering at her.
They've made up their minds and suddenly I'm mad at them,
mad at all of them – for Dad's sake, for my sister's, and
now for Gabby's.

I get up and start moving towards Miss Farley. What am
I gonna do? Push her away from Gabby? Doesn't matter cos
a second blast, bigger than the first, erupts from the surging
cloud. A bolt of lightning, crooked and forked like a dead
tree branch, explodes above my head and strikes the antenna
above the doors that lead back into the school.

I'm thrown off my feet as the whole building starts to
move, like a sleeping giant waking up. People run in all
directions, teachers and students pushing and shoving for
the doors. The screams and wails in the panic drown out

my thoughts, but I can hear the building groaning, beams and brick struggling to hold together.

Besides me, Gabby Vargas is the only other still body on the roof yard.

'Pat!' Ollie's running for the door. 'Come on, man!'

My eyes are on Goobs, down on all fours at the edge of the yard, her face buried in her hands. And all I can think of is Maggie – *variety of behaviours.*

'Pat!' Ollie again. 'We've gotta go, now!'

That's when I hear it – the cracking.

The roof yard begins to split, the whole north side separating away. Gabby is alone on the north side.

I sit there, helpless, as she frantically looks for something to grab onto. I can't process it, can't think; all I can do is watch the cement beneath her crumble, the protective fence at her back lean and fall away over the side, and Goobs – Gabby – disappear from sight.

Before I know what I'm doing, I'm scrambling to my feet, running to where she fell.

'Are you crazy?!' screams Ollie.

She can't be gone. She can't.

I approach the destroyed edge of where the north piece fell away. The Eventualies are intense and whip around me, whistling in my ears as I inch closer. A wave of vertigo threatens to make me faint when I see the street below. My knees buckle and for a second I think I'm going to black out, but Ollie's voice snaps me out of it.

'What the hell are you doing?!'

Deep breaths. This is going to take huge monster breaths. I force myself to open my eyes and peek down, over the edge. *Gabby*. I almost laugh with relief. She's there, clinging to a metal beam, her hands turning white from the strain of taking the weight of her body.

'Hang on!' I call to her. I look back at Ollie. 'Help me!'

He's fighting the Eventualies to keep the door open. The last of the other students disappears inside and it's just us now. Ollie doesn't move.

'Forget her!' he yells back. 'She's dead anyway!'

Something cold crawls its way up my back and I stare at Ollie. The wind whips through his shaggy hair, his clothes. The Movers' wind. And now I realise what it is I'm looking at.

A Nowbie.

A frightened Mover-hating Nowbie.

The wind picks up suddenly, and Ollie loses his grip, the door slamming shut. It takes all of his strength, frantically scrambling to prise it open again.

'Pat,' he screams, 'we gotta go now.'

But I can't. Dad's words are all I can hear in my head: *You need to take care of her*.

Maggie. What if it was Maggie?

I won't leave her.

I turn my back on him and scoot even closer to the edge.

Ollie screams, 'You're crazy!' and then I hear the slam of the door.

I'm on my own.

My body starts to tremble as I edge forward, beads of sweat pooling on my forehead. I'm half hanging over the side, doing my best not to look at the 1,300-foot drop below me. Gabby's there, hugging her beam and staring down at the street that's waiting to smash her up. Anchoring myself to the roof with a vice grip on a twisted piece of iron cemented into the wall, I reach out my hand.

'Come on!' I yell to Gabby. 'Grab it!'

She glances up, the *I'm about to die* terror that was all over her face briefly replaced by surprise.

'Gabby,' I beg her, 'come on!'

Those eyes of hers lock onto mine, huge and glistening with tears. For a second there is just those eyes and the feel of the wind, and then another crash of thunder breaks them away from me.

'Gabby!'

She squeezes her eyes tight, trying not to look down, and when she opens them again they are focused on my outstretched hand. She tries to reach but her arms are too short.

I lean as far as I can while my eyes fight against what my brain is telling them and, without permission, look down. The world is in miniature from up here. Everything below looks microscopic, like mould on bread. My body freezes and my vision starts to go wavy. That's when the ground moves.

Another blast sends tremors rippling through the building. The cement begins to give way under my right foot and there's nothing I can do. My body is in freefall and I cry out. My brain shuts down, and there's only one thought – I'm so dead – but my hand still has a grip on the metal bar.

I dangle there, scream-crying with Gabby while the rough rusty bar cuts into my palm. My vocal cords feel ready to snap while the rest of me is consumed by fear. No Gabby, no Movement, just – falling.

My temples start buzzing, like the lightning has shot right through them, and I can feel him, my Shadow, suddenly aware of me. He's angry, overwhelmed by the emotion flooding out of my body and suddenly I'm furious too.

Stop screaming! Pull yourself up!

The anger surges through my muscles like fire. I hold tight to the bar and hoist myself up, my fingernails clawing into metal. I get my elbows up onto the broken concrete, dragging the rest of myself back onto solid rooftop. I lie there, my cheek resting against the hard ground, trying to keep my pounding heart from exploding.

That's when I hear Gabby. She's screaming my name.

Another blast sounds above us. We're running out of time. Another tremor could knock Gabby from her perch and anyway, she can't hang on for ever. I'm back at the edge, trying to find something to anchor myself while I reach for her.

To my left, the roof-yard fence dangles over the side but some of it's still cemented to the roof. I look out to Gabby. There are broken beams, tattered wires and chunks of concrete branching to where she's hanging. I grab the dangling part and pull it towards me. It's still attached to the cemented part of the fence, but there's enough give that I can make it to her. I step out onto the strongest-looking beam, my fingers cramping up from the grip I have on the fence.

After three carefully placed steps, I'm almost beside Gabby and I reach down to her.

'Take it!' I tell her.

I can see how much she wants to, but it's clear from the tears in her eyes she's too afraid to let go of her grip on the beam – her arms are the only thing keeping her from falling.

'Gabby!' I scream. 'Do it!'

I don't know if my voice gave her the courage or scared her more than the threat of falling, but she reaches for my arm. My hand clamps down on her forearm and her fingers dig into my skin.

'Pull!' I shout.

Gabby pulls on my arm and her weight is more than my muscles can handle. My teeth are grinding into paste as Gabby drags herself from her armpits to her stomach onto the beam.

'Now use my hand,' I tell her. 'I'll steady you. You have to stand up!'

She whimpers and makes a shaky effort. As she pushes and pulls on my arm, in my mind I see what happens if she loses her balance: she'll pull me down with her.

She's on her hands and knees now, barely daring to breathe as she makes an attempt to stand.

'You can do it, Gabby!'

She stays statue still, her gaping mouth practically kissing the beam as she stares at the street below.

Another blast, then another. The lightning shoots around us like fireworks.

'Gooba!' I scream. 'Move your fat ass!'

She does her best and struggles to her feet through the tears. I guide her across the splintered bones of the broken building, her hand in mine, my other on the fence.

When we're back on the rooftop she falls to her knees and I want to let her catch her breath, but the lightning above us is crackling and hissing so much that the roof is no safer than where we just were.

'Follow me, Gabby,' I shout over the noise.

Her dark eyes, red from crying, look up at me and she reaches out for my hand a second time. I force her to her feet and she stumbles a bit. 'You can do it, Gabby!' I tell her again, and she lets me drag her across the roof, through the doors and out of the storm.

FIVE

When homeroom is on the fifty-second floor, you don't find yourself taking the stairs much. In fact I've never taken the stairs before now. It smells like old paint and dust, and the emergency lights offer just enough to let us know it's really friggin' dark in here. Gabby's breathing is loud behind me as we fly down the empty south stairwell, our footsteps echoing so that I'm painfully aware it's just me and the Gooba.

Floor after floor we make our way down, leaping four steps at a time, getting dizzy with each turn. The air is thick with what looks like white smoke. But it's not smoke. It's pieces of Romsey, flaking into nothing as the storm works to bring it down.

Everyone left. They just left. Left me, left Gabby. They didn't care. Ollie left. I shouldn't be surprised. Not when I really think about it. We were never friends, not in any real sense. We were just convenient to each other. Loners together. Movers don't have friends, I remind myself. Not really.

I leap onto the next landing – floor 48 – and stop. Gabby's a good three flights behind so I wait.

'You all right?' I ask when she finally catches up.

She says nothing, just nods and makes her way past, moving as fast as she can manage.

'What the breezes happened up there, Gabby?'

She stops and looks back at me, her head tilted like she's confused by the question.

'Did you do this?' I ask.

Her eyes drop then, and she shakes her head no. She shakes her head so hard the elastic that's clinging to what hair is left in her ponytail drops out, and strands fall into her face.

And I hate myself for asking. Because of course she didn't do this. She couldn't do this. She's only Phase 2.

But so was Dad.

'Gabby,' I say, 'I need to know. Are you sure? I mean, maybe BMAC got your phase wrong? Are you sure you're not . . . Phase 3?'

Her wet eyes meet mine, and her mouth is pulled into such an anguished frown it hurts to look at. She looks up at the ceiling, as if she can find some answer in the air above her. 'I didn't,' she squeaks.

The look on her face, the sound of her voice, so hopeless – I believe her. In my gut I do. Who did make the Move, though?

Gabby sniffles quietly into her hands, and I want to tell her I'm sorry, that she doesn't need to cry, but a man's voice cuts me off.

'Teacher says she's with some boy.' The voice echoes

up the stairs from somewhere below. 'Another Mover, wearing a baseball hat.'

The way he says it kicks my heart into panic. *Mover*. Like he can't stand the taste of it.

'Another one?' A second voice. 'What phase?'

Gabby's shaking behind me, her breath coming in panicked gulps. I put my finger to my lips and she nods.

I creep up to the railing and peek down between the spiralling stairwells. I can see movement, just shadows in the white, but there are definitely people coming.

'Phase 1, but even still. We'll have to bring him in,' the deep voice says. 'BMAC policy, you know that.'

BMAC.

'We're going to need to talk to him.'

'The girl?' asks the other.

'What's to talk about?'

Gabby. They're here for her.

Something pokes into my back, and when I turn round Gabby nods at the door to floor 48. Slowly she pushes it open and we both wince at the quiet click. We listen. BMAC's still talking, which means they didn't hear it. Quietly Gabby pushes further but it stops. She pushes again. There's something blocking it on the other side. She pushes harder, and there's a bang. I jump on her, pulling her back from the door. 'They'll hear you,' I hiss.

I grab the door and try to push, but it won't go. I can feel there's something holding it shut.

'Help me!' I order in a whisper, and Gabby uses all her strength against the door while I try to budge it with my shoulder.

And then I hear BMAC. 'Who's there?'

Frantically I lean back on the railing and slam my foot into the door, again and again as Gabby groans from the strain on her shoulder.

'Stay where you are!' the officers shout.

Whatever is blocking the door budges inch by inch until finally there's just enough room to squeeze through – well, for me to squeeze through anyway.

Gabby keeps pushing while I wiggle my way out, doing her damnedest to make enough room for herself.

As my lower half pulls free of the tight opening, I trip over a chunk of wall and land on a pile of broken school. I've seen a lot today, but I wasn't expecting to see this – floor 48 is unrecognisable. I'd have a better shot navigating the surface of Mars. It's dark; I can't even see the red glow from the exit signs. But the flashes from outside blaze with light and I can see everything clear as day in split-second intervals. Across from me is a classroom, sort of. The wall separating it from the hallway is gone. Lockers lie scattered and crushed beneath more broken cement. The windows are all shattered and the stormy wind blows through, cooling my cheeks. The lightning weaves outside like blue ribbons, and it kisses the walls and floor every so often. I flinch as lightning strikes the teacher's desk and the whole thing jumps and lands back down with a crash. The ceiling is slanted low, and there are sinister cracks branching out above me. If I stand on my toes I can touch it with my head.

How did this happen? A Move, but this is all too much. This can't be just any Move. I'm eight years old again and the wind's tickling my ears. Dad's yelling at me to get away from the window, but I don't listen. The lightning's dancing above our apartment building and I'm wrapped up in the show.

The floor below me is steady, stable. Dad wraps his right arm around me and hoists me off my feet to join Mom, who's soothing the screaming baby beneath the kitchen table. The storm rages, but I'm safe in Dad's grip. It's loud and it's noisy and the windows shatter, but the ground is stable.

This is so different.

So *powerful*.

The sound of Gabby's grunting pulls me back from the memory and I see her head trying to poke through the little gap in the door. One of the fallen, crunched-up lockers lies in front of it, barring her way.

I can hear the officers' voices, both of them shouting for us to stop.

'Hang on,' I say. The locker is weighed down by rubble and with all my might I can barely drag it a couple inches, but it's enough for Gabby to squeeze through. When she's finally out, I try to move it back to block the door. 'Gabby, help me!'

Her hands are over her mouth. Floor 48's a shock for Gabby too, but we don't have time for her to take it all in. BMAC is coming.

'Gabby!'

'Don't run!' The officers' voices are clear and loud, just beyond the door.

Gabby jumps down beside me and the two of us growl against the weight of the locker as the officers appear in the window. It budges forward and the door clicks off the latch and collides with the locker so there's nothing but a tiny crack that BMAC can't fit through.

Their furious faces scowl at us through the tiny window. 'Open this door,' shouts one of them, pounding on the glass.

The second officer isn't wasting time negotiating. There's a loud wham, wham, wham, as he throws his shoulder against it. The locker won't hold them long.

A nagging tingle in my skull begins to grow. My Shadow tries to connect, confusion swelling and shrinking at his end.

There's another locker on my left. It's leaning forward. With just a bit more weight . . .

I jump and grab the top of the leaning locker, pulling it down with a crash on top of the other, dust and rubble raining down as pieces of the ceiling come away.

'Run, Gabby! Run!' I grab her hand and drag her along as I race for where I think the north stairwell should be. There's junk and busted school all over the place and I trip and scrape my knee on a chunk of wall. I bite through the pain – no time to slow down – and pull Gabby along, hurdling fallen lockers and broken beams as I sprint down the hallway, but I'm not sure where I am. I'm just hoping the stairs are somewhere in this general direction.

My arm nearly gets ripped from my body as Gabby comes to an abrupt stop in front of a collapsed library room.

'Come on!' I order, yanking her after me.

She jerks her hand out of mine and points to a grey door hanging crooked on its hinges. 'The stairs.'

She's right.

I leap over what's left of the library wall and kick the crooked door aside.

The north stairwell is as bad as the rest of 48. The flight down to 47 has split in half, the lower half fallen down on top of 46.

'Gabriela Vargas?'

BMAC.

A surge of stomach juice shoots up from my gut, burning my throat.

I look up and there are two new agents, flying down the stairs at least five floors above us.

'Move Gabby, move!'

And then there's a *pop*.

I know that sound.

It doesn't sound like it does in the movies.

It's louder.

Sharper.

BMAC is shooting.

Pop.

Another shot and I cover myself, dropping to my knees. Hands are on my back, pushing me to keep going, and I'm surprised when I look back to see Gabby, nudging me on.

'Stop right there!' bellows the officer.

We don't.

'Go, Gabby, go!' I scream. She stays on my heels, prac- tically throwing her body down the staircase. We leap four stairs at a time, like maybe we can stay ahead of the bullets.

'Don't stop!' I yell, and Gabby's not about to. We have to get out of here.

And then there's a blast – an explosion – of blue-white

light somewhere above us and Gabby and I drop to the floor, arms over our heads as debris rains down. Lightning? How would lightning get in here?

I glance up, and I can hear the officers shouting, the pop of their guns firing wildly, but at what? Not us, something else. Something on one of the landings above them.

Birds. Dozens of ugly black crows circle above the screaming agents as a spark ignites somewhere in the middle of the flock.

And then, the rush.

A scream of wind fills my ears just before a whip of lightning explodes from the centre of the circling crows, striking out at the officers and splintering the staircase.

They fall. It's the last thing I see before I have to cover my eyes, the brightness nearly blinding me – BMAC, falling, crying out as they plummet in a blur of grey.

And then there's nothing. No shouting, no pop, no nothing.

Gabby peeks down over the railing while my blood thunders beneath my skin.

'BMAC?' I whisper. 'Are they . . . dead?'

Gabby ignores me and looks up, and I copy her. The BMAC agents are gone, but there's someone there – a tall, dark-haired man with square shoulders, dressed all in black. He's like a ghost, his face shrouded in the cloud of white. He's too old to be a student and he's definitely not wearing the usual grey of a BMAC agent. He stands there, staring down at us, and all I want to do is keep running, to get out before whoever that is up there blasts us the same way he did the agents.

Her muscles have locked up, but still she's shaking,

trembling. Her mouth hangs wide open as she stares up at the man.

'Gabby?'

She gasps at the air, trying to find her breath, gulping, hyperventilating, and for a second I'm worried she's about to have a stroke or something.

I look back to the figure leaning over the railing. He's just staring down at us, birds circling, like he's in no hurry to be anywhere else.

The man lifts his hand, and I brace myself for the blast. But there isn't one. Just the man's raised hand. A wave.

I hear Gabby gasp. When I turn back she's already running down the stairs, the fastest I've ever seen her move.

I hurry after her, looking back over my shoulder at the figure above us. The lightning. What kind of person can control lightning? From the look on Gabby's face, I think she knows the answer.

At the ground floor, the lobby is a mess. Half the school is running around, teachers barking orders, students looking for friends, BMAC agents and policemen trying their best to herd the masses of people out the door. It'll only take one person to recognise Gabby and we're screwed.

I hand her my hat but she doesn't notice, her eyes dead as she mutters to herself and wrings her hands.

I put the hat on her head for her and pull the bill over her face. I want to look back, to see if the man's behind us. But I don't. We had a big head start and we're in the crowd now. There's safety in the crowd – so long as no one stops us.

We keep our heads down and make our way to the doors, and I can feel a cold sweat beading along my back. Gabby's pretty easy to spot. How could anyone miss her?

To the right I see Mrs Dibbs and my heart nearly stops, but she's not even facing us. She's yelling at a bunch of the football team who are throwing around a bunch of school trophies that have fallen out of the shattered display case.

I can feel the breeze from outside on my cheek, and when I look back I'm standing in front of the doors. Gabby's already outside.

There's a tickle at the base of my neck, a mild irritation, and I know it's him – my Shadow – trying to get a feel for my emotions. I shake my head, shoving him away, and he tunes me out immediately. I'm over the *I'm-about-to-die* panic, and I guess that's good enough for him.

And then I see Ollie. He's standing over by the sign-in desk with Miss Farley and a bunch of BMAC officers. He's talking to the officers, his arms flailing wildly, and one of them scribbles down whatever he's saying. I duck my head and turn away before he can see me. *Movers don't have friends*.

My arms reach out and I push the revolving doors. The familiar wind of the Eventualies wraps itself around me and I breathe it in through my nose until my lungs can't take it any more.

SIX

Gabby and I make our way through the busy city streets. It's chaos. People running everywhere as the thunder blasts overhead. BMAC vehicles plough through the crowds, rushing to get to the school. I notice a woman with arms full of shopping bags; she's not looking at the sky like everyone else – but at Gabby, who hasn't stopped mumbling to herself since the stairwell, since the lightning man; her eyes have barely focused at all and she's still shaking.

'Gabby, pull it together, will you?'

But it's not just her. I knock shoulders with some business-suit man, and his eyes follow me, looking me up and down like I've just arrived from outer space. People are noticing *us*.

I look down at my shirt – it's practically white it's so covered in dust. My arms, my jeans, my shoes. Gabby's the same. We're filthy, scraped up, bruised and smothered in white chalky stuff.

'We have to get off the main road,' I say.

I don't need to say it twice. She's already ducked into a narrow alley, scurrying away from me and mumbling more. I follow after her, the sound of thunder drowning the echo of BMAC sirens back on the main road.

Gabby stops beside a dumpster that reeks of rotting food and pee, and digs around in her pockets.

'What are you doing?'

She acts like she hasn't heard me – maybe she didn't, she's so busy talking to herself – and pulls out a silver droidlet.

'Are you calling someone?'

No. She isn't. Before I can blink, she spikes the little sphere into the asphalt, shattering it into pieces.

'Gabby!'

She drops to her knees, sifting through the shards.

'What are you doing?!'

She reaches for a tiny plastic square of green and snaps it in two between her fingers, then scrambles to collect the rest of the pieces and drops it all into the dumpster before she whirls on me.

'Where's your droidlet?' She looks wild, crazy, as she glares me down.

I take a step back. 'Why? What do you care?'

Her hands grab hold of my collar. 'They'll track us! BMAC monitors droidlets!'

'What?' I can feel my heart rate kick into high gear and I reach into my back pocket. 'How do you know that?'

'*Everyone* knows that,' she growls.

I didn't. I bet a lot of people don't. But Gabby's not like a lot of people. She's a brainer.

'Your droidlet,' she says, holding out a demanding hand.

I feel around in my jeans and there's nothing there. 'It's gone,' I realise. 'I must have lost it back at school.'

Gabby looks at me for a moment, and when I guess she decides I'm not lying she backs off, leaning against the dumpster. She stares up at the sky, her chest rising and falling so quickly it looks almost painful. Whatever's scared her has scared her good.

'Gabby,' I say, 'what the breezes was that back there? The lightning, I mean. That guy just – he killed them with lightning!'

'It didn't feel any different.'

'What?'

'During the Move!' she says. 'I should have felt myself do it. I should have chosen to do it! But – nothing felt any different. For a Move to happen, the pungits have to get excited. If they're attached to me, I'm the one who has to decide to Move.'

'Pungits?' She's rambling about her Mover particle. 'Gabby, forget your stupid experiments. This is serious!'

'It's not stupid!' she screams at me. 'Pungits are the whole key to everything. Don't you get it? They are the tiny fragments of the universe that make a Mover Move! They reach through time and space and connect you to your Shadow and that's the whole reason this is happening!'

I don't have time to debate her theories. I don't even understand them anyway. 'Gabby, what are you talking about? What are you saying?'

'It's the whole reason he's here!'

Her mouth clamps shut, like she's just said something she shouldn't, and she turns away from me.

'You know him,' I say. That much is obvious. If I wasn't sure before, I'm positive now. I move in front of her and she tries to step around me but I'm faster. 'Gabby, I just put a whole lot on the line for you, so I think you need to start talking right now. Who was that man?'

'I think he . . .' Tears fill her eyes and she looks down at her feet to hide them. 'No, I know it. That man, he's my . . .' She stops, like she can't decide how to finish her sentence. Like she doesn't *want* to.

And then I understand why. 'Your Shadow,' I finish for her. 'Gabby, you think that guy on the stairs was your Shadow?'

She nods weakly.

'Your Shadow,' I say again, trying to get my head around the idea. 'Your Shadow?! But you told me – you *told* me you didn't do this!'

'I didn't!'

I grab my head, suddenly wanting to rip out all my hair. 'That doesn't make any sense!' I slam my foot against the dumpster, stubbing my toes, and the sting makes me bite down on my lip. 'Gabby,' I say, taking a deep breath, 'you either did it, or you didn't. It's not a grey area.'

'I didn't,' she insists.

'Then *what* are you talking about?'

She shakes her head, struggling for an explanation, and I'm mad at her for it. Mad at her for being so weird. For not talking to me, having a conversation, like a normal human being. She slides to the ground, pulling her knees up.

'Gabby! Just *answer* me!'

'I didn't feel anything,' she says finally. 'Not when the Move happened. The pungits that make up my connection, their energy levels should have skyrocketed. I would have felt that, if I'd done it. I would have *made* that happen. Shouldn't I have felt myself doing it?'

'How should I know?!' It's not like I've ever done it.

The Eventualies whistle as they funnel down the alleyway, rippling through my clothes, and I take another breath. You'd think she would have felt *something*. Even if her pungit theory was wrong. Whenever my Shadow pays attention to me, there's a tingle, a light burning in my head. And something else, swelling in the pit of my stomach, expanding kind of. I would have thought that when a Mover Moves someone it would feel like that, but . . . times a billion.

'You figured out the pungits,' she says suddenly.

'What?'

She looks away from me, drawing into herself the way she does at school. 'You messed with my pungits so you could get back here, didn't you? You did something to the connection on your end,' she goes on, and suddenly I feel like I'm alone in this alleyway. She's not talking to me at all. She's talking to—

The answer splits through my brain like lightning and all at once relief swells through me, so much that I crouch down in front of Gabby, grabbing her knees to get her to look at me.

She flinches.

'Gabby! Are you talking to your Shadow now? Is that who you've been mumbling to this whole time?'

She watches me, frowning, tears staining her cheeks.

68

'Can you feel him now? Can you feel where he is?' It's like the fog. I can tell how far away my Shadow is. And I'm only Phase 1. Not the exact year or anything, but still, I know my Shadow's not *here*, in this time. He's ahead of me. I *feel* him ahead of me. Shouldn't it be that way for Gabby? 'Is he far away or nearby?'

She thinks for a minute, and then her frown slides off her face. 'Far,' she says. 'But also close. But it's all messed up somehow. Noisy inside my head. I can't—'

Close. The thought scares me. Shadows are supposed to be in the future. That's where they belong. 'Gabby, he can't be in two places at once. If you can still feel him in the future, then he can't be here. Maybe you're wrong about the guy on the stairs. You're just confused. Maybe the guy just *looks* like whatever you think your Shadow looks like.'

Her eyes are huge, like an owl, as she looks at me. Finally she shakes her head, as if it hurts her to do it, tears falling down her cheeks. 'My head hurts too much. I don't know what I feel. But I do know it was him on the stairs. I know it. He was older, but it was him.'

And it's right there in her eyes. The truth of it. The truth of a Mover who knows her own Shadow.

'He's my Shadow, Pat,' she says, her voice breaking. 'I wish he wasn't, but . . .'

But he is. It's all over her. The guilt of it. I want her to be lying because it doesn't make sense. 'How . . .?' I start. 'How can he be here if you didn't Move him?'

She shakes her head. She's just as confused as I am. 'He must have done something to the pungits. Messed them up somehow.'

'Gabby, pungits aren't—'

Her wet eyes meet mine, like she knows what I'm going to say, and I stop. I don't want to debate the existence of her Movers particle right now. It's not helpful.

'You could still be wrong . . .' I tell her instead.

'I'm not,' she says. 'My Shadow's here.'

But my brain doesn't know how to process it. What she's saying is nonsense, pungits or no pungits. She either Moved him or she didn't.

'My Shadow's here,' she says again. 'What will BMAC do to me?'

There's an ache in my throat. What have I got myself into? I want to scream, groan, cry, laugh. I don't know what to do. If Gabby's right, if the lightning man on the stairs *is* her Shadow, then BMAC is going to be on the warpath. He killed two of their agents. Because of Gabby. Everyone was there, on that roof yard. They saw me help her. I just put myself between BMAC and a guilty Mover. Why did I do it? Why the breezes did I let myself get involved in this?

I slam my foot against the dumpster and the whole thing rattles.

And Gabby sniffles into her arms.

Because she's scared.

And when I look down at her I remember exactly why I helped her.

Because of Dad.

Since Sibichendosh's letter – Gabby could just as easily be Maggie.

I hear sirens and look back to the mouth of the alleyway.

Two more BMAC vehicles rush by on their way to Romsey. 'We need to get off the street.'

'And go where?' she says quietly.

Good question. BMAC's on the hunt for her. They've probably got a dozen officers at her house already. They might even be looking for me, if Miss Farley and Ollie told them who I am. This is big, I realise, and my brain feels like it's swelling, trying to sort out what we need to do. This is too big.

And then the East Grove lady is in my head – what Maggie asked me the other day on the fire escape. *Could Mom have helped her?*

Yes.

'We'll go to my place,' I say.

Gabby looks up, surprised.

But it's the best place to be. This is something Mom knows how to handle.

A distant rumble of thunder echoes over the sirens and I bite my lip.

If anyone will know what to do next, it's Mom.

SEVEN

'Mom!' The apartment's dark and silent. Everything's still and quiet just when all I want is noise. I want to hear her voice call out, nag me to fix the tank again, or pick up my clothes off the floor. There's only silence. 'Mom?' She's supposed to be here. She can't still be with Sibichendosh, can she?

I grind my teeth together to stop the floaty feeling.

'She might've gone to the school. Went to pick me up when she heard what happened,' I say. Or maybe she's still yelling at Sibichendosh. The walls of my stomach feel hot with nerves. 'I guess we'll just have to wait for her to get back.'

Gabby stands outside in the hall, staring at her feet.

'You coming?'

She doesn't acknowledge me. She's clawing at her finger, and the sound of her nails on her skin is grossing me out.

'Gab!'

She stops mid-scratch and her dark eyes meet mine.

'You wanna hang out in the hall all day?'

Without answering, she squeezes by me and into my home. I can't help but shake my head when she plops herself down on the doormat and tries to wriggle out of her tan leather cowboy boots. Gabby 'Gooba' Vargas is in my apartment.

'You, uh, want to call your parents?' I ask. 'They'll be freaking out.'

She shakes her head. 'No. They won't.'

Before I can ask what she means, there's a *thunk*. It's coming from the window. Another *thunk*.

It's Maggie's stupid bird, tapping on the glass.

I ignore it, watching Gabby free her left foot and start struggling to release the right. The effort's too much for her, I guess, and she takes a break, leaning her head back against the wall.

'You can use my mom's smartdesk,' I tell her. 'They'll want to know you're OK—'

'I don't want to call them, all right? It's fine.'

I shut my mouth. I don't understand, but she clearly doesn't want to explain, so I leave it alone.

Gabby pulls my hat off her head and a cloud of dust falls off. My own skin feels choked and sticky from being covered. I want a shower.

She shakes her head to let more dust fall away, then holds the hat out for me without looking up.

My throat is dry and ticklish – I can taste that chalky dust clinging to the back of my tongue – and I need water.

'You want a drink?' I ask, taking back my hat.

She acts like I haven't said anything. Just goes back to struggling with her boot. She does that a lot, ignores what I said. I wonder if it's just cos she's not used to talking to people.

73

I sigh and figure that's a yes.

Another *thunk* from Beauty.

I head over to the cupboards and grab a blue plastic cup for myself. 'Water OK?' Gabby just sits there on the floor, scratching anxiously at her finger. At least she's not talking to herself. I reach in for another blue cup and turn the tap. The pipes groan and a sad brown drip trickles out.

Right. The tank's still busted. So I guess a shower's out.

I pull open the fridge, looking for something else. All we have is Pretty Pruny's Princess Juice – some purple lemonade junk that Mom buys for Maggie. 'Do you like Pruny's?'

Gabby shakes her head. No. Me neither.

Frustrated, I toss the cups into the sink and lean against the counter. The tickle in my throat is strangling me. I try to clear it, hacking and coughing.

Gabby glances in my direction.

I guess that was gross.

'Sorry,' I say, and she goes back to scratching her finger.

'You think I'm crazy, don't you?'

Her voice is so quiet I'm not sure I heard her. 'What?'

'You think my experiments are stupid,' she says.

I just stare at her, not sure what to say to that, or why she wants to talk about it, considering we've got bigger problems.

'It's OK,' she says. 'Everyone thinks it's stupid. Even Mrs Dibbs.'

Her chin is in her chest while she picks harder at her finger, and I find myself feeling a bit bad that I've never really bothered to listen to her presentations. But that was only because I could never understand them.

'I think the stuff you say is just over Mrs Dibbs's head.'

I can tell from the curious look on her face that she's never considered that as a possibility. So I figure it's best to just be honest. 'No one really knows what you're talking about, so we all just kind of zone out. Price you pay for being too bright, I guess.'

Gabby smiles and blushes. I don't think I've ever seen her smile. I hadn't meant it as a compliment. It's always just been a fact. Gabby's smarter than everybody. I guess the only person who didn't know that was Gabby.

She looks back at her lap and tucks her hands away beneath her. At last she's stopped the scratching.

The two of us are silent then, alone in the apartment together. I still have that chalk taste on my tongue, and I try to clear it as quietly as I can. I feel it on my skin too. And it's starting to itch. I need to get out of these clothes.

I head to the bedroom – Beauty squawking at me from the other side of the glass – and dig through the hamper. I pull out a red sweatshirt and lay it on the bed, then peel off the dust-caked T-shirt, using it to wipe what's left on my arms. Another *thunk* from Beauty, and when I look over at the window I see Gabby reflected in the glass. She's leaning forward, watching me from her spot on the floor. She jumps when she sees me looking at her and goes back to staring at her lap.

Heat rushes to my cheeks. Quickly I throw on the sweat-shirt.

'You, uh, want to change?'

She pulls at her shirt, letting the dust puff off it with each pull. She nods without looking at me.

Beauty pecks at the window again. *Damn bird.* I lift it open for her, just to make the pecking stop.

The bird makes a beeline for the bathroom door and slams into it so hard it knocks her to the floor.

Gabby frowns, confused.

'That's Beauty.' I shrug. 'Can't get rid of her.'

Gabby nods, as if she gets it, and Beauty shakes her feathers and squawks at me.

Stupid.

Gabby's eyes flick to me, expectantly.

'Right! Clothes.'

I open the drawer to Mom's dresser and root through what she has. Mom clothes. Fitted work stuff. The heat in my cheeks gets warmer. This was a mistake. Nothing of Mom's is gonna fit Gabby.

I hear a creak and turn to see Gabby standing in the bedroom, leaning against Mom's smartdesk. Her face is red. 'It's OK,' she says.

And I feel like it's really not OK. I'm so uncomfortable and mad at myself for making the offer that I throw open drawer after drawer, throwing Mom's clothes as Beauty rams herself into the bathroom door a couple more times. 'I'm sure we have something,' I say.

But I'm not.

Sweat prickles my forehead as I throw open the bottom drawer – my last shot – and the crisp folded clothes looking back at me make me freeze. Dad's clothes. I didn't even know Mom still had any.

I reach for a blue checked button-up – I remember him wearing this.

Gabby clears her throat, and I realise she's waiting for me. Beneath the blue checked shirt is a paint-spattered T-shirt. His weekend work shirt. I snatch it. 'This should do.'

I spin round and toss the shirt to Gabby. She doesn't catch it. She picks it up off the floor and opens it up, holding it against herself. It looks big enough. Her fingers run over the paint stains.

'Sorry, it's all I could find. My dad was kind of a messy painter.'

She looks at the checked shirt still clutched in my left hand. 'I didn't know my mom kept any of this stuff.' I fold it up quickly and place it gently back in the drawer. 'I haven't seen most of it since—' I stop. I don't talk about Dad to people. I don't even like talking about Dad with Maggie.

'—he was Shelved,' Gabby finishes.

She inhales suddenly, like she can't believe what she's just said. I can't either.

'You know about that?' I mean, it's not like what happened to Dad is a secret. But it was so long ago, and I don't ever talk about it. I didn't realise kids at school knew anything about my dad. Or cared to know anyway. But Gabby knows.

'I just . . .' She shifts on her feet, not daring to look at me. 'I just, I remember reading about it.'

'It happened forever ago.'

'Yeah, but I read a lot, cos of my research.' She waves a hand, like *You know, that stuff.* 'I um, I saw your last name on an article and so I . . .' She trails off, her cheeks as red as two stop signs. And she does stop. She bites her lip and glances at me quickly and then at the shirt in her hands.

The two of us stand there, both of us staring awkwardly at the floor.

Beauty rams against the bathroom door and the sound is deafening in the silence between me and Gabby.

It's too quiet in here.

I reach over and swipe the surface of Mom's desk and tap the TV icon. The screen is projected on the wall above the desk. *Avin News*.

There it is. Romsey.

Helicopter footage of a skyscraper in the middle of a chaotic city. It's our school – sort of – if it had just been through a battle. Whole chunks have fallen away and pretty much all the windows are gone. The sky above it is cloudy, but the storm has definitely passed. *Movement activity at the Romsey Institute for Academics* flashes along the bottom of the screen.

'. . . with the Eventualies reaching speeds of up to 182 kilometres per hour,' says the newscaster. 'The highest recorded wind speed of any Movement activity in history, beating the previous record of 174.'

I flinch. 174 was Dad's record.

The damage looks even worse from the outside. I've never seen a Move do anything like that. Not even Dad's. Busted windows, sure. But never that.

'While BMAC has acknowledged the irregularity of such a violent Move,' the anchor drones on, 'they have yet to comment on what could have accounted for the change. Some Movement experts have theorised that this could be evidence of a new, more powerful phase.'

I nearly choke.

A new phase?

Gabby practically collapses, taking a seat on the bed, mouth gaping at the screen.

What does that mean? A 'new phase'? Is that even possible?

And then Gabby gasps.

Because her face is on the screen. And my gut drops into my feet. Her face is on the screen next to mine. 'BMAC has provided these images of the suspects and has asked that anyone with information regarding the whereabouts of Gabriela Vargas and Patrick Mermick contact the BMAC hotline.'

Suspects?! They're calling *us* suspects? They think Gabby's this new phase? Is that what they think?

I remember what she said in the alley, about her Shadow being two places at once. Is that part of it? This new phase? Could that explain it? She said she thought he messed with her pungits things. Could this be some new phase where your Shadow can Move without your permission?

I think I'm going to throw up.

Mom needs to get home. *Now.*

Something cool spreads across my mind, my Shadow, feeling the terror that's firing through my head like firecrackers.

I *am* going to throw up.

I scramble out of the chair and throw open the bathroom door, lifting the lid on the toilet. Beauty flaps in behind me and rests on the tap. I stare into the still, clear water, the sloshy stomach juices rising and falling but nothing comes out. *Suspect.* What does BMAC do to suspects?

They'll come for me. This is the first place they'll look.

'Pat?' A new voice takes me by surprise, and I fall back as the cupboard under the sink opens up.

Beauty lets out a triumphant squawk.

There's Maggie, covered in dirt, her hair a mess of tangles.

'Mags!' All I want is for Mom to open the front door. 'What are you doing here!? Where's Mom!'

Her eyes are swollen and her face is blotchy. She's been crying. A lot.

'They took her,' she says.

'What? Who?'

'Officer Kelley.'

BMAC.

My brain seizes and I can't even think.

Maggie starts pulling on her braid, nervously. Mom's not coming.

Maggie's chin starts to quiver and she squeaks out, 'I think I'm in big trouble.'

EIGHT

I hurry into the kitchen and grab a pink cup. Maggie's melting down. She can't even speak through the gasps and the tears and I need for her to keep it together long enough to tell me what happened to Mom. I fling open the fridge and there it is – Pretty Pruny's Princess Juice. With my thumb I flick off the cap and pour half a cup's worth, nearly spilling it as I sprint back to my sobbing sister.

Gabby's standing in front of the bathroom door, and I shoulder past her and join Maggie on the floor.

'Here, Mags.' She's shaking too much and I have to hold the cup to her lips. 'It's Pruny's.'

She guzzles, eventually calming down enough to hold the cup herself.

Her little throat throbs with each glug and her cheeks are filthy. Her hair is a mess too, still in her braid but the rich bronzy brown is dull.

She puts down the cup and gasps like she's just come up from the deepest dive of all time.

'OK, Mags,' I say, sounding entirely more steady than I feel, 'what happened?'

Her eyes are still glossy, but she's got her breath back. 'Officer Kelley was at the school with Mr Sibichendosh. They said I had to go for tests.'

'Tests?'

'Tests for what?' asks Gabby, standing in the doorway.

The blue envelope and Sibichendosh's handwriting flash across my brain. 'For an upgrade?'

She nods. 'Mom said no, she wouldn't let me. But . . . but Officer Kelley said she had to take me, said it was the law. '

Variety of behaviours.

'Then what?'

'Mom – Mom said she'd take me to BMAC herself, but Officer Kelley said no. That's when Mom picked me up. She never picks me up!' It's true. Mom always told her she was too big for that. 'So Mom told Officer Kelley she was coming with me, no matter what.

'Officer Kelley put us in the back of her car and was going to drive us to BMAC. The car slowed down. We stopped at a light. Mom – Mom told me to run.'

I blink. 'What!?'

'I didn't know what she meant at first. She went like this—'

Maggie opens her mouth really wide and says, *Run!* without making a sound.

'I wasn't sure what she wanted me to do, so I – so I just sat there. Officer Kelley's our friend, BMAC is our friend!'

She's young enough to still buy BMAC's stupid primary song.

'The light turned green,' Maggie continues. 'The crowds started moving out of the way, and she reached over me. She opened the door and she shoved me out. It hurt. I scraped my hands on the road.' She inspects her palms and I can see they're scraped up and red. 'And then Mom screamed, *Run, Maggie girl! Run!* And Officer – Officer Kelley – shouted at me to stop. I got scared. And Mom kept yelling, "Run!" So I did. I ran.' She's gasping again, the tears overwhelming her. 'I saw your school and I ran inside to find you. I didn't know what else to do! But your school was too big and some teacher yelled at me so I went and hid in a locker.'

'You came to my school?'

She nods. 'That's when the storm started, and I got so afraid. Everyone was running and screaming and saying we had to get out of the building. So I came here.' She gasps a few times between sobs. 'It's all my fault! This is all my fault!'

The rest of her words are drowned in phlegmy sputters and I grab her and hug her tightly to me. She cries on my shoulder and I feel a lump rising in my throat. Mom's not coming. She's really not coming.

'Do you think Mom got Shelved?' Maggie wails.

I hope not. I mean, she's not a Mover, so why would they? But she's definitely done something really bad. And BMAC isn't going to be happy about it.

'Why would she do that?' The question tumbles out of my mouth all on its own. 'Why would she make Maggie run away from BMAC? Running is so much worse than being upgraded, isn't it?'

Maggie just goes on crying and Beauty perches protectively on my sister's head.

'Maybe she was afraid of the tests,' says Gabby. 'Afraid BMAC would discover something.'

I look up at Gabby, who's leaning against the door frame, staring at her finger.

'Discover what?'

Gabby shrugs. 'Something scarier than an upgrade.'

The tremor in my bones feels like a quake, and it's like I'm back on the roof yard. 'What's scarier than an upgrade?'

She shrugs again. 'I don't know.'

Gabby turns back to the news, completely oblivious to the tornado of questions she's set off in my head.

Maggie lifts her head off my shoulder, wiping away stray strands of hair from her eyes as Beauty pecks lovingly through her tangled curls.

'What do we do, Pat?'

I have no idea. No Mom means no plan. We're on our own. I bite my lip and try not to scream, pulling my hat over my face.

BMAC has Mom.

BMAC's calling me a suspect.

And Maggie.

BMAC's looking for Maggie.

They'll come looking for us. They are probably already on their way.

Dad's voice echoes through my head. *You need to take care of her . . .*

It's up to me now.

'Pat—' Maggie's cut off by a knock at the door. Beauty screeches.

The muffled sound of a man's voice is on the other side.
'Patrick Mermick—'

My breath catches on my ribs.

'Maggie, sweetie—' a woman's voice now – 'it's Officer Kelley.'

My blood drains down into my feet.

BMAC's already here.

NINE

'If you're in there, open the door, honey,' says Officer Kelley's singsong voice.

Open the door. I glance at the screen, my face, Gabby's face, *PHASE 4???????* scrolling across the whole of it. BMAC will Shelve us for this.

'Maggie, please open the door.'

I hear a snap of fingers and look over at Gabby. *Droidlet,* she mouths, and points at my sister.

That's how BMAC monitors you.

Beauty flaps her wings anxiously as Maggie pulls the little purple device out of her pocket.

'They *know* Maggie's in here,' Gabby whispers.

I snatch it out of her hand, creep over to the window and chuck the droidlet out onto the street below.

'Patrick Mermick?' The door-knocking turns to banging and this time the man speaks. 'This is Officer Simpson with the Bureau of Movement Activity Control. This is your first warning.'

Part of me stupidly hoped they'd just disappear as soon as the droidlet did.

'It's in your best interest to co-operate, young man.'

But they're still here.

BMAC is here.

I'm seven years old, BMAC swarming our tiny apartment. They took Dad. They Shelved him.

You have to protect her . . .

'This is the last chance I am giving you, young man. Open this door.'

Run. That's what Mom told Maggie to do.

We have to run.

Run where?

'If you do not comply in the next five seconds, we have the authority to open this door ourselves.'

I glance at the window – maybe we could climb down the fire escape. Head down to the street, make a run for the underground.

No. The fire escape is the only way out of here. It's the first place they'll check.

We can't run.

'One . . .'

We need to hide.

'Two . . .'

I lunge for the closet, pushing through the hanging clothes and storage boxes, running my hands along the back wall. My heart hammers in my chest so hard it might explode. It's too dark, I can't see. But the panel's here, I know it is.

'Three . . .'

My Shadow's picking through my brain, annoyed and

nervous because I'm radiating panic again. My fingernails catch in a narrow slit and I dig in, the panel coming away with a quiet crack.

'Four . . .'

I turn back to Maggie, whose eyes are wide with surprise. Mom managed to keep the second closet a secret from Mags at least.

'Five!'

The sound of the bangs gets louder. BMAC is ramming the door with what I assume is Officer Simpson's shoulder.

Gabby's the first to move, squeezing herself into the little space behind the panel.

There's a sound, like a drill, back at our front door and Maggie jumps. A ping as the hinges fall to the floor. BMAC's coming in.

'Mags,' I whisper, calling her attention back from the door.

She reaches out for my hand, ducking into the closet, Beauty flapping in after her. I'm not sure that's a good idea but there's no time. I nearly trip over the boxes on the floor as I squish myself between my sister and Gabby. I grab hold of the closet door and close it carefully as the front door falls in with a bang.

BMAC's inside.

My head screams with panic and I breathe in too quick and too fast, in time with my rapid heartbeat, and pull the panel closed. It's pitch black. My sister's hand is hot, wrapped around my index and middle fingers. Gabby's breath brushes my cheek in short fast bursts. And my Shadow, he's pinging against the walls of my skull like a nervous fish in a bowl.

He doesn't understand what's happening. He can't under-stand. I shove him out of the front of my mind, all my focus devoted to breathing as quietly as I can.

The three of us listen, but there's nothing to hear except for the nervous clucking coming from Beauty, who's sitting on my sister's shoulder. I'm not sure how much we can hear from outside, hidden in the wall. I'm not sure about a lot of things. And they all come rushing at once. I'm not sure how long we'll have to hide here. Not sure how long it will be before Officer Kelley and her friend figure out where we've gone. I'm not sure what BMAC does to *suspects*. What they'll do to us if we're caught. Would they take us to Mom? I doubt it. And what's worst of all is I don't know what they've done with her.

No. That's not worst of all. What's worst of all right now is not understanding why Mom made Maggie run away. And Mom's not here to explain it to me.

Maggie squeezes my fingers tight as we hear a soft thudding. Feet on the carpet. BMAC's in the bedroom.

Beauty's clucking stops.

I hear voices. Officer Simpson's hums through the walls, along with a higher-sounding voice – Officer Kelley. It's a muffled conversation but I can just make it out.

'Someone's been watching the news,' announces Officer Kelley.

'Because they're here. The signal from the girl's droidlet was coming from inside,' growls Simpson.

There's the sound of footsteps as BMAC steps further into the room. Officer Kelley's calling out for Maggie while the footsteps move ever closer.

'It seems to be coming from outside.' Officer Kelley's voice is easy to hear now and Gabby's noisy breathing has stopped. 'No one out on the fire escape.'

'Message the street unit,' snaps Officer Simpson. 'If they are already outside I don't want them getting away.'

I hear a lot of rustling, cupboards opening and closing.

'Afraid of Special Agent Hartman, are you, Simpson?' Officer Kelley laughs.

'The Mermick woman should be afraid of Hartman,' he grumbles.

Mom.

'Hartman's going to have those kids Shelved faster than Mermick can scream *Shelf-Meat.*'

Shelved.

Maggie's little fingernails dig into my hand, her whole body trembling beside me.

The click of the closet door. A sliver of light where the panel meets the wall, practically blinding, it seems so bright now. I just hope it's not as obvious to BMAC as it is to me.

'They're still just children, Simpson,' says Kelley.

'And I'm just doing my job, Kelley.' Officer Simpson's voice is clear as a bell as he rifles through the boxes and clothes on the other side of the wall. 'Besides, they're not *just children*. They're Movers.'

I feel Maggie and Gabby press closer to me and my eyes close on their own. *Please, oh please, don't find us.*

More rustling. A shadow moves across the sliver of light and my muscles twitch, ready for a fight.

And then the sliver's gone. The closet door clicks closed.

'All clear,' says Simpson, his voice safely muffled.

Maggie's grip relaxes just a bit and I can feel Gabby's breath on my cheek again.

'I've got some pretty grimy clothes here,' says Kelley. 'Looks like the brother came home with the Vargas girl. Maggie's probably with them. Check if the neighbours have seen them?'

Simpson grunts what I guess is agreement and their footsteps move away from the closet. Their voices fade to murmurs as they head back towards the kitchen. It sounds like they're getting ready to leave.

And then there's silence.

The three of us stand there, frozen in the dark.

And I can't hold it in any more.

My stomach twists, and I spew bile down the front of my hoody.

TEN

We haven't heard a sound for – what? – fifteen minutes? Twenty? The three of us just stand there in the dark, listening to our frightened breaths and Beauty's clucking. The smell of my puke is sour, burning my nose. I can't stand it any more and reach out for the panel.

'No!' squeaks Maggie, pulling my arm back.

We can't stay here for ever. 'It's OK,' I whisper.

Her grip on my arm loosens, and quietly I crack open the panel. There's no light. Officer Simpson closed the closet door before he left. I step out of Mom's secret hideaway, my ankle rolling as my foot slips on an old sneaker, and reach for the closet door. Slowly I pull down on the handle and nudge it open barely an inch.

I wait, listening for BMAC.

Nothing but the sound of the news channel.

I dare a bit more, peeking just my head through the opening, and look out at the empty bedroom. The beds are crooked, shifted from their usual spots. One of the mattresses has been flipped. The drawers of Mom's dresser are all open, and the hamper's been dumped all over the floor. They tore the place up.

There's a squawk and a flutter of wind as Beauty suddenly lands on my shoulder. When I open the door enough, she takes to the air, circling the room, and I hold my breath, afraid I'm going to hear Simpson or Kelley call out.

Nothing.

Heart thumping, I take a step out of the safety of the closet and creep over to the kitchen doorway. The front door lies on top of the mat, but the apartment hallway beyond it is empty. The cupboards are all open, pots and pans tossed all over the floor.

And I feel him creeping in – my Shadow, wondering what the hell is going on.

BMAC is what's going on.

I take another breath and the smell of my puke makes me dizzy.

'Pat?'

The room is spinning. And my Shadow's presence buzzes through my temples with worry.

'Pat?' Maggie says behind me. 'Is it OK?'

No. None of this is OK.

I look back at the closet, Maggie and Gabby's heads poking out, frightened eyes looking at me.

My stomach lurches and I grab my knees, dry heaving onto the carpet. There's nothing in me, but my gut wants to vomit anyway. My insides strain, it hurts so bad. Maybe I'm gonna puke up my heart, who knows?

A little hand falls lightly on my back.

93

Maggie.

The tingle of my Shadow fades as he retreats from me – I'm alive, and that's good enough for him, I guess. I wipe the drool from my chin with the back of my wrist and turn round to face my little sister.

How am I supposed to protect her?

There's a thud and the sound of things falling as Gabby trips on her way out of the closet. The door swings open and she falls to the floor, a box toppling over and spilling out onto the rug.

Gabby looks up at me, embarrassed.

But I'm not looking at her. I'm looking at what's behind her – Mom's secret panel, open. A stack of boxes are tucked in the corner, just like the one Gabby knocked over.

And droidlets.

Dozens of them have rolled out onto the carpet, one resting against my shoe.

I bend down and hold it up. It's dead. A plastic film is stuck over the eye – the camera part. *Strip to activate*. It's a blank. Brand new.

Gabby hoists herself off her knees and stares at the object in my hand, 'How does your mom have a stash of blank droidlets?'

When you need a new droidlet you put in an application to the Service Avin offices. They program it with your FIILES and tell you when it's ready for pick-up. You can't just get your hands on a blank droidlet. And even if you could, it's useless without someone to program it.

I frown in the reflection of the droidlet's smooth plastic surface.

Someone to program it.

Mom grabbed three droidlets from the closet this morning – *one, two, three* – and popped them in her bag. It was right after that guy called, the one from Hexall. Mom's programmer guy.

'Leonard.'

Gabby frowns. 'What?'

Three droidlets. Mom, Maggie, me. That's what Leonard was calling for. She must have been planning to get us new FIILES. Mom was getting ready to run.

And Leonard would help her do that.

Maggie tugs gently on my arm. 'Pat?'

Run from BMAC? That's insane! That's criminal! Crazy! My eyes flick to Gabby, remembering what she said about Mom being scared. Scared of what? What could be so bad she'd risk something like this? I think of Dad, of Oscar Joji, and BMAC swarming the apartment. She wanted to run then. I remember. Mom begged Dad to run.

Whatever Mom's afraid of, it's big. Big enough to get new identities for.

'We gotta go,' I say, snatching up two more loose droidlets.

'Where?' says Gabby.

'Hexall Hall.'

Maggie gasps. Because she knows what I know. She knows what everyone knows. Hexall Hall isn't safe. It's all Movers – runaways who've been kicked out of their homes, or kids whose parents were Shelved and left them with nothing. They survive by gambling, fortune-telling and busking. And the forebrawls. I've never seen a forebrawl in real life, and I don't think I want to.

But forebrawlers aren't what make people afraid. It's the others that scare them – wanted Movers and Shadows. Criminals. Hiding from BMAC.

Gabby's expression doesn't change. There's no fear there. 'Why?' she says, her voice even.

I hold up one of the blank droidlets. 'My mom has a friend. He makes phoney . . .' I stop. How do I explain this? I've spent so long not talking about it – not wanting to talk about it. So long pretending not to know. My tongue practically knots in my mouth, so conditioned to bite when it comes to Mom and what she does.

'Phoney what?' says Gabby, her forehead crinkling as she looks at the droidlet. 'Not FIILES?'

I bite my lip. Gabby will know now. She'll know Mom's secret.

But she needs to know, if she's going to trust me on this.

I nod.

Gabby's eyebrows spring up, surprised. Or maybe horrified. And she takes a step back.

'My mom helps Movers,' I blurt out. 'Movers and Shadows who need to get away from BMAC. I think this Leonard knows how to do this stuff. He's my mom's friend. She was going to go see him today. Whatever made Mom tell Maggie to run, whatever she's afraid of, it upset her enough to risk getting us new FIILES. Her guy called this morning, I think because she wanted him to set them up. They were going to meet today, at Hexall Hall. He can help us, you see?'

And maybe he knows, some part of me hopes, he *has*

96

to know what this is all about, what Mom's so worried about. This guy, this Leonard, he can tell me what I need to know.

Gabby stares at the droidlet in my hand and I can see the gears in her mind working to process what I've said.

'What choice do we have?' I ask her.

Gabby's black eyes meet mine, staring into them so hard I want to look away. But I don't. I'm right about this, about Leonard. It's the only option. And I need Gabby to believe me.

Finally she nods. 'OK,' she says. 'We'll go.'

We'll go. A sense of relief moves through me, as though having Gabby agree makes my plan more real. But I shouldn't be relieved. No one I know has ever been to Hexall Hall. No one I know would ever want to go down into that place.

No, I realise, that's not true. Mom's been there. Maybe more than once. And she was planning to go there again. But she can't now. Only I can.

'Hexall Hall,' whispers Maggie through her bitten finger-nails. She shakes her head, Beauty bobbing anxiously on her shoulder. 'It isn't safe.'

Gabby scratches at her finger and looks up at the screen above Mom's desk. There we are again, me and Gabby, our faces side by side on *Avin News*.

Not safe?

'Right now,' I sigh, 'Hexall Hall is the safest place to be.'

ELEVEN

The daylight's fading by the time we're scurrying down side streets to the Crossline Path that leads to the east end of the city. I'm wearing a pair of Mom's giant sunglasses and they're tinting everything so dark in the dwindling light I want to rip them off my face. But I don't. With our pictures all over the place, I can't risk someone recognising us. The three of us look ridiculous – me in an oversized hoodie and lady's sunglasses, Maggie with her hair tucked up under my baseball hat, wearing a pair of overalls and one of my old T-shirts, with Beauty perched on her shoulder. She looks enough like a boy in that get-up to keep her from being recognised, at least. And Gabby. She's wearing my dad's paint-spattered shirt and a blue scarf wrapped around her head. It's not really a scarf. It was part of my Nano Ninja Halloween costume from a few years ago. But it hides her hair, and if we really need her to, she can pull the mask part up over her mouth to cover her face, though that would probably call more attention to her than anything.

So far the disguise has been enough to foil BMAC. Simpson and Kelley posted guards at every exit of the apartment building. We figured if the three of us left together, they'd notice. So I went first. I slipped through the side door, the two officers posted there too busy answering nosy old Mr Carrol's questions to notice me. I waited around the block for the other two. Maggie and Gabby came a little while later, after they'd blended into a family of four on their way out to dinner.

I keep my hood up and my head down, my hand gripping Maggie's firmly. I've never been further east than the Upway Path and I'm starting to wonder how many people have actually visited this part of the city. The neighbourhoods are dark thanks to busted streetlights and the buildings are shabby and worn. The smell is awful – like hot sour farts, thanks to the garbage. It's piled up high in heaps beside the road. I guess sending it to the dump just means making the city dump bigger and it will end up overflowing here anyway. Easier to leave the mess and move away than clean it up. It's like everyone just decided to forget this part of town exists – as if there were an invisible wall around it, cutting it off completely from the rest of Avin.

Movers are best forgotten.

I look back at Gabby, who walks with her head down, her arms wrapped around her middle. I don't think everyone will be able to forget about her so easily. Not after what happened at school. What she did. What *did* she do? Her Shadow's here – that's what she told me. After huge, wildly violent Movement activity, Gabby's Shadow is here. But she says she didn't Move him. Not on purpose, I guess. Is BMAC right? Is Gabby some kind of new phase? Some new phase where they can Move someone from the future without even feeling it? Without even trying?

What'll that mean? Will doors start opening up all the time now? If there are people out there who can't control their Moves, we could have Movement happening at any given moment, new Shadows arriving every day. There's no way BMAC can allow that. BMAC *won't* allow it. If there are more people out there like Gabby, BMAC'll hunt them down and Shelve them all. I know it. And Gabby will be first on their list.

Gabby's Shadow is here. But she said he was ahead of her too. A Shadow here *and* in the future?

'My head hurts,' Maggie whines. She scratches at her hair, frowning up at me. 'Can we take a break?'

'No,' I say.

I look back for Gabby. She's facing the Avin Turbine.

I stop, noticing it for the first time since we left my apartment. I don't think it's ever looked so far away.

'Gabby?'

She jumps, a squeal escaping her as she whirls round.

'What's wrong?' I ask.

She quickens her step until she's walking alongside me. 'N-nothing.'

I don't buy it.

Gabby starts shaking her head, like there's water in her ear that she can't get out.

I glance down at Maggie, her lips pursed. She doesn't buy it either.

'Gabby.' There's an edge to my voice that I can't hide. But she's doing Gooba-like things again, and I need her to keep it together. 'Just tell me.'

Gabby chews the inside of her cheek, like she's holding back whatever it is she wants to say. She turns and looks back at the Avin Turbine, spinning in the distance.

'He's mad at me,' she says finally.

'Your Shadow?'

She nods. 'He'll find me. I know he will.'

'Why do you say that?'

She doesn't say anything, just scratches harder at her finger.

Maggie shifts on her feet, her grip on my hand getting tighter. She's scared enough about going to Hexall Hall. This kind of talk from Gabby isn't making anything easier on her. Or me. A rush of cold works its way up my spine as I remember the two BMAC agents on the stairs, their screams as they fell fifty flights.

Because of Gabby's Shadow.

'Gabby,' I say, 'why do you think he's gonna find you?'

She shakes her head again, knocking loose the imaginary water.

'Hello?!'

She sucks at the cut she's made on her finger, her eyes blank as she thinks. 'I just . . . I can feel it. Like you said, about feeling him in the future . . .?'

'Yeah . . .'

'I did, I mean, I still do . . .'

I wait, watching her look back the way we've come.

'But,' she says finally. Her hands go to her head and

she winces. 'But it's like there's two of him. One far ahead but one . . . right up close.'

'You only have one Shadow, Gabby,' I say, as if I'm explaining how Shadows work to a little kid. But Gabby knows how Shadows work. She knows more about it than I do.

'It feels strange,' she says, ignoring what I said. 'It's all so muddled – like, like being in a room full of shouting people.'

'Like listening to two songs at once?' asks Maggie.

'Yeah,' agrees Gabby, and I look down at my sister, surprised at the insight. Maggie just scratches her head.

'What does that mean?' Gabby asks.

'I don't know,' I say. 'Maybe that's just what happens in your head after your Shadow comes to your time,' I try. 'And maybe that's a good thing. If it's muddled for you, it must be muddled for him, right? It'll make it hard to find you. Maybe he won't even bother.'

She shakes her head and starts to walk. 'You don't know him like I do.'

No, I don't. And after what he did to those BMAC officers, I don't want to. I watch Gabby walk ahead of us and I give Maggie's arm a gentle tug to catch up. If Gabby's Shadow is looking for her, then all the more reason to get to Mom's Leonard friend as fast as possible.

The light grows dimmer the further we walk. The tight apartments are steadily more dumpy, boarded up and falling apart.

There's a strong smell of skunk as we walk by a group of older kids sitting on a stoop, smoking.

'Don't make eye contact,' I mutter to Maggie.

One of them stops the chitchat and points in our direction, and I quickly look at the ground.

One after another, in groups or alone, the people of this neighbourhood watch us make our way through the streets. Everyone seems surprised to see us, and I pull my hood down over my eyes, uncomfortably aware of how much we must stick out. Covering our faces doesn't matter much here – our age, our clean clothes, even the way we're shuffling along all give us away as nervous outsiders.

Then again, we probably look the same as everybody who comes to hide out at Hexall Hall for the first time.

Gabby stops suddenly and points across the street. 'Is that it?'

My eyes follow her finger to a massive grey building – pillars, boarded windows, the whole lot. In the brick above what must have been an impressive open entrance once upon a time are carved chipped letters: Hexall Hall.

It's busy, like Fellows Junction Train Station in the middle of the Upway Path, only this place is harsher. There are crowds of people moving in and out, huddled in groups, laughing and talking, but the feeling is nothing like Junction. It's buzzing with something darker, greasier, like it's suffocating under the same stinking film that's clinging to the rest of the neighbourhood.

There's a white glow leaking out between the cracks in the window boards and I can hear music, a heavy drumbeat and some mechanical, rhythmic rattling noise.

'It smells funny,' says Maggie. 'I don't wanna go in there.'

It does smell funny. Like barbecue, salty cheese and dirt.

I shrug and step out onto the road. 'We can't just stand here all night.'

A *ka-caw* from Beauty stops me.

I turn back and Maggie's standing on the sidewalk, rubbing her left arm nervously, her chin quivering.

'Pat,' she says, her voice choked. 'No.'

'It's OK, Mags.' I hold out my hand. 'I promise.'

She still doesn't move, her big eyes begging me not to make her do this. I don't want to make her do this. It physically hurts, in my chest, to see her so afraid. But there's nowhere else for us to go. Leonard is our only shot and he's here, in Hexall Hall. Somewhere.

The match, that's all he said on the phone. Probably a forebrawl match. I just have to find it, which shouldn't be too hard. Forebrawl matches are big business down here. Hexall Hall is always on the news because of their trouble at forebrawls – fights between Movers. People gamble on them. Supposedly the fighters listen to their Shadows, who read the forebrawl books. Every time a fighter takes a swing, the judges record the strike in the forebrawl books, which the Shadow allegedly reads in the future. That way, the Shadow is supposed to help their Mover anticipate their opponent's next Move. It's all a big scam, but enough Nowbies and Phase 1s don't seem to realise that, and they sink a lot of money into it. And just because it's a scam doesn't make the fighting part any less real.

'Come on, Maggie,' I say. 'We don't have time for this. Let's go.'

'But—' her voice squeaks, right on the edge of tears. 'But Mom wouldn't want us to go in there. We need to wait for Mom.'

'We've been over this, Mags.' We did. Before we left the apartment. Maggie was afraid to leave in case Mom came back. But Mom's not coming back. Not so long as BMAC's got her.

'Maybe we can go—' she swallows hard, trying to get control of her voice. 'Maybe we can go to Officer Kelley. I can do the test. That's all they want. I'll do the test!'

'Maggie, Mom doesn't want you doing the tests. Mom wants us to go see her friend. I explained this!'

She rubs her arm faster, her eyes wandering over the strange crowds gathered outside Hexall Hall. She shakes her head and bites her lip. 'Pat, I'm scared.'

I look up at the sky, doing my best to hold back a groan. I don't know how to make her understand. Don't know how to get her to just suck it up and deal with it. She's only six.

'I'm scared too,' says Gabby.

When I look back, Gabby's standing beside my sister, the two of them staring into the crowds, Beauty's head bobbing up and down.

'But—' she looks down at Maggie, who's wiping tears from her cheeks – 'I bet they're just people too.'

'They're *bad* people,' says Maggie.

'I used to think Movers were bad people.'

Maggie's brow furrows. 'But you *are* a Mover.'

'I know. But my parents still said Movers were dangerous. So I figured they were right.'

This doesn't make sense to Maggie, and even I'm confused. 'Don't they know you're a Mover?'

Gabby nods.

Maggie and I wait for her to say more, but she just shrugs and her eyes go blank and I wonder what it is she's remembering. What kind of parents tell their Mover daughter that Movers are dangerous? Gabby didn't want to call them. We're on the run from BMAC and she's never even tried to let them know she's all right. Gabby picks at her bloody finger and a question that I'm worried I know the answer to creeps into my head; do her parents even care?

Beauty flaps up to Gabby's shoulder, calling her back from inside her own head.

'I never met another Mover till I went to Romsey,' she says. 'And it turned out Movers weren't so bad.'

I have to look down at my feet. She's lying for Maggie's sake. Because I know what life at Romsey's like for Gabby. It's hell. Everyone makes fun of her. Even Movers. Me. My cheeks flush hot with shame when I realise I can't even count how many times I've called her 'Gooba'.

'It's probably the same with Hexall Hall,' says Gabby. 'Can't know what they're really like unless we find out for ourselves.'

Maggie sniffs, wiping her nose on the back of her wrist, and nods. She looks up at Beauty, perched on Gabby's shoulder, and holds her hand out for Gabby to take. Gabby stiffens, surprised, like she doesn't know what to do with it. So Maggie just grabs her hand anyway.

'We have to stick together though,' announces Maggie, holding her other hand out to me. 'Promise, OK?'

'Uh, promise,' I agree, wrapping my hand around hers.

And Maggie steps out into the street, allowing me and Gabby to guide her into the thick of the crowd.

What just happened? Gabby rarely says much at all, even when I beg her to. And she managed to convince my baby sister to get over her fear of Hexall Hall. All with what she said. I steal a sideways glance at Gabriela Vargas. Her parents taught her to be afraid of Movers. What kind of life is that? And her Shadow. He killed two BMAC agents. Killed them with lightning. That's the sort of person she's had haunting her brain since birth? I've been going to school with Gabby since kindergarten, and I'm only now realising how little I know about her.

The smells get stronger as we're swallowed up by the crowd and Maggie covers her face. A couple of guys are roasting chicken over a flaming garbage can, a woman squats on the ground cleaning more. My nose wrinkles when I'm close enough to see it's not chicken. Above me Beauty lets out an angry squawk. Because it's a pair of fat black crows lying dead in the woman's lap, her hands furiously ripping out the feathers. She grins a toothless grin at me.

Gabby might've been wrong about people from Hexall Hall not being so bad.

The woman's glassy eyes linger on Maggie, at Beauty landing on her shoulder. Her grin fades to a dumb-looking open mouth, and she smacks her lips as if Beauty might be next on the menu. Or Maggie. She notices me glaring and her eyes narrow.

'Come on, Mags,' I say, pulling her along.

The front doors to Hexall Hall are boarded up, but the crowd seems to be flowing up and down a large ramp to our left that leads to an underground entrance. 'We can get in there, I think.'

Maggie's too busy watching the people moving around us to care what I've said, but Gabby nods and I lead them down the ramp towards the doorway.

Maggie lets out a sudden squeal as a man waddles past her. Beauty screams and swoops between her and the man, who grunts at us. My stomach flips when I get a look at his face – covered with scars, like someone came at him with a blade once upon a time. His right eye is swollen shut and bruised and his ear is warped and bubbly.

He grumbles something and Maggie gasps when he takes his fist and bumps his forehead with it. I'm shocked too, having never seen anyone do it in real life, only once in a bad movie that Mom caught me watching. She freaked out and turned it off right away. Because that's how they Shelve you – a shot to the forehead.

'What happened to his face?' says Maggie, mouth gaping in horror.

I shake my head because I don't want to answer. But I'll bet he's a forebrawler. Which means we're heading the right way. I give my sister's hand a reassuring squeeze as we pass through the open entrance to Hexall Hall.

In here, the crowd has dispersed a bit because the ramp opens up into a massive dark chamber filled with still more of these strange forgotten people. It's a train station after all, old and rundown, seeming to stretch into forever. Floodlights, strung up haphazardly at the tops of giant marble columns, flicker and struggle to stay on. Beauty lets out a nervous garble from her spot on Maggie's head, wings flapping all anxious-like and I see why. The columns stretch up fifty feet at least, and at the top are crows. Hundreds of 'em.

'Whoa,' breathes Maggie, and Beauty lets out a rattle of agreement. What are they all doing here?

The roar of a crowd brings my attention back to the ground. Between the massive posts there's a giant blue canopy, which seems to be where everyone's heading. The sour smell of beer and other harsh boozes stings my nose as men and women shout between gulps.

There's a sound of a bell somewhere inside the crowd, and arms fly into the air as they howl together and they start to climb all over each other.

The forebrawl match.

'Where is she?' Maggie asks, looking up at me, waiting for me to answer.

'What?'

'Gabby,' she says, shaking my arm with urgency. 'She's gone. We said we'd stick together and she's gone!'

I whirl round and Maggie's right. Gabby's not with us. People in soiled tattered rags stumble around singing and cheering. They pile into Hexall Hall by the dozen, but there's no sign of Gabby in the bunch.

And I'm here alone.

Alone with Maggie.

She tugs on my arm, hard. 'Stick together, Pat. You promised. We gotta find her!'

Beauty squawks at me. Motion seconded.

My teeth feel soft in my gums, and I bite down to stop the feeling. And something Gabby said before gnaws at my gut. *He'll find me.*

TWELVE

Everyone's coming while I'm trying to go. The droves of people piling into Hexall Hall don't even glance at me as they shoulder by, knocking me and Maggie around. I pull my little sister in front and keep my hands on her shoulders, guiding her back up the ramp to street level.

And I feel my armpits getting hot.

Where the breezes did she go? And it's in my head again – the BMAC agents' screams as they fell. *He'll find me.*

Beauty screeches, taking to the air, and I see there's someone blocking Maggie's path, a young guy with hair down to his elbows.

'Looking for a decent dinner?' he asks. Maggie jumps as he holds up a couple of naked crows by their tails. 'Plucked 'em myself, I did.' Then he turns his mouth to his shoulder and starts shouting as if someone's there: 'Shut up! You didn't tell me how. I know how to clean a buzzard. You were no help!' He takes a breath and turns back to us, smiling pleasantly, 'Five dollars!'

I shake my head and pull Maggie close. The man throws the crows back into his cart with an angry slam and wheels away, cursing under his breath. 'Don't interrupt me again! You ruined another sale! Just shut it! Shut it!'

I move to take a step but Maggie pulls me back. She's watching shopping-cart man.

'Maggie, come on. We gotta find Gabby.'

She doesn't move. 'Do they always fight like that?'

'He's just some crazy person, come on, Mags!'

Maggie's rooted to the spot, staring, and now the guy's got his head in his hands, stomping his foot. 'No, he isn't,' she says, turning back to me. 'It's like Gabby said. He's not so bad, just upset. Upset with his Shadow.'

I stop, and look back at shopping-cart man. He's rocking now, his hands buried in his hair. My eyes drift through the crowd and I notice there's more of them, more men and women, muttering to themselves or yelling at nothing. My Shadow's so quiet I never think of him as someone to talk to. But these Movers . . . they must all be higher than Phase 1.

I tighten my grip on Maggie's hand. She figured out what all these Movers were doing. She figured out they were talking to their Shadows. And I hate that she did. Because it makes me remember seeing her in the bathtub talking quietly over the drain to no one. *Strange behaviours*. Phase 2.

My brain sees it all – Maggie, she's filthy and her clothes are limp and worn. She's talking to herself, just like she did in the tub. She's talking to her Shadow. Whoever it is, I hate them. I want to scream at them to leave her alone, to never talk to her again. I want to scream at Dad's Shadow, Oscar Joji, for coming here and tearing up our family. And at Gabby's, to tell him to go back to whatever the breezes time he came from. *He'll find me. I know he will.* I want all Shadows to disintegrate into nothing, just spontaneously combust and leave us all alone, and at that moment I'm seething with resentment at my own.

I can feel him, somewhere far away but always there, like a constant stink. My brain starts to tickle and I know all this hostility has caught his attention. There's confusion · on his end. I can feel it and I'm glad. If I can't scare away Maggie's Shadow, then mine's the next best thing.

There's a shift in his attitude, like when the shower decides to freeze you without warning. He's shunning me, doing his best to block me out, and I back off. I'm tired. I don't want to remember he's there anyway, remember any of them are there. But I'm not allowed to forget—

'There!' Maggie points to a flaming garbage can. 'She's over there!'

Maggie sets off at a run, dragging me after her and scurries up to Gabby, who's leaning against the ramp railing, Beauty landing beside her. Gabby's attention is focused on the street. Just leaning there. Warming up by the fire, like she didn't come here with us at all.

'Gabby!' says Maggie. 'Stick together! You promised, remember?'

Gabby doesn't turn round.

'Gooba,' I bark at her, furious, 'what are you doing? Are you insane? We've been looking everywhere for you.'

She glances at me quickly and there's hate there – I

shouldn't have called her that; she just scared me is all. I feel like punching myself for letting the stupid nickname come out of my mouth. I think about saying sorry, but she's already turned her attention back to the street. 'Over there.' She nods towards a group of three or four Hexall Hallers hanging around a streetlight.

'So?'

'The one in the middle,' she says. 'Watch his hand.'

There's a man standing in the middle of the group, wearing a grubby floppy hat and a raincoat about five sizes too big. He's definitely the centre of attention, as the rest of the group all seem to be talking at him and no one else. He brings his fist to his mouth for a minute and lowers it as one of the others starts pointing at the ramp and his hand goes to his mouth again.

'See it?' says Gabby.

'What?'

'It's a droidlet.'

I watch as he lifts his hand again and this time I see his mouth moving. He's talking to someone. Definitely a droidlet. 'So?'

'BMAC,' she says. 'Look at his shoes.'

Through the group I catch a glimpse of the man's feet – clean black boots. New. The same kind Officer Dan wears.

The skin on my neck starts to tingle. 'We need to find Leonard,' I tell her.

Maggie looks up at me. 'Is BMAC here for us?'

I shake my head, for Maggie's sake. But honestly, I'm worried about the same thing. 'We should get out of here.'

The three of us hurry back down the ramp, Beauty leading the way into the throngs of Hexall Hall. The ring in the centre of the tent, the one everyone's crowding around and screaming at, has two forebrawlers in the middle, beating each other up. And I let myself hope BMAC's just here to break it up.

But we can't operate on hope.

I stare uselessly into the buzzing tent, not sure how to go about finding Leonard. He said someone would be here. He said the name. I can't remember what it was.

There's another loud roar from the crowd as one of the fighters goes down. A ding of the bell.

'Pat,' shouts Maggie over the crowd, 'what are we supposed to do?'

'He said someone would be here!'

'Who did?' asks Gabby.

'Leonard!' He said the name when he called. He said it. What was it?

The roar of the crowd merges from a mess of voices into one single sound, all of them chanting, fists in the air as someone new steps into the ring.

An R. It started with an R.

The new fighter is a woman, tall and slender, toned brown skin and a long black braid that hangs down to the middle of her back. Her eyes are dagger-focused on the last match's winner – a muscle-scarred bald man, easily four times her size. But she doesn't look worried.

'The Leonard man is here?' asks Maggie.

'No!' *Not Leonard. The name! The name that starts with R.*

And then it's there, rising up and around the pillars, thundering in my ears.

Rani! Rani!

The crowd's chant bellows the name that's been hiding in my memory. The someone Leonard said would be waiting.

Rani! Rani!

The girl in the ring. The crowd bellows for her.

THIRTEEN

There's a ding of a bell and the giant bald man starts shifting on his feet while the crowd roars. The woman – Rani – just stands there, watching him dance. She's the one, the one Leonard said would be waiting, but how am I supposed to get to her?

Gabby's hand is on my shoulder. She squeezes hard. 'Over there.'

When I look, I see the disguised BMAC officer standing by the door with the crow-plucking woman from before. She's latched to his arm, gesturing wildly at her shoulder and then flapping her arms like a bird.

Her head swivels from side to side while she speaks to the officer, who surveys the crowd with a cool, hard expression. The woman's eyes catch mine, lighting up with recognition, and she thrusts a pointed finger in our direction.

'Ouch,' complains Maggie as my hand instinctively tightens its grip on hers.

The BMAC officer glances our way as the crow woman

goes on yakking in his ear, flapping her arms and pointing. I pull my hood tighter and turn my head away. 'Follow me,' I order, making a hard line for the safety of the crowd.

'Pat,' says Gabby quietly, nodding at a couple of young women leaning against one of the pillars, shiny shoes poking out beneath grubby skirts that aren't quite grubby enough. One's got her hand pressed to her ear, the other lifting her hand to her mouth to speak.

BMAC.

My feet want to run, but I don't, forcing myself to keep a brisk pace. I don't want to give BMAC a reason to investigate whatever crow lady's telling them. My pulse pounds in my neck and I pull my hood a little lower. Did she recognise us? Our faces are everywhere, but there aren't a lot of news screens in Hexall Hall, from what I've seen. I remember how crow lady stared, her open hanging mouth, her eyes hungry for Beauty. I glance back and the bird is sitting on Maggie's head, beady eyes blinking rapidly. What does crow lady's interest in Beauty have to do with BMAC? I should have scared the stupid thing off back at the apartment.

The crowd's so tight it's like a wall of people, swaying and bumping into each other as they holler at the fighters. I shoulder my way into the mass, pulling Maggie behind me, and Beauty takes to the air, circling above us. Everyone's taller than I am so I can't see the ring. But I have to get close to it, close to Rani. She's waiting for us; that's what Leonard said.

An elbow comes down on my ear as the crowd erupts with applause and cheers.

'Ow! Pat!' Maggie's grip on my hand falls away, and when I look back she's being tossed around by the bodies jumping all around her.

I lunge for her, but another sweaty body bumps me back. 'Maggie!'

Gabby forces her way through the mess of torsos and spilling beer cups, and her hands reach out for Maggie's shoulders, pulling her close and covering them both.

'Go!' yells Gabby. 'We'll follow!'

Back towards the centre ring I can just make out the tops of the forebrawlers' heads, and as the crowd shifts and moves I get a glimpse of a tight path I can wedge myself through to the front. Gabby's right. It's faster if I go alone.

I squeeze myself through the lines of people. Someone slams me on my left, sending me flying into an angry skinny guy who nearly goes over. 'Watch it!' he growls as his drink – it smells like antiseptic – splashes onto my hoodie. He shoves me forward and I slam into another person's back, a fat woman, her shirt wet and stinking with sweat. She turns to glare at me, her one yellow snaggle tooth snarling above rolls of neck flab.

'Think you can worm yer way to the front of the fore-brawl, do you?'

She's right. I'm nearly at the front. I can see the fighters clearly just behind this mountain of a lady. A foot slams into the bald man's face and he's on the ground, covering his bleeding mouth. He's lost. Rani leans back against the ropes, lips tight, eyes hard. She's younger than my mom, but still a grown-up. In her twenties maybe?

'Rani!' I shout.

Snaggle Tooth shoves my shoulder. 'Think yer gonna steal my spot, do you?'

'What? No!' I say. 'I just—' She shoves me again as her friend turns to see what the fuss is about. 'I just need to get to the—' I reach forward, pointing at Rani, when Snaggle Tooth's friend, a bony man with sagging skin, smacks my hand back.

'You think yer better than us, Shelf-Meat?'

'No, no! I just need to talk to Rani!' I try to push my way through, but they both shove me back. There's something about them that turns my stomach – the way they move, almost in unison, the way they speak without having to look at each other, like they know what the other is thinking. I've never seen two people like them before, but I know what they are, know it in my gut the way I know when it's going to rain. Maybe I know because I have one too. But looking at them, there's just nothing else they could be.

A Mover and a Shadow. Here. In one time. Together. It's so wrong. So not allowed.

'Talk to Rani Nair?' the woman cackles. 'What's Rani gotta say to a little turd like you?'

That's when Rani's head turns, lazily noticing our discussion as she waits for the match to start up again.

'Rani!' I shout. 'Rani Nair!'

She looks me over slowly, then frowns. 'No autographs.'

Any feelings of hope that I had immediately drop through my sneakers. She doesn't know me. Doesn't recognise me at all. Leonard said she'd be waiting, but she's not expecting me at all, just waiting to fight in the next match.

Snaggle Tooth explodes with laughter. 'Aw, poor widdle baby isn't gonna get his precious autograph.'

'Go on,' growls Saggy Skin. 'Get on outta here, boy.'

Mom wanted to go to Leonard. Rani can take us to Leonard. I can't just turn back now.

'No! Rani!' I try to squeeze by, and as I do my shoulder knocks Snaggle Tooth's beer. She screams like I've just made her drop a baby, and Saggy Skin gasps in horror.

'Look what you done!' She smacks my head, knocking off my hood and grabbing a fistful of my hair. It feels as if my scalp's gonna rip off in her grip.

'You're gonna be dead sorry you ever done that, boy.' Saggy Skin kisses his knuckles and winds back his arm as Rani watches placidly out of the corner of her eye.

'No!' I squirm against Snaggle Tooth. 'Rani! I'm with Izzy! I'm here with Izzy!'

Saggy Skin drives his bony knuckles towards my face and I wince—

But the blow doesn't come.

'Hey!' barks Snaggle Tooth, her grip on my hair loosening as the crowd starts chanting for Rani.

I open one eye and Rani is standing in front of me, twisting Saggy Skin's arm behind his back so that he cries out. 'Takes a brave man to fight a child,' she growls into his ear. She shoots an angry glare back at Snaggle Tooth. 'Let him go.'

Snaggle Tooth's grip tightens a moment and I groan,

until she finally releases me, shoving me into Rani, whose hand wraps roughly around the scruff of my neck. 'Let's go,' she says through gritted teeth, and drags me around the side of the ring, where a metal barricade separates us from the sea of people.

'Thanks,' I say, rubbing my stinging scalp.

She takes a swig from a water bottle. 'Don't mention it.'

Up close she's even more intimidating. It's her eyes. They spark with something angry. Afraid to look directly at them, I stand on my toes and scan the crowd for Maggie and Gabby. They're standing on the far side, just outside the crowd, closer to the pillars. They're safe there. For now.

Shouts and heckles rise up as another bell sounds and a new fighter steps into the ring. Rani watches him with an appraising eye and cracks her knuckles. 'You're not supposed to be here,' she says, her back to me.

'No, I am,' I explain. 'I'm Pat Mermick. I'm Izzy's son.'

'I know who you are.'

Her tone is sharp, and I feel like I'm making her angry. 'Uh, Leonard told us to—'

'He changed his mind.'

My heart sinks. 'What? What do you mean? Why? Why would he do that?'

Rani shrugs. 'I don't know why Leonard does what he does. I just got the message that I'm not supposed to take you to him.'

'But he called this morning—'

'He's been trying to get in touch all day.' She spits again as the man in the ring bares silver teeth, the crowd roaring

122

with approval. 'Maybe if Izzy would answer her droidlet once in a while she would have gotten his message.'

'She can't answer,' I say, my cheeks flushing hot. 'BMAC took her.'

Rani turns, her brown eyes flaring with that spark she has. 'Took her? The girl too?'

I shake my head. 'Maggie's with me. We . . .' My chest feels heavy, my head too, and my Shadow's poking around in there while I swallow a lump forming in my throat. Changed his mind? How could he change his mind? Mom's gone and Leonard's name is all she left us. This one name, this one plan. If Leonard's changed his mind then . . . 'We don't know where else to go.'

I look back into the crowd to where Maggie's standing with Gabby, both of them craning their necks to see me. There's nowhere else for us to go. No Leonard means no plan. How am I supposed to go back and tell them that we came all the way down here for nothing?

I can feel Rani's eyes on me, and when I look back she turns away, watching the man who's taunting her from the ring. He points at her and drives his fist into his other palm and the crowd laughs and cheers. Rani twists her hands on the ropes. She doesn't say anything more. And I stand there, not wanting to make my way back through the crowd, back to Maggie and Gabby, with bad news.

'Why did Leonard change his mind about you?' Rani says.

'What?' How does she expect me to know that? I've never met the guy.

She lets go of the ropes and turns to face me, resting

a hand on an impatient hip. 'Izzy's the only friend Leonard has. He wouldn't just give up on her and her children unless he had a good reason. What is it?'

I have no idea how to answer that. The first and most obvious reason is in my head immediately. He's seen me on the news, knows BMAC is after me for what happened at school, and decided it's too risky. But I don't want to tell Rani that. She hasn't mentioned it so she might not know. I don't imagine she gets a lot of access to news down here. If I tell her, it might scare her off too.

'I don't know,' I say quietly.

She raises a doubting eyebrow and I look down at my shoes.

'Rani!' roars the man with silver teeth. 'Get in here so I can ring that pretty little neck of yours!'

There's a mix of laughs and boos from the crowd, but Rani's eyes don't leave mine. She bites her lip again, then shakes her head. 'If Izzy was with you . . .' She trails off, her knee shaking as she stares into nothingness. 'But leaving a pair of kids to fend for themselves doesn't sit right . . .'

We're a trio, not a pair. But I'm afraid to let her know about Gabby. I wait, trying to keep my hopes in check.

'My Shadow's got your number, Rani Nair!' yells the man in the ring. 'Is that why you're scared to face me?!'

'Get your sister,' says Rani, hoisting herself up into the ring. 'Wait here for me.'

'You'll help us?'

'After the match,' she says, her voice drowned out by the roar of the crowd. They start their chant again, their chant for her, and my chest swells with so much relief I start to chant along with them.

Until the voice.

'People of Hexall Hall,' it booms through the crackle of a loudspeaker, *'this is a surprise inspection.'*

BMAC.

FOURTEEN

The crowd explodes into screams as the BMAC officer's amplified voice rises above the chaos. '*We want to see FIILES! Anyone without proper documentation will be taken into the custody of the Bureau of Movement Activity Control.*'

'Breezes,' spits Rani, hopping down from the ring. 'Raid.'

Through the running bodies I see their uniforms – BMAC – head-to-toe in riot gear. There's a steady drumming as the officers beat their shields with stun staffs. Stun staffs – long black wands that slam you with a strong current of electricity when they touch your body.

It *is* a raid.

For us? Or the forebrawl? Not that it matters.

'Patrick,' barks Rani, 'where's the girl?'

I don't know. I can't see them – Maggie or Gabby. And panic ignites my limbs. Did BMAC find them? I plunge into the fleeing crowd, shoving through to where I saw them last.

There's a tingle at the base of my skull – my Shadow. He's frantic, coiling himself around my brain to get a sense of what's happening, but he can't be here. He can't be in the way. Not when I need to focus. I'm trying to shove him back, grunting from the effort, when a fleeing Hexall Haller knocks me off balance and I'm thrown to the floor.

My Shadow surges in my head as feet scramble all around me and I cover myself to keep from getting trampled. I need to force my Shadow out, need him to back off so I can think!

'Pat!' Maggie's voice screams for me through the chaos.

I can't see through all the legs, but a pair of hands yanks me to my feet.

Rani.

'Is that her?' Rani points over by the pillars, and I see Maggie, waving her arms beside Gabby.

'Come on.' Rani grabs me by the scruff of the neck and drags me to my sister, who leaps at me, gripping so tight around my middle that she knocks the air out of me.

'Who are you?' demands Rani, looking angrily at Gabby.

'She's with us,' I say.

'Not any more she isn't.'

Gabby looks nervously to me.

'What do you mean?' I say. 'She came here with us. She's—'

'You there!' Two officers standing back by the ring, shields up, each one brandishing a nasty-looking stun staff crackling and spitting with electric current. The shorter one points at us. 'Stay where you are.'

'Right,' says Rani. 'Argue about it later then, shall we?'

She takes off at a sprint as the officers yell for her to

stop. She doesn't. Neither do we. I grab Maggie's hand and charge after Rani, Gabby struggling to keep up.

'Come on!' I yell at her.

As we pound across the hard cement floor of Hexall Hall, I notice the crowd has thinned out – half nabbed by BMAC, being organised into single file by the doors, bound with current bindings, and the other half milling around the pillars because a line of officers is blocking the dark hallway that leads deeper into the Hall.

Rani huddles up against one of the pillars, and I bounce on my knees as the two officers that were chasing us close in.

'Rani!' I yelp. 'We're trapped.'

'Wait for it . . .' she says.

'Wait for what?!' and that's when I notice she's staring at a man on the far side of the hall, a large bird sitting on his hand.

I look back at the two BMAC officers approaching with current bindings ready in their hands. 'Miss Vargas,' says the older one, 'Mr Mermick, I'm gonna have to ask you to come with us.'

My heart pounds and the sound of it is like a booming drum in my own ears. There's no question now. BMAC's here for us.

Rani doesn't even acknowledge the officers. 'We've got a system,' she says, and points a finger to the ceiling. 'See them crows? They may like Movers but—' she points to the man with the bird, then at a woman crouched low by the pillar on our right. She's got the same kind of bird on her hand too, a big one, with a cap covering its eyes – 'they sure hate hawks.'

The man on the other end of the hall gives a nod, and the crouching woman tears the cap off the hawk's eyes, releasing the bird into the air. Three more take flight from different spots around the massive chamber, soaring up into the rafters.

A gloved hand grabs me hard by the shoulder. 'GOTCHA!' shouts the officer.

And then the explosion.

The crows in the ceiling scream in unison, all of them spiralling into the air as the hawks chase after them.

'What the . . .?!' The BMAC officer lets go of my shoulder, shielding himself against the hundreds of black blurs flapping around our heads, screeching and shrieking in fright, the beats of their frantic wings tickling my cheeks and hair.

'Follow me!' hollers Rani, grabbing hold of Maggie's wrist. Maggie takes my hand and I reach out for Gabby, though it's hard to see her through the swarm. She finds me and grabs hold as Rani guides us deeper into the dark recesses of Hexall Hall.

She stops at a boarded-up archway.

'Through here,' she says, prising the bottom board open a tiny crack.

Maggie doesn't need telling twice and she wriggles her way through the hole first. A crow flies low with a screech, and it's only when it ducks in after Maggie that I realise it's Beauty. And then two more, no, three – three crows dive after Maggie into the hole, just as eager to escape the frenzy as we are. Gabby and I scramble in behind them. And it's black inside. I can't see anything. I trip over myself, flying forward and down, down, down, Gabby crying out beneath me.

And we stop.

We've come to the bottom of what felt like a very long staircase, the two of us lying in a crumpled mess together, knees and elbows good and bruised. It's quiet, the chaos back behind us muffled by the walls.

There's a slam at the top of the stairs and a beam of light explodes from Rani's torch.

'Crows,' she says. 'Dumb pests hang around because they're attracted to the Movers. But they do come in handy, now and again.'

Attracted to Movers?

My nose is in Gabby's cowboy boots and she's pulling me to my feet.

'What do you mean they're attracted to Movers?'

'They sense it.' The heels of Rani's boots click as she makes her way down the stairs. 'Same as dogs sensing earthquakes, I guess. They feel the pull through time that's hanging around all of us like a bad stink. Especially those of us who've opened a door. They love that stink best. Strongest, I suppose. That's why they flock to Hexall Hall. What with all the guilty Movers hiding out here, it's like moths to flames.'

I look back at Beauty, perched on Maggie's head. I've never heard this crow theory before. Still, with the way the birds were all hanging out in the rafters in the main hall – hundreds of them – I don't have a hard time believing it.

Six shiny dots on a beam above my sister reflect the light from Rani's torch. The three crows that followed us.

They rattle and caw nervously together. What are they telling each other?

Rani points her torch in my eyes. 'So I think it's safe to say we know why Leonard doesn't want to see you,' she says. 'What have you kids been up to that's got BMAC on the warpath?'

'Nothing,' I say a little too quickly.

Rani frowns.

'They've got it wrong,' I insist.

Rani shakes her head. 'Sure they have.' She flicks the light away and now it's Gabby's turn in the spotlight. 'I assume BMAC's got you wrong too?'

Gabby opens and closes her mouth as she struggles to answer. When nothing comes Rani sighs. 'Listen, guys, I've got my own issues with BMAC so I'm not judging. I'm just asking you to be straight with me. Does this have to do with that Move this morning?'

'How do you know about that?' I ask.

'People in the Hall have been talking about it all day. Supposed to have been a big one. Do you know something about it?'

Me and Gabby stay quiet, squinting into the torchlight. *Be straight.* I'm afraid to. Afraid to confess to what Gabby's done. Afraid Rani is going to panic and bail on us, leaving us stranded in the bowels of Hexall Hall. But she saved us. She deserves an answer. And once we find Leonard and start sorting out what to do, she's going to find out what happened anyway.

It's best to answer.

'Yes,' I admit.

I see Gabby out of the corner of my eye, surprise and horror on her face.

Rani clucks her tongue once. Then, 'Your Move?' she asks.

I shake my head.

Gabby shifts on her feet and Rani watches her squirm in the light of the torch.

'Right,' says Rani, rubbing the back of her neck. She drops the light at her hip and I can hear her groan.

'It's complicated,' I tell her.

'Always is,' she says. She holds out her hand to Gabby. 'Where are your parents? They must be worried sick, if BMAC's—'

'They don't care,' mumbles Gabby.

But Rani isn't convinced. 'Because if they're out looking for you, they probably won't be too happy to find you down here with someone like me. And I don't want any trouble.'

'Trust me,' says Gabby, her eyes meeting Rani's. She swallows and I can see she's grinding her teeth. 'They don't care.'

That's the third time I've heard Gabby mention her parents. And the third time they haven't sounded great. How can they not care?

Rani's glare softens and she watches Gabby for a moment. 'WAN brat, huh?' she says finally.

Gabby nods.

So does Rani. 'Takes one to know one, I guess.'

I have no idea what they are talking about. But it seems to put an end to Rani's interrogation because she holds her light out ahead, into the blackness of the tunnel.

'Well, let's get moving then. Faster we get to Leonard, the better.'

Gabby moves to follow but I stop her. 'What's a WAN brat?' I whisper.

She chews her cheek a moment and watches after Rani. 'A Mover with WANs for parents, obviously.'

I still don't understand.

'WAN,' she says again. 'We Are Now.'

I nearly choke on my own spit. 'Your parents are We Are Now?!' My voice gets away from me, echoing through the dark.

Gabby scowls and storms away as Rani shines her light in my eyes.

'Believe it or not, Patrick,' she says, 'not everyone is as lucky as you in the parental draw of life.'

FIFTEEN

We march our way through what look like abandoned subway tunnels, dark and leaking with the smell of sewer water. Everyone's quiet, except Maggie. Talking about crows.

'What makes them attracted to Movers?'

She hasn't been able to drop this subject the entire time we've been walking. Rani's answered mostly with grunts, focused more on finding our way through the twists and turns in the dark.

'Dunno,' she says, annoyed. 'Something to do with radiation, so I'm told.'

'Radiation?'

Rani grunts again and waves a hand above her head. 'From the Movement activity, you know, through time. It's like the Eventualies and the storm clouds. Movers just sort of pull them in.'

I think about Gabby's Shadow – the way he stood on the stairs, the flocks of crows swirling around his head. A fresh Move. They swarmed him. *They sense it*. The idea gives me the creeps and I can tell Maggie's not feeling good about it either because she swats Beauty away – I've never seen her do that. Is that why Beauty hangs around our apartment? Is there some remnant of Dad's Move, even after all this time? A part of me hopes so. Even though it was the worst day of our lives . . . it means some piece of him is always around, doesn't it?

The bird squawks – offended, I bet – and flies ahead through the dark, the other three following after her.

Maggie moves in closer to Rani and for a second I think she's going to grab the forebrawler's hand, but she stops herself. 'Is that how come they like it in Hexall Hall so much?'

I decide to let Maggie badger Rani for a little longer and drop back a bit. Gabby's fallen behind, dragging her feet from exhaustion. The light from Rani's torch barely reaches this far back so I can only really make out Gabby's outline.

'I'm sorry,' I tell her, 'for how I reacted.'

She doesn't say anything.

'About your parents, I mean.' As if I needed to clarify. I can tell I offended her and I didn't mean to. I was just so surprised to find out Gabby's parents are We Are Now.

'Don't worry about it.'

'No, I am,' I say. 'I just . . .' Just what? I breathe in a big nose full of sewer stink, trying to get a handle on what I want to say. *We Are Now*. Gabby's parents are part of the Anti-Movers cause. They don't teach much about it in school, but Mom's told me plenty and I've seen the odd documentary to know how twisted they are. When BMAC implemented phase testing thirty years ago, people started singling out identified Movers. And attacking them . . . sometimes killing

135

them. The We Are Now vigilantes targeted Movers' homes and places of business, setting fires and small bombs in the name of 'protecting' the present. They *hate* Movers. They blame us for everything bad in the world, even the bad in their own lives. For them, Movers are the enemy.

That means for Gabby's parents – Gabby is the enemy.

I think about what Gabby told Maggie, about her parents teaching her that all Movers are dangerous. What other horrible things would a couple of We Are Now fanatics tell their Mover daughter?

'I mean, what would that even be like?' My teeth clack as I slam my jaw shut – did I say that out loud?

'What do you think it's like?' There's an edge to Gabby's voice, and I hate myself for not keeping quiet.

I can feel her waiting for me to say something, and I can't think of anything better than the truth. 'Scary?' I say quietly.

'I'm not scared of *them*.'

The way she says *them* makes me stop. 'What are you scared of?'

Gabby's quiet, but I can feel the answer crawling up my spine. *Her Shadow.*

I hear the scrape of nails on scabby skin and I know Gabby's scratching her finger again. I've been around her enough now to know she does it when she's nervous.

'You feel him still, don't you?' I say.

She nods. 'Like a fist . . .' Her voice is raspy, strangled by what sounds like the tears she's trying to hold back. '*His* fist. Wrapped around my brain, all the time. And he just squeezes, tighter and tighter until I can't . . .'

'Can't what?'

'Until I can't tell the difference between his anger and mine.'

'Your anger?'

'Yes, mine,' she says. 'I've had to put up with the Gooba name most of my life. I have to sit through classes with teachers like Mrs Dibbs. My parents are—' She stops, and I can see her throat throb as she swallows.

'Aren't you angry?' she asks quietly.

I don't answer that. I guess so. Phase forms, BMAC . . . Dad. I've never really thought about being angry about it. Never let myself, I guess.

Gabby doesn't need my answer. 'It's the same with my Shadow,' she says. 'But . . . bigger. His anger, I mean.'

I nod, thinking of the screams of the BMAC agents he blew away. So much bigger.

'He's always been that way.'

'It's not like he's not a morning person, Gabby,' I say. 'He killed two people. No one's just *that* way.'

The light on Gabby's face grows dim, and a squawk from Beauty echoes its way down the tunnel to us. We're too far behind, and Gabby speeds up. We walk together, neither of us saying anything, both of us trying to think of what there is to say.

'He hates anyone who's not a Mover,' she says.

'Why?'

'It's bad in the future, from what I can tell. Between Movers and Non-Movers. Much worse than now.'

'Worse how?'

'It's bigger,' she says. 'The tension between Movers and

Non-Movers must snap eventually. Because from what I can tell, they're at war with each other.'

War. The word steals the breath from my lungs. I'm surprised, and not at all, at the same time. I'm surprised to realise that some part of me always guessed it would come to that. War. What happens between Movers and Nowbies that brings us to that?

'My Shadow said we could keep each other safe,' she says. 'Said that together we were stronger. It's the way nature wanted it. Why else would it go to so much trouble to connect us through space and time if we weren't supposed to be together?'

I hate that I see her Shadow's point. That I feel it. And I notice my Shadow. He's been hiding in the corners of my mind all day, monitoring how I'm feeling. And there's a twitch, way down deep in my gut, like a muscle that wants to flex. The part that wants to Move. If the law didn't tell me I couldn't, if I didn't work so hard to ignore him and stay Phase 1 . . . would I try to get stronger and Move my Shadow?

'But . . .' says Gabby, 'because of how my parents are . . . well, you know – I just wanted him to leave me alone. So I kept telling him that. That's when the thoughts started.'

'Thoughts?'

'I started thinking things.' She glances sideways at me, embarrassed for some reason. 'Angry, ugly things. I'd just be sitting in class, or having dinner with my parents, and then – I see them.'

'See what?'

She frowns, deciding if she should tell me. 'I dunno.'

'It's OK, you don't have to say. I shouldn't have asked.'

'No, no. I just . . .' She sighs through her nose before she continues. 'You know how Mrs Dibbs gets, at phase-form time?'

'Yeah.' Crabby. Nasty. Angry. Mean. Although really she's always that way. It just gets worse then.

'There was this one time,' Gabby goes on, 'last year. She'd said my name in that awful voice of hers. The class started to laugh. And those hideous eyebrows of her dipped down so far between her eyes, like she was accusing me of something. And, I just hated her for it. When I didn't answer her fast enough, she said, "Just like you Movers – holding up the world with your unnatural condition." She used that word. *Unnatural*. And as soon as she said it, I saw her in my mind – her head in my hands, my fingers gripped in that silver frizzy ponytail, and I slammed her forehead down on the desk, so hard she just dropped.'

I'm stunned. Who would have thought that quiet, loner, brainiac Gabby was so violent inside? It doesn't fit; it's so unlike her.

She swallows again, and in the dim light I can see her eyes are getting wet. 'Thoughts like that are in my head all the time. But they aren't my thoughts.'

'They're his?'

She nods.

I'm quiet, trying to think of what that must be like for her. My Shadow and I, we aren't like that. The connection's too weak. I can feel him there, in my head. But he can't do stuff like that. Can't make me see things, think things I don't want to. It sounds so . . . invasive.

'Anyway,' she says, trying to sound brighter than

we both feel, 'now you know why I'm trying so hard to find pungits.'

'What?'

'Pungits,' she says, searching my face for understanding. 'The particle I've been talking about.'

I stare at her blankly, feeling a bit embarrassed. 'I told you, I have a hard time understanding—'

'They're what connect a Mover to their Shadow,' she says.

'OK.'

'If I can find the pungits, find the connection,' she says, her voice lower, 'then I think I can get rid of him for good.'

I stop walking. 'Get rid of him?'

She turns back to face me, and I see from the look in her eye that she's serious.

And then I understand Gabriela Vargas like I've never understood her before. 'Gabby,' I whisper, 'is that what all those projects were about? You're trying to cure yourself?!'

She steps back from me and looks away.

'Gabby, you can't cure yourself from being a Mover. That's impossible.'

She nods, her eyes on the ground. 'Maybe. But can you blame me for trying?'

No. After everything she's told me about her Shadow, and her parents, I can't blame her at all. He scares me, this strange man that just appeared on the stairs at school. Without Gabby's permission. Without her say. How can he be here without her permission? Phase 4. That's what the news said. Whether she wanted to Move him or not, the fact remains: Gabby's Shadow is here.

And I remember something else. Something that makes me worried.

I glance up at Rani. She's so busy trying to ignore Maggie's questions and lead the way through the tunnels, she hasn't noticed we're lagging behind.

'Is the connection still messed up though?' I whisper. 'Cloudy, I mean.'

Gabby shakes her head. 'He doesn't know where I am, I can tell. Just like I can't tell where he is.'

Good, I think, and release a breath I didn't realise I'd been holding.

'But,' she says, 'he's frustrated. I can feel it through all the . . . murkiness. It's making him really upset.'

That's less good. And I start to worry about what happens if he ever does manage to find Gabby. *Natural*, he told Gabby, for them to be together. Maybe. But after what he did back at Romsey, someone like that, linked to someone like her – I can't see anything natural about the two of them being paired up.

She glances at me again, that embarrassed look. 'Sorry.'

'Sorry for what?'

'I don't know,' she says. 'It's just that I've never talked about this. About him. Not to anyone. Ever.'

'Sure.' I shrug, as if it's no big deal. But the weight of what she's just confessed starts to sink in. She's never told anyone. And I can't understand it. I can't understand living with something so big, so frightening, all by yourself and not asking for help. I think of Mom and I know that even if I tried to hide something, she'd sniff it out and make me tell me what was wrong. And she'd move mountains to make it better.

141

Like she'd do for Maggie.

And a black hole of sadness opens up inside my heart as I watch Gabby, silhouetted by the flashlight. It's a sadness for Mom. For what she did for Maggie with BMAC. And because I don't know what they've done to her.

And it's also for Gabby.

Who has no one to move mountains for her.

SIXTEEN

After what feels like hours of walking, I can see a light out in front of us that isn't coming from Rani's flashlight. There's an opening in the darkness, an archway of dim fluorescence and the murmurings of people.

Gabby and I step into the light and I can see we're still walking on subway tracks, the platform raised high on our right, with people, Hexall Hall types, huddled in little pockets. It's a subway station – 'Dunedin', according to the chipped faded mosaic decorating the wall to my left.

'"Dunedin",' reads Gabby. 'Where's that?'

I shake my head. I've never heard of it. I can't be sure what part of the city Rani has walked us to. Or if we're even in the city any more.

Rani hops onto an unsteady stack of trashcans and boxes in the middle of the tracks – some sort of makeshift staircase – not seeming to mind that the whole thing's about to topple over as she skips her way up onto the platform. 'It's under what used to be the old Auto District,' she says.

And that's no help because I've never heard of the old Auto District either.

'What's it under now?' I ask.

'Garbage,' she says, helping Maggie up the wobbly steps. 'Same as everything else outside the city limits.'

A dump site. I look at Gabby – she chews her lip. We're definitely not in the city any more.

I follow them up the precarious staircase. Each jumbling piece of junk teeters in a different direction, pulling my limbs in all kinds of ways I'd rather they didn't go. When I finally manage to step up onto the platform there's a whole tattered and lumpy neighbourhood nestled on the speckled station tile. The people of Dunedin Station sit in spaces they've claimed for themselves, marking their territory with turned-over shopping carts, old news-paper dispensers, garbage cans, soiled boxes and bottles. Some of them have even gotten a bit sophisticated, rigging up struggling garden lights and monitors with wavy screens.

Who are all these people? Movers, I know. Most of them runaways, or kicked out by their families. But there are so many. Each one with their own reason for heading underground.

Something clatters as Gabby loses her balance on the trash-stairs and I give her my arm for balance. She takes my hand and wobbles her way to the solid platform and I feel that hole opening up in my chest for her. Because a Mover on their own, a Mover like Gabby, is the kind of Mover that ends up here.

Her sweaty palm releases my forearm and she readjusts

her shirt, which has gotten twisted funny from the climb –
Dad's shirt. She notices me staring. 'What?'

'What?' I repeat clumsily. 'Nah, nothin'.'

I hurry after Rani and Maggie, avoiding sleeping lumps
and wires as best I can.

Rani leads us to the far end of the platform, where
someone's strung up a couple of sheets as a screen. Beauty
and her new companions land on the ropes and Rani throws
back a corner. 'Through here.'

On the other side I see where the stairs up to street level
would be if they hadn't been boarded up. There's a camp set
up here too, though it looks more like a command centre.
Dusty flickering monitors, some cracked, all of them so old
Mrs Dibbs probably wouldn't recognise them, sit on top of
shopping carts and rusted public benches. Bottles, take-out
wrappers, crow feathers and bones litter the ground.

Sitting on a desk chair with a missing wheel is a guy
in a raincoat, frantically tapping away at what I guess is a
keyboard from a long time ago. I've never actually seen
one.

Gabby, Maggie and I stand together by the sheet curtain
as Rani reaches out for the man's shoulder. 'Leonard—'

He jumps, swinging around like he's expecting a punch.
He's old. His face is thin and long, as if the weight of his
jaw is pulling the whole thing down. His skin is like leather,
spiked with rough five o'clock shadow, tanned – or maybe
just dirty. Down here, I guess it's more likely he's dirty. And
his hair is slick with grease.

This is Leonard?

'Thank God you're back.' He leaps out of his chair and

145

reaches behind the desk, pulling up a giant duffle bag and throwing it at Rani. 'I've got all your stuff packed—'

'What?' says Rani.

'I'm just finishing up with the hard drive and then we can go.' His voice is strange, a funny accent that runs his words together so that the whole thing sounds like one long word.

'Go?' Rani puts the bag down. 'Leonard, go where? What are you . . .?'

He's back at his monitors, typing away, the tickety-tick-ticking making my eyes twitch with nerves. 'We have to get out of the city!' he says. 'Soon as we can. We can take the—'

Maggie coughs, and the man spins round in his chair, realising finally that we're standing here.

'No,' he breathes. His mouth hangs open, skewed to his left as he squints. I tug awkwardly at my own jeans leg while he studies the three of us.

'They turned up at the forebrawl,' says Rani, and Leonard jumps up from his chair, tearing at his hair and pacing around. 'BMAC has Izzy and they were alone, and I—'

'No, no, no, no, no,' Leonard goes on. 'I told you! I told you not to bring them here! Do you know what will happen if we're seen with *her*?'

Gabby looks at me and we realise he must have seen us on the news. We need to do something before Leonard tells us to leave. I step forward, hoping I can convince him to do for us what he's done for Mom's Mover friends in the past. 'Uh, Mr Leonard, my name is Patrick Mermick. I'm Isabelle Randle-Mermick's son—'

He throws up an arm to stop me. 'Yeah, I know who you are. I think the entire city knows who you are at this point.' He motions at one of the monitors and I see *Avin News* is on. And there's my picture, right next to Gabby's.

Yup. He's seen it all right.

Rani stares at the footage for a moment before her head snaps in my direction. 'You should have told me about this.'

I swallow. 'Look, I'm sorry, but my mom—'

'I've been calling your mother all day!' Leonard says, throwing his hands in the air. 'I've left her a thousand messages telling her *not* to come here!' He looks past me, trying to see around the draped sheet. 'Where is she?'

'BMAC,' says Rani. 'Like I said.'

Leonard stops, taking a minute to process that information. Finally he collapses into his chair, his fingers pinching the bridge of his nose.

'Uh . . .' I say, pulling harder on my jeans leg. 'She said you could help us . . .'

'Before!' he says, leaning forward in his chair. 'Yeah, sure, I could help *before*, when the situation was manageable! Before *this*!'

He waves at one of the monitors over his shoulder, and there's the Romsey Institute for Academics, scarred and chewed up, standing in the middle of the city.

I look over at Gabby, who shrinks a bit into the curtain at her back.

'But *now*,' Leonard goes on, jumping to his feet and pacing again, 'it's all got out of control and I don't want to be anywhere near it! Particularly near *you*.' One crooked finger points squarely at Gabby and I feel like stepping in front of it.

'Why?' I say. 'I know what kind of work you do for my mom. You help wanted Movers all the time. Why not Gabby?'

Leonard wags his finger at her like I don't know where she's standing. 'Do you *know* who she is?'

'Who is she?'

'Who am I?' Gabby rasps.

Leonard shakes his head, his icy blue eyes staring at her like he's looking at a bomb. 'You and that big brain of yours,' he tells her. 'You're Gabriela Vargas, the Commander's little Mover girl.'

Gabby and I just stand there, stunned into silence while Leonard goes back to tickety-tapping at his keyboard. Then he pulls up another duffle bag from under the desk, dumping in his meagre belongings that just look like garbage.

'The Commander?' repeats Rani, staring at Gabby like she's seeing her for the first time. 'You mean the guy who starts the war?'

War. That's what Gabby said. In the future, between Movers and Non-Movers. 'You know about the war?' I ask. 'How do you know about the war?'

Leonard doesn't even look up from what he's doing when he answers me. 'Because I was there.'

'Wait,' I say, suddenly understanding. 'You're a Shadow?'

'I'm *her* Shadow.' Leonard nods at Rani. 'Came here from 2343. Me and Oscar Joji.'

There's a flutter in my stomach. No. More like a tsunami, a typhoon. At hearing that name a tremor quakes my knees. 'You *knew* my dad's Shadow?' I say.

Leonard's cool eyes look blue as they fix on me, but then I see they aren't really blue. They're foggy, like clouds are brewing inside them, swallowing the pupil and whatever colour his eyes used to be.

He looks away and a curse hisses through his teeth. 'Your mother *still* hasn't told you?'

'Told me what?'

'Your father didn't Move Oscar Joji here from the future.' He looks past me and nods over at my little sister who huddles in beside Gabby as if to hide from those cloudy eyes. 'She did.'

SEVENTEEN

A laugh shoves its way from my throat, forced so hard it hurts. But I have to laugh. That's the only way to respond to something so outrageous. 'You're insane. Maggie's only Phase 1.' And then I think of Sibichendosh and the letter home. 'OK, *maybe* Phase 2, but she's never Moved anyone.'

Leonard's eyes stay narrowed on my sister, not bothered at all by my reaction. 'She did.'

'Pat?' says Maggie nervously.

I step in front of her, hiding her from that gaze of his. 'Don't listen to him, Mags. He doesn't know what he's talking about.'

'I do know,' Leonard insists. 'Better than anyone. *I* know.'

Gabby's frowning, eyes flicking from Leonard to Maggie. '*How* do you know?' she says.

'He doesn't,' I snap, annoyed that she'd even entertain the idea of something so stupid. 'He's a crazy person.'

She holds a hand up to stop me, steps away from the curtain and stands in front of Leonard. '*How* do you know?'

'Because I know your Shadow, girly,' he tells her. 'I was there when he started stealing people's pungits.'

That word smacks me in the face.

Gabby stiffens. 'You know about pungits?'

'Gabby's pungits?' I say.

'Everyone in the future knows about pungits,' Leonard says. 'What do you think your mother wanted to run for, huh? She didn't want BMAC getting a look at the pungits on your sister's head and knowing what I know.'

Blood drains from my face. Mom. Why *did* she want to run? *Something scarier than an upgrade*. But pungits aren't a real thing! They're just Gabby's crazy project.

'BMAC knows about pungits?' Gabby's fists ball at her sides. She looks as if she'd like to shake information out of Leonard, but she stays rooted to her spot, questions pouring out of her mouth one after the other. 'Does BMAC know how to see them? Can you see them? Do you know how?'

'*You* know how. They're your discovery,' says Leonard.

Gabby doesn't say anything. She hasn't been able to see them. That's the whole point of all her experiments, to *see* her pungits.

I notice the fists at her side start to quake. Leonard's wrong. Gabby doesn't know how.

He watches her for a moment and must realise it too, because he grunts. 'Well,' he says, shrugging, 'you haven't figured it out yet. But you will, I know that. When you're twenty-eight. That's how we all end up in this whole mess.' He swings his chair back to his monitor and starts tapping at the keys again, not caring about the questions he's sent swirling through our heads.

BMAC knows about pungits? Gabby's pungits? How? And how did Mom know about pungits? What does any of this have to do with Maggie? I don't understand. I look at Gabby for help, for some way to make sense of all this.

Gabby doesn't notice. She's staring at Leonard's back, her forehead crinkling while her mind works.

'Show me.' It's like a command, she says it so flatly.

Leonard ignores her, grabbing the duffle bag at Rani's feet and slinging it over his shoulder. And I'm suddenly afraid he'll leave. Afraid he'll disappear and take the things he knows with him.

'Show her!' I say, standing at Gabby's side.

'Leonard.' Rani grabs hold of his bag and pulls him back down into his seat.

'There's no time for a time-travel lesson,' he tells her. 'We have to get out of here.'

'Just show them,' she says, fixing him with that fore-brawler stare that must make her opponents think twice about stepping into the ring.

He growls, 'All right!' and throws up his hands before he starts rooting through the piles of junk on his desk. He pulls something up from the clutter, a cylinder of some kind.

'Is that a torch?' asks Maggie.

'No,' snaps Leonard, a bit shortly. But it sure looks like a torch – an old one, with lots of wires and things hanging from it. 'Well,' he checks himself, 'it used to be. Now it's a pungit ray.'

'Like X-rays,' Gabby breathes beside me.

'That's right,' he says. 'Only you don't need to take a picture with this.'

I watch Gabby, her mouth pursed in concentration as she stares at the contraption in Leonard's hand. She's bouncing slightly, bending her knees. She talked about X-rays the other day in her presentation when no one was listening. And here's Leonard, repeating it. She's so excited she looks as if she can barely contain herself.

'Now,' Leonard explains, 'when the pungit rays come from the torch and pass over the person, the pungits absorb the rays. Patrick,' he says, waving an impatient hand at me, 'go stand over by the sheet.'

Uncertain, I move away from Gabby and Maggie and do as he asks.

'Hold still,' Leonard warns as he clicks the flashlight to on. I expect light to explode from it, to blind me, but it doesn't happen. Nothing happens.

Maggie shifts on her feet. 'Is that it?'

'Is what it?' I say. 'Nothing happened!'

Gabby's stepping closer to me, leaning forward with her eyes squinting.

'Voila!' says Leonard triumphantly.

There's a quiet laugh from Gabby, and her eyes have started to water as she stares.

'What?' I ask her. 'What do you see?'

With an annoyed growl, Leonard fishes a mirror from the piles on his desk – the kind the girls have in their lockers at school – and throws it at me. I catch it, and as soon as I hold it up to myself I see them. Tiny black particles, like some kind of sinister fairy dust, fan out from my head as if they are riding invisible conveyor belts to nowhere.

Gabby places a hand over her gaping mouth and it's

like she's never seen anything so beautiful in all her life. But they aren't beautiful to me. The opposite. They are ugly. Dangerous. And I'm afraid of what they mean for my sister.

'Now,' says Leonard, 'the minute you were born, those pungits of yours ripped through space and time and latched on to the first person they liked,' says Leonard.

'So Movers *do* establish the connection?' Gabby checks, like a scientist sharing data with a colleague. 'That's one of my theories, but without the pungits I didn't have any way to prove it.'

'They do,' says Leonard. 'Same way lightning looks for the path of least resistance to strike the earth, your pungits sniff out the poorest sap they can find and *bam!* You're locked together.'

That's a weird thought – that I grabbed onto my Shadow. It's strange to think that our being stuck with each other is my fault.

'So, what you have there are the pungits of the average Phase 1 Mover,' Leonard goes on. 'A sparse dose of rigid pungits, pulled tight by the distance through time between you and your Shadow, yes? The pungits are what connects Mover and Shadow. Right?'

Gabby nods.

'Marigold?' says Leonard, looking at Maggie. 'Kindly stand beside your brother for the class, will you?'

My sister obeys, and hurries to join the experiment, excited to be participating like we're volunteers in a magic show. There's nothing I can do and as soon as she's beside me, the pungit ray is on her and it's like her head is covered in a swarm of angry bees. They zip around her head in a chaotic mess, and there are ten times as many specks as I have.

Gabby frowns. 'So many,' she says. 'So many pungits.' She looks back at Leonard. 'She *is* Phase 3.'

Leonard nods.

I swallow. 'What?'

'My theory was,' says Gabby, 'that the more powerful the Mover, the more pungits they'd have.' She bites her lip and looks apologetically at me before turning back to Leonard. 'Pat only has a few, because he's Phase 1. Maggie has more because she's Phase 3, right?'

He nods again.

The swarm of black specks dances above Maggie's head, swirling and spiralling. There are so many compared to the ordered ones fanning out from my head. Phase 3.

'But . . . but why are they moving like that?'

'Pungits get like that,' explains Leonard, 'after a Move. Imagine the pungits like a string of beads. Stand far away from the person holdin' the other end of the string, and the string is tight, right? Like Pat's. But bring that person close and the string goes all loosey-goosey, pungits floatin' around on floppy spaghetti. After a Move, the pungits are excited, flying around all speedy crazy like.'

'I said that would happen!' Gabby's grinning ear to ear, looking at me like she wants me to smile with her. But I can't. I'm too nervous to smile.

Leonard nods. 'That's just how they looked after she Moved Oscar Joji.'

After she Moved Oscar Joji. So that's it. Evidence. Right there above my sister's head. I want to fight it, to say, *No, it isn't true*. But I'm too afraid. 'BMAC knows how to see these?'

'I would bet that they do,' Leonard says.

So this is what Mom was afraid of.

'But how?' I ask. 'Gabby hasn't even discovered how to measure them yet.'

Rani folds her arms, leaning against Leonard's desk. 'You don't think BMAC Shelves immigrant Shadows before questioning them, do you? Whenever they apprehend a Shadow, they scare that person into telling them everything they can about the future.'

I have to believe that. I've filled out the Sworn Testimony box in enough phase forms to know how much BMAC wants to know everything they can about the future. Nowbies don't like that they are stuck in one moment in time.

'But,' I say, 'if they know about pungits, why haven't they started testing Movers for them?'

Leonard sighs. 'Probably because what they know is pretty useless. They're sort of stumbling around in the dark, trying to figure pungits out, because any Shadows that do come back either won't tell them what they want to know, or just don't have the scientific understanding themselves. You couldn't explain DNA to a caveman, could you?'

No. I shake my head. I glance over at Gabby. She might be able to.

'BMAC knows pungits exist,' Leonard goes on. 'Maybe can even see them, with a lot of effort. But whatever contraption they got is probably mighty expensive to run, if they're using the metals I think they're using. They just don't have the right technology yet, or the know-how to test for pungits on the entire population of Avin on a monthly basis.'

'Why doesn't BMAC in the future just tell BMAC in the past how to do it?' asks Gabby.

He smirks. 'Probably because they're afraid of messing with history. BMAC in the future is afraid to introduce pungits to our time because that's not how it's supposed to happen. They think they have to wait for Gabby to do it.'

'Why?' says Gabby. 'What do they think will happen if they don't wait?'

'The world will explode?' he laughs. 'Who knows?'

'Will it?' I ask.

'I just told you about them, and we're still here, aren't we?'

Yeah, I think miserably, here we are.

Leonard shrugs. 'It's just easier not to think about it.'

I watch the pungits dancing above my sister's head. So Sibichendosh was right. Maggie did need an upgrade. 'But' I say, 'even if she's Phase 3 now, no baby is just born Phase 3. They're too weak.'

'Yeah, well,' huffs Leonard, 'experiments like the Commander's don't adhere to the laws of nature.'

'What sort of experiments?'

'The ones that let him steal your sister's pungits from Oscar Joji.'

EIGHTEEN

The things I'm hearing from this Leonard man are impossible to understand. How can a person steal pungits? What would that do? 'You're saying,' I say slowly, 'that Gabby's Shadow stole Maggie's connection?'

Gabby walks over to the desk and picks up the pungit ray, turning it over in her hands. 'Why would my Shadow want to steal pungits?'

'Because not long after Miss Gabriela Vargas 2097 discovers pungits,' says Leonard. 'She figures out how to sever her own connection.'

Gabby drops the pungit ray, but Rani is quick to catch it. 'I cure myself?' she squeaks.

That's all she's ever wanted. Everything she's been working for.

'You're not sick,' Leonard says angrily. 'But yes, you sever your connection.'

And I can't help but feel happy for her – this future adult Gabby who finally does it. Who finally frees herself from the nasty thoughts and angry images her Shadow has forced on her all her life.

'Which is why,' Leonard goes on, 'your Shadow's trying to get back to you. He needs to get his hands on you so he can re-establish the link. But the only way to get back to where you are, in the past, is by using someone else's Mover to bring you here. Her Mover. My Mover. Didn't matter, so long as they lived in this time.'

'Wait, you're saying—' No, I don't understand. 'What are you saying?'

'I'm saying, Pat, that your little sister Moved your friend's Shadow to now. I'm saying that she's the first Mover in history to Move two people.'

'That – that – that doesn't make sense.'

'Look, you saw her pungits, didn't you? The way they were flying around all speedy and messy right now? They were like that after she Moved Joji. But over time the pungits lose some of that energy, slowing down and getting lazy.' He turns the ray on Rani and she flinches back, annoyed, but we can see what he means. There are a lot of pungits, like Maggie has, but they aren't moving as fast. They look tired, sluggish in comparison. 'See that? Rani Moved me five years ago. Old Move, slow pungits. Your sister's pungits are excited because she Moved someone recently. And that someone is Vargas's Shadow, because he's the one who stole Oscar Joji's pungits!'

Gabby's watching Leonard carefully. 'Steal the connection? You mean, you've seen him do it? In the future, where you come from? You saw it happen?'

He lets his chin drop to his chest and he taps his toes. Finally he nods.

'The world changes a lot,' Leonard says, 'when the Vargas girl discovers pungits. Becomes more . . . hostile, I guess would be the word. When BMAC introduces pungit testing, and more and more studies are published, it doesn't take long before pungit rays can be bought pretty much anywhere. Soon anyone who wants to know what you are just has to shine a light at your face and that's it – no hiding. People start deciding how many pungits is too many to come over to dinner or work in their offices. How many pungits is too many pungits to be friends with a person, marry a person, even live next door to a person. By the time I was born, the lines between Movers and Nowbies were pretty thickly drawn. And when the lines are drawn, that's when the fighting starts.'

'The war,' says Gabby.

'The war,' Leonard agrees.

'Leonard signed up for the Shade Unit,' says Rani.

'Shade Unit?'

'The army,' says Leonard quietly. 'Made up of Movers and Shadows who were fed up of answering to BMAC. And led by Commander Bram Roth.' He throws open his arms, in mock reverence. 'Liberator of Movers and Shadows from the oppressors. A true hero!' Leonard shakes his head. 'God, was I ever an idiot to have believed that.'

'What did you do for them?'

Leonard sniffs, as if he can't decide how to answer. Finally he busies himself with the duffle bags instead.

'A hacker,' Rani answers for him. 'Leonard's job was to crack into the Nowbies' weapons and defence systems and shut them down.'

160

Leonard rubs the bridge of his nose again and I watch him wince, like the memories are hurting his brain. He worked for this Roth man. A hero for Movers, he called him. What kind of hero does the things he did to Gabby?

He lets out a long sigh before he speaks again. 'Anyway, Roth made this pungit test mandatory for all personnel. And so I went. They hit me with the ray and wrote some stuff down and that was it. Till I got a call that I had to report to Commander Roth himself. Wasn't till I got there that I found out the pungit tests were created by Roth to measure how far back their Movers were. He was looking for Shadows with Movers in the years 2070 to 2098.'

'Shadows like you,' I say, making sure I'm following.

He nods. 'Turns out there were three of us. Myself, a woman named Misha Stern—' He stops, and I can tell from the way his forehead wrinkles, it's not a good memory. Then he points to Maggie. 'And finally some brand-new recruit. This poor twenty-something kid who went by the name Oscar Joji.'

There's a twitch in the corner of his mouth, like he's fighting to keep it from frowning. He licks his lips and goes on. 'The first day, Roth brought us to this secret lab the Shade Unit had been operating – researching weapons, chemicals, serums, anything that would help in the fight against the Nowbies. But mostly what he was having them experiment with was pungits. He brought us there: me, Misha and Oscar Joji. Said it was our objective to learn how to manipulate pungits to our benefit. If Roth could strengthen all the Phase 1s and 2s to Phase 3s by manipulating their pungits, all the Movers in our time could Move their

Shadows to our time and double the size of our army. He also wanted to learn how to reverse the flow of pungits of the Shadows we had in the army, people like me, like Joji and Misha, so we could Move our Movers. Imagine that. If we could do that, we'd outnumber the Nowbies four to one.' He shrugs. 'Sounded all right to me.'

It should sound all right. But I can't help but feel nauseous. What Gabby told me about Roth, about his anger. What he did to those agents. With him in charge of an army that big, who knew what kind of damage he could do?

'I asked Roth once why his Mover didn't know how to do it,' says Leonard, 'since she discovered 'em and all. He told me to shut up and mind my own business. I should have known something was off then. But Roth was my hero – I didn't want to upset him – so I stopped asking questions and just did what he wanted. I never guessed his Mover had cut him off.'

'So how did you figure it out?'

He gets a faraway look in his eyes, and whatever he's seeing in his head looks like it's hurting him. 'This one day,' he says, 'Roth brings us to the lab and it's empty. Typically there'd be assistants and nurses, other scientists. But that day – that day, no one. There was an operating table, and he ordered Misha onto it. She did as she was told, and then he asked me and Joji to secure the straps that were hanging by her arms. And I saw in his hands he had this crown – a silver band that he placed around her head. He looked at me and asked me to strap her ankles, so I did.' Leonard rubs his face and his breathing has got heavier. 'I had no idea what he was about to do to her.'

Leonard leans forward in his chair, hunched for a moment, and all we can hear is the sound of him breathing. Finally he takes a deep breath and looks up. He holds out his hands. 'The Commander had these metallic circles strapped to his palms. And he stood by Misha's head, holding them on either side of the crown. Poor Mish, she started wriggling all of a sudden, and whimpering, and I didn't know, I couldn't know. Then the pungits started showing. They fanned out from her head, charged with this electric blue glow. I'd never seen them look like that. Suddenly she started screaming and thrashing, fighting hard against my hands and the restraints, but I held her down. I held her down and I watched as the pungits reversed direction. They weren't moving out from her head, they started moving in. It was like her brain was sucking them all back, and the crown around her head started to glow the same blue as the pungits. And then, when the pungits were all gone, she was shrieking. The Commander, he didn't even flinch; it was like she wasn't making a sound.' He looks at his hands as though he doesn't even recognise them. 'And then she stopped fighting. She just lay still and quiet. The band around her head was so bright. And the circles in the Commander's palms – they glowed just the same. And when they were just as bright as the crown, I saw the pungits again. Flowing from the crown into the circles. He was taking them. He was stealing her pungits from her.'

Maggie hugs my arm tight as we watch Leonard together. I don't know how much she's understood, how much I understand what he's just said. What would something like that do to a person? What would it feel like to have your connection stolen from you?

'And she died,' finishes Leonard, his voice shaking. 'Right there in front of us.'

We all wait in silence, watching Leonard, whose eyes are blank, unfocused, lost in the memory.

'What . . .' says Maggie quietly, 'what did the Commander do with her pungits?'

Leonard shakes his head. 'Not a thing. They burned out right there in his palms. The experiment was a failure.'

Leonard sighs. 'After Misha, he had a meltdown. Trashed the lab and vowed that he'd make the Move, no matter what. Vowed to go back and find his Mover. That's when I realised what all these experiments were about. It wasn't just for the Shade Unit, for fighting the Nowbies. He wanted to go back in time and get his Mover back. Wanted to re-establish the connection. He was the leader of the Shade Unit. How was he supposed to lead an army of Movers and Shadows if he wasn't one any more? If any of his generals found out, well, it wouldn't be long before they overthrew him.'

'So what happened?' I ask. 'How'd you end up here?'

'Well, I told the Commander,' says Leonard, 'told him that I wouldn't let him do to me what he did to Misha. He couldn't have my pungits, couldn't have Joji's. And you can guess Commander Roth didn't like that much, so he called in a goon squad to haul me and Joji off to some cage where he could keep us prisoner until he was ready to try his experiment again. What made it worse though was the goons that carted us away – they were Shade Unit. So much for "all for one", huh?'

I can see the hurt is still fresh in his face. These people were supposed to be on his team. Until they weren't.

Leonard steals a quick glance at Rani, and when her eyes drop to the floor he looks away. 'So I begged. I'm not proud of it. But I begged my innocent Mover girl to open a door and bring me back so Roth couldn't do to me what he did to Misha. I begged her to risk arrest. I begged her to choose a life on the run from BMAC. I begged her to save my life.'

Rani reaches out and squeezes Leonard's hand, but Leonard can't even look at her. That's the first time I see it, the closeness between them. More than family. It's the kind of closeness that can only come from being in each other's head. The closeness between a Mover and a Shadow.

'What about Oscar?' I ask.

'Once I'd been Moved, there wasn't a lot I could do for him, was there?' says Leonard. 'When it had been just the two of us, alone in that cage, I told him he had to try, that a Move was the only way to save his skin, but he had such a hard time connecting to his Mover. I mean, he couldn't make heads or tails of what was being transmitted on his Mover's end. Wasn't till I met your mother and little Maggie that I finally understood what the issue was.'

I nod, understanding. 'She was just a baby.'

'Exactly. Anyhow, after the Move I kept looking for Joji. If he Moved, I knew from the measurements of his pungits he would have arrived a year before me. It didn't take long to find articles about what happened to him, and to your family. Way I figure it, whatever experiments Roth did on Joji to fix what went wrong with Misha ended up strengthening Joji's connection to Maggie – supercharged the pungits somehow. That's probably why her Moves are so big. They're not natural.'

I look down at my sister, who's chewing on a strand of her own hair. *Not natural.*

'Then when Commander Roth had Joji on the table and was trying to steal his pungits,' says Leonard, 'the baby must've felt how frightened Joji was and opened a door without knowing what she was doing. Poor girl just wanted to make the fear stop.'

'So Roth failed then,' I say. 'Joji died, just like Misha.'

'No, not just like Misha,' says Leonard. 'Joji Moved. He didn't die until he came here. So I think that when Maggie opened the door for Joji, it was right in the middle of Roth's experiment. Roth must have managed to take some of Joji's pungits before Maggie made the Move. She closed the door behind him, leaving Roth in the future, but still, Roth had her pungits. It's the only way he could have stayed connected to Maggie all this time.'

'But still, I don't get it,' I say. 'Maggie's Phase 1.'

'Well, she was just a baby. Not a lot of communicating a baby can do. The connection atrophied and she showed the symptoms of a Phase 1 Mover. Till now. Roth had to wait until she was strong enough before he could make the Move again.'

Strange behaviours. She looks up at me, hair still in her mouth.

'That's how you knew how to fix the water tank,' I realise, remembering the concern on Mom's face. 'Your Shadow told you how to do it.'

She nods, her eyes glossy, and I can see she's worried she's in trouble.

I hate the idea that this crazy Roth man has been inside my little sister's head. Hate that he wanted to use her to bring him here. And I think of the Move, the storm above me and Maggie and the man on the stairs as the crows swirled around him. 'Wait . . . no,' I say. 'I don't understand. The Move happened at school, *my* school! Maggie wasn't even there!'

'She was,' Gabby says. 'She told us she was there, remember?'

Gabby's right. It was when she was in my arms, sobbing on the floor of our bathroom back home. She said she came to Romsey looking for me. She was there, making it happen. 'Mom knew,' I groan, my hands on my knees. 'Mom knew this would happen.'

'Well,' says Leonard, 'she knew it *could* happen. We both did.'

Why didn't she say anything? Why didn't she tell me that Dad – oh, Dad! *You need to take care of her.* All this time that he's been sleeping. All this time he wasn't with us. He gave it up for Maggie.

Everybody's quiet then, and Leonard gets to his feet, finishing up packing whatever trinkets from the junk pile he's decided are important enough to save.

My sister watches me, hands still on my knees, and I don't know how to stand back up. She Moved him. She Moved Gabby's Shadow. What am I supposed to do now?

Gabby's not listening any more, her eyes focused on one of Leonard's monitors. 'Those are my parents.'

NINETEEN

Rani leans over Leonard and taps the keyboard a couple of times until the sound crackles out of a tiny dusty speaker.

'. . . *seen here at a We Are Now rally back in July of 2071,*' says the newscaster. '*The victims were found dead in their home this afternoon, after neighbours called BMAC to report a strange man dressed in black who allegedly blasted his way into the quiet apartment complex.*'

My legs start to shake. Dead. Gabby's parents are dead. Killed by her Shadow. He was at her house. He found out where she lived.

Gabby said it would happen. *He'll find me.*

'*Witnesses tell* Avin News *that the weapon they saw the man use appeared at first glance to be a simple droidlet. But as you can see from the damage behind me, it was anything but.*'

It looks like a bomb went off. Scorch marks and shattered walls and splintered furniture. And I know what caused it. It's like what I saw on the stairs back at Romsey.

The lightning. He went to Gabby's house. He was there. Him and his lightning.

There's a tingle at the base of my skull. My Shadow. The fear swelling in my head has caught his attention.

'BMAC has told Avin News *they believe the killer to be the fugitive Shadow of the victims' own daughter, Gabriela Vargas, a Mover wanted in connection with events at the Romsey Institute earlier today. BMAC Special Agent Beadie Hartman addressed the media moments ago.'*

A woman stands on a podium in front of a microphone, looking older than she probably is. Special Agent Hartman. The name is familiar and I remember it's the name Officer Kelley said back at the apartment. *You're afraid of Hartman.* Her hair is pulled back so tight she looks bald at first glance. Her scowl is deep and hard, like it's been carved into her face. 'Gabriela Vargas is wanted by BMAC for causing the Movement activity at the Romsey Institute for Academics earlier today. Anyone with information on her whereabouts is asked to call BMAC immediately.'

I watch Gabby, her eyes glued to the monitor. Her face is blank. Unreadable. The splinters of her home are right there on the screen for her to see, but she's blank.

'See that?' says Leonard, finger jabbing at the monitor. 'What'd I tell you? Roth's after you, Vargas.'

'Shut up, Leonard,' spits Rani, before turning a concerned gaze on Gabby.

'Gabby?' My hand reaches out for her shoulder, and as my fingers graze Dad's paint-spattered shirt she flinches away from me. Her eyes never leave the screen. I stand there helplessly, while she watches the images of her destroyed apartment flick by, each one worse than the last.

'This is because of me,' she whispers.

'No,' I tell her. 'Gabby, this isn't your fault.'

She closes her eyes, shutting the images out. 'It is, Pat.'

'It's *his* fault, Gabby.' Without my realising it, my hand reaches for her again, but she pulls away and I stop. She doesn't want to hear me. Not right now.

'Look, I'm sorry,' says Leonard. 'Sad, it's all very sad. But this thing isn't over. And I for one don't want to be near Vargas when Roth finds her.'

'Why her?' I say. 'He's here now. Why can't he just leave her alone?'

'She's his Mover,' he says plainly.

'So what?'

Leonard rolls his eyes. 'I told you. Without his Mover connected to him, he's not a Shadow any more. Not really. The war is all about pitting people against each other. Movers and Shadows versus Nowbies. How long before his own army turns on him? Think about it. Without Vargas, Roth is nothing but a Nowbie.'

'But he's got me,' says Maggie nervously.

And he used her. And I hate him for it. Because if BMAC finds out – if BMAC sees my sister's pungits – what will they do to her? She's Moved twice. What kind of punishment will they come up with for something like that?

'That's right,' Rani agrees. 'Why bother going to all this trouble for Vargas when he managed to get himself a new Mover anyway?'

'What would you rather use?' he asks. 'Your own toothbrush,

or someone else's? Gabby is *his*, as far as he's concerned. It's not just about his status as a Shadow any more. It's moved well past that. Gabby's humiliated him by making him the only Shadow to be cut off by his Mover. He wants her back because she's *his*. It's an obsession. He's not gonna give her up without a fight.'

She's wrapped her arms around herself, rocking slightly the way I've seen her do so many times alone at school. So many times, curled up by herself on the roof yard, facing this Roth man in her head all by herself. But she's not by herself right now. I won't let her be by herself.

'And if he finds us?' I ask Leonard. 'Even if he gets his hands on Gabby, and re-establishes a connection somehow, what's to stop her from severing it again?'

Leonard laughs. 'Oh, he's not just gonna leave her here.'

My fists clench at that – if not here, then where?

Gabby's tear-filled eyes turn away from the monitor. 'What do you mean?'

'If I know Roth,' says Leonard, 'he's not gonna risk leaving you all by yourself to just sever the connection as you please. He's gonna take you back to the future with him and make sure you never have a chance to cut him off again.'

'How?' I ask him.

Leonard shakes his head. 'Beats me, but if he's come here, then you can bet he knows how to do it. And I'll bet my brain it's got something to do with that Punch of his.' Leonard holds up his hand, pointing to his palm.

'Punch?' I say. 'You mean that thing that makes the lightning?'

Leonard nods. 'Seen it, have you? His proudest creation.

He was still ironing out the bugs when I saw him last. Looks like he got it working.'

'What's it supposed to do?'

'Never said,' says Leonard. 'But it was important enough to keep secret. And if it has the power to do that—' Leonard points at the images of Gabby's apartment that *Avin News* keeps showing – 'I'd rather not get between him and this girl.' He holds up the droidlets to Rani. 'Look, I've got new FIILES ready to go. All I have to do is load 'em up and we're out of here.'

'To go where?' she says, folding her arms.

'Killberry Beach. Burton Hills. Tokyo. Who cares?' He flicks on the droidlets so their screens bloom to life, *ready for upload* blinking in white light. 'First TLJ out of Avin we can get, we're gone.'

TLJ. A Transit Land Jet – they leave from Fellows Junction for places pretty much anywhere in the world. You can get to the other side of the country in an hour. Other side of the planet in a few. With new FIILES, you could disappear. BMAC wouldn't even know where to start looking. That's what Mom was planning to do.

'And what do you suggest we do with them?' says Rani, waving at me, at Maggie – at Gabby, who's gone back to staring blank-faced at the images on the news.

Leonard takes a seat at the keyboard. 'They're not our problem.'

Rani throws her arms up into the air. 'Just whose problem do you think they are?!' She moves closer and lowers her voice, but still we can hear her say, 'It's not as if their parents are coming to get them, Leonard.'

I watch Gabby, but if she heard, she doesn't show it. She's gone back to rocking herself, her eyes closed and tears spilling down her cheeks.

My fingers fidget in my pocket, rubbing the smooth hard surfaces of the droidlets I brought with us. Mom wanted to run. To leave town. BMAC's looking for me and Gabby. And from the look of Gabby's home on the screen, so is Roth.

And what about Maggie?

How long can I keep her safe from BMAC like Mom and Dad wanted?

I'm scared. Because I know Leonard's right. As long as we're in Avin, it's only a matter of time before BMAC or Roth finds us.

'Take us with you,' I blurt out.

Leonard makes another *pfffft* sound that I know is not a yes.

'We don't have to take the same TLJ as you,' I tell him. 'In fact, we'll go somewhere completely different. Just help us get out of Avin.'

'Kid, even if I brought you to Fellows Junction, you need a droidlet to buy a ticket. And the second they scan your FIILES we'll have BMAC on us faster than you can say *crow pie*.'

I slam the three droidlets down on the desk. 'So give us new ones.'

His eyes narrow as he looks up at me and I stare right back. My pounding heart is ready to break through my ribs, but I don't look away. I don't want Leonard to see how frightened I am. Leave Avin. It's what Mom wanted. But leave without her?

You need to take care of her . . .

173

Leonard watches me, frowning, and it feels as if he can see what's going on in my head.

'Leonard,' says Rani. 'Think of Izzy.'

Leonard's gaze drops and he runs a thoughtful finger along his silvery stubble. 'All right,' he says, grabbing the droidlets. 'But if Roth is looking for you, we've stayed here too long as it is.'

TWENTY

We're standing beside a garbage pile behind a nice looking-office building, waiting for Rani. She and Leonard led me, Maggie and Gabby out of Hexall and back into the city centre. I have no idea what time it is, but it must be late, because there aren't a lot of people in the streets, and the ones that are around are too busy laughing and shouting so they don't pay much attention to us anyway. Still, my nerves are buzzing from being so out in the open, the fresh winds of the Eventualies tickling my hair. I watch the Avin Turbine blink blue and red, its blades slicing at a thick, billowy black sky. The lights of the city shine off the underbellies of the clouds, making what looks like an upside-down sea of black and orange cotton candy. I think we're pretty close to Fellows Junction, based on how close the turbine is. Other than that, I have no idea where we are.

'What are we doing here?' I whisper to Leonard.

He's balancing some kind of tablet on his lap, typing away at a glass screen that's so cracked it looks like a spider web. He looks up to check the street nervously. That has to be the hundredth time he's done that. Like he expects Commander Roth to show up any minute.

'Leonard?'

His eyes flick to me briefly, before he looks back at his tablet. 'Hiding.'

'But what is this place?'

Before he can answer, there's a click of a lock and the door in front of us swings open. Rani stands there, a droidlet in her hand. 'This way,' she says, beckoning us inside.

Maggie and Gabby duck through the door, Beauty swooping along behind them. Leonard managed to scare off the other birds that had been following us back at Hexall Hall. But Beauty wasn't having any of it and followed us the whole way here. I can't decide whether to be mad at the thing or impressed. She's stuck with us this long. Part of me thinks it's because her interest in Maggie isn't just about the Movement. Maybe the dumb bird really does love my sister.

The door slams behind me and Leonard, and I look around trying to get a sense of where we are.

An old parking garage.

I frown, looking at Rani. 'How did you get in here?'

'Idiots haven't changed the entrance code since I was a kid. No one's used it since then, I'll bet.'

'What? Wait, aren't there cameras?'

'Not any more.'

'Well,' says Leonard quickly, tapping his cracked tablet screen. 'Not for five more minutes anyway. So let's go.'

Before I can ask more questions, Rani is speed-walking

across the empty lot to what looks like a panel for a circuit breaker. She clicks it open easy enough and we see it's not a circuit breaker at all – it's a door. A little door into a hidden room.

Rani helps Maggie through, and I follow behind. The door is so small it's a bit of a squeeze even for me. After I'm through, I hold out my hand to Gabby but she ignores me, acting like I'm not there at all. Her eyes are red and swollen and she looks like she's in a daze, like she's not even awake. She's deep inside her own mind now. Probably thinking about what happened to her parents.

'Gabby?' I say, trying to call her back.

She wipes her eyes with the back of her wrist and shakes her head. She doesn't want to talk to me, so I step back. I'd want to be left alone too, I guess.

The stale dusty air in this hidden room makes my nose wrinkle. There are cobwebs hanging from thick iron supports, and boxes of canned food line the walls. Against the far wall are four camp beds; an LED lamp sits on the end of the first one, providing the only light.

'What is this place?' I ask.

Rani has another lamp in her hand, and with a click it blinks to life, lighting up her face. 'A safe house,' she says. 'For We Are Now.'

And now I notice the signs and photos stuck up all over the walls. Framed pictures of burning buildings and giant protests, anti-Mover pamphlets from twenty or thirty years ago. *We Are Now* is written in big letters on every single one. My mouth feels dry and I try to swallow. On one of the posters behind Rani I recognise the BMAC symbol, or an early version of it anyway. It shows cranes and trucks and framework because the picture was taken when it was still under construction, but there's enough of it built to see; it's the Movers' Prison. The caption reads: 'Movement is a *Choice*. Choose to shut the door on tomorrow. BMAC: Patrolling your Present, Protecting your Future.'

Rani cranes her neck around to see what's caught my eye. She huffs, and rolls her eyes. 'Mother and her charming We Are Now chapter used to meet in the restaurant upstairs to plot whatever awful anti-Movers rally or attack they felt would help their cause. When I was little, Mother always made me come along. She didn't tell the others what I was, of course. She was too humiliated. But she wanted me to see how the rest of the world saw my *unnatural* ability. Wanted me to know there were consequences if I ever decided to use it. Anyway, whenever a chapter member was wanted by police for burning down someone's home or place of business, they'd hide out here.'

I feel claustrophobic. It's like the anxious feeling I get every phase-form day, but all of them compounded and piled on top of each other. With all this anti-Movers crap, who knows? There might even be a Shelving facility somewhere around here. Rani grew up around these people? She must have been frightened every single day.

There's a scream of springs as Gabby takes a seat on the furthest bed, facing the wall. Was growing up like that for her too?

'What if someone comes down here?' Maggie's chewing her hair again, ignoring Beauty, who's pecking lovingly at her feet.

'Look at this place,' says Leonard.

'It hasn't been used in years,' says Rani, offering Maggie what looks like a can of fruit cocktail. Maggie slurps the whole thing down in one gulp and my stomach grumbles. We haven't eaten all day. Rani tosses me a can and I pull the tab and crack it open. The juice is sweet and the fruit hits my belly with a cool splash, quenching my hunger pains.

Rani smiles and tosses me another can. 'BMAC does a good enough job keeping the Mover 'threat' under control for We Are Now, so they haven't been as active lately.'

I guess that's true. The We Are Now attacks happened in the days before I was born. Before BMAC was up and running. Now they mostly just protest to make BMAC implement stiffer Mover policies and penalties.

'Besides,' says Leonard, setting up his computer on top of a few jars of spaghetti sauce, 'we'll be gone first thing in the morning. Before anyone even knows we're here.'

First thing in the morning, we'll leave Avin behind. My fingers fumble for a piece of pineapple as Maggie takes a seat on the bed beside Gabby's. Tomorrow morning, we'll leave Mom behind.

A gentle hand rests on my shoulder. 'You should get some sleep,' says Rani. 'All of you.'

Maggie's all too happy for a rest and she lays down, asleep before her head even hits the pillow. I wish I could do that. My body weighs a thousand pounds right now, my limbs are rubber. My eyes feel dry and swollen. But I know I won't sleep. My head is too full to sleep. Full of Mom.

And Dad.

And Oscar Joji.

And Roth.

Gabby sits on her bed, staring at the wall, her face unreadable as ever. She hasn't spoken since Dunedin. Since she found out about her parents. I guess, after everything that's happened today, sleep won't come easy to her either.

A light tingle interrupts my thoughts as my Shadow tries again to get a feel for me. I guess he hasn't been zapped by a jolt of terror from my end for a little while and he wants to make sure I'm not dead. I reach out into the fog with my mind, trying to show him I'm still here, that I'm all right. No sooner does he sense me than he retreats back into himself, satisfied that I'm OK and happy to shut me out. Because that's our normal. Ignoring each other. I made it hard for him to ignore me today.

Leonard's on the floor, leaning against one of the iron beams. He's hunched over his tablet and computer, hands working furiously. He's emptied his duffle bag, and the contents are strewn around him. I recognise the pungit ray on his left. The droidlets for me, Maggie and Gabby sit on his right, blinking with white light, ready to be loaded.

I sit down beside him with my can of fruit, trying to get a look at the screens. 'You think you can finish?'

'Hmm?'

'The FIILES,' I say, chewing on a cherry that tastes like sugary heaven. 'You think you can get them done tonight?'

Leonard lets himself grin – only half. 'Is there another option?'

I don't answer that. He knows there isn't.

'Then I guess I'd better get on with it.'

I know he's patronising me, but it makes me feel better. I'd rather he was confident than unsure. Though I guess he ought to be confident by now. After all the FIILES he's made for Mom.

Mom.

I beg myself not to think about her. Sitting alone in some BMAC cell. Worried about Maggie. About me. Which of course only makes me think about her.

'My mom,' I say quietly, 'she knew about all this?'

Leonard doesn't look up. 'All what?'

I reach for the pungit ray, turning it over in my hands. There's a panel missing on one side of the metal tube, a mess of delicate wires and tiny cylinders assembled carefully inside. 'About you. And the war in the future. About Roth and Oscar Joji. You know, all of it.'

He nods.

'So she knows about Gabby then?' I say. 'That she discovered pungits?'

Leonard scratches hard behind his ear. 'I mean, she knows Roth had a Mover that managed to sever the connection. I don't know that I ever mentioned the name Gabriela Vargas to her.'

No, I don't think I did either. No one seems to talk much about Gabby.

'She should have told BMAC,' I say, suddenly angry with her. 'In the future. She should have told them how she severed the connection and then they could just cure all of us once and for all so this sort of thing doesn't happen again.'

Leonard stops typing. '*Just* cure us? You think you need to be cured?'

I drop my eyes to the pungit ray, trying to get away from that stare. Do I think I need to be cured? All I can do is shrug, because I don't know. I guess things might be easier if I wasn't a Mover any more. I shrug again.

Gently Leonard takes the pungit ray from my hands. I watch him connect one of the wires to one of the tiny cylinders, then another, before he finally clicks the on button. There's a quiet hum from the little machine and he points it towards me. He grabs the mirror from among the strewn contents of his bag and holds it up so I can see myself, the pungits fanning out above my head.

'You're not sick, kid,' says Leonard. 'You got something that makes you special. A power. Don't let BMAC take it away.'

Power? I've never thought of it that way.

After what Maggie's Move did back at school, I guess maybe Leonard has a point. What Maggie did when she Moved Roth – *that* was powerful.

No wonder Mom didn't want BMAC to find out.

I watch my sister, curled up on her side and fast asleep. First Dad gave up his life for her. Now Mom.

There's a click as Leonard turns off the pungit ray and unhooks the little copper wires.

'What about you?' I ask him, knocking back what's left of my fruit can. 'Why do you want to help my mom?'

'Because she helped me,' he says, putting the ray into the duffel bag. 'After Rani Moved me, the two of us were on the run from BMAC. I came here with nothing, no FIILES, and Rani was just a kid. I knew if we didn't set up some bogus FIILES fast, BMAC would find us easily. We needed help. When I managed to track down the articles on Joji and your family, I read about your mom's job. She was working for the government, in the Service Avin offices.'

Setting up marriage licences and liquor licences and stuff like that. That was a long time ago. I can't even remember Mom going to a normal job.

'I needed droidlets, and she could get 'em,' explains Leonard. 'So I told her what I knew about Joji and her baby and Roth.' He stops there, looking uncomfortable.

'And what happened?'

He sighs. 'Look, kid, you have to understand that when you're desperate, you do things you don't want to do.'

'Like what? What do you mean?'

He shakes his head and clears his throat. 'I, uh, well, I blackmailed her. I told her that if she didn't get us the droidlets, I'd tell BMAC about the baby.'

I frown. 'You threatened Maggie?'

'Well, I'm not proud of it.'

'You must have terrified her,' I say, thinking of Mom, alone with two little kids, facing this strange Hexall Hall man at her door.

Leonard smiles warmly. 'She was scared, sure, but your mom's pretty sharp. She figured I couldn't go to BMAC without getting myself into trouble in the process. So she told me that if I ever went to BMAC about her daughter, she'd rat on me as soon as they came for her.'

I grin. That sounds like Mom. 'Is that why you do all that droidlet stuff for her? Cos she can turn you in whenever she wants?'

He laughs. 'Well, that's certainly one of the reasons. But really, I think she comes to me because she knows she can trust me. After I failed at threatening her to get us the droidlets, she helped us anyway. I think she took pity on us, to be honest. It was a big risk. And it saved Rani and me. I owe your mom.'

Owe her. Guilt pricks at my heart. That doesn't really sum up all the things Mom's done for me. For Maggie. How can I just leave her behind?

I guess Leonard can see how the gears in my head are turning because he nods at the camp beds. 'Kid,' he says wearily, 'get some sleep.'

I know I'm not going to. But I also know Leonard doesn't want me sitting over his shoulder all night. I push myself off the floor and carry my empty fruit can and my sluggish body over to where Maggie's sleeping. Rani is fast asleep on the bed beside hers. And Gabby sits facing the wall, staring at nothing. Her shoulders tremble and I can hear her sniffling.

'Gabby,' I say, standing beside her camp bed, 'you OK?'

She wipes at her face, keeping her back to me. Obviously not. After what Roth did to her parents. They may have been We Are Now. But still. They were her parents. I don't know what to say. I try to think of something, but all that comes out is, 'I'm sorry about your parents.'

Gabby presses her palms into her eyes and groans.

I bite my lip. That was a stupid thing to say. *Sorry*. It's too small a word. Too insignificant. What good is sorry to Gabby? Sorry can't help her.

I try to think of something else to say, something better, but Gabby speaks before I can.

'They were right,' she says. 'Movers *are* dangerous. My parents are dead because of me.'

'That's not true.' I sit down on the end of her bed, but she doesn't turn to face me. 'Gabby, this happened because of Roth. Not you.'

She stares at the wall and I can see the left side of her face – tear-stained and glistening. Her shoulders rise and fall as she breathes deeply, trying to control the tears. And then I notice her fingers. She has her hands in her lap, her fingers smeared with blood as she scratches mechanically at them.

'I didn't mean for any of this to happen.'

'I know that, Gabby.' Of course I know it. But she looks at me doubtfully and I wrack my brain, trying to think of something to reassure her, something to make her believe that this isn't her fault.

'I should never have tried to find pungits.' Her voice swells with what I know are more tears, and my heart hurts to hear it. 'I just want to make him shut up! I want him out of my head!'

I watch her as she grabs her head, her eyes squeezed shut like she's trying to squeeze him out of her mind.

'You can hear him still?' I ask.

'Both of them,' she says, opening her eyes. 'I didn't understand it at first, why there were two voices in my head. There's my Roth. The one I know. The one who's younger, in the future. The one who hasn't been disconnected yet. But then there's this older version. The one Maggie Moved here, the one who has been disconnected. He's close up. Real loud. It's like what Leonard said about lightning striking. I think when Maggie Moved Roth here, my pungits were attracted to him. They got confused and some of them diverted from my Roth in the future to the Roth that's here now. The path of least resistance.'

My eyebrows go heavy. 'You're saying . . . are you saying he *did* it? He's reconnected? Just by Moving here?'

She nods sadly. 'I think so.'

'Can he feel where you are? Does he know where we are now?'

She shakes her head. 'No, it's like I said. The connection is loud, just a mess of noise. Like it's overcrowded.'

'Because there are two of them?'

'I think it's more like three.' She looks past me, over to where Maggie's sleeping.

'Maggie?' I ask.

'I think her pungits are getting in the way of mine.'

Because Roth stole them.

Like listening to two songs at once, Maggie had said. When we were walking to Hexall Hall. I didn't think much of it at the time, but . . .

'Roth's connected to both of you?'

Gabby nods.

My heart skips a couple of beats. 'Can he tell where Maggie is?'

'I don't think so. If I can't sort through all the noise, I doubt he can.'

'Maggie hasn't said anything.'

'She probably can't make sense of it either.'

No, I guess not. I can't imagine what that would even feel like. It's got to hurt their heads, having someone else in the mix. There's just not enough room for that. Even for me and my Shadow, and I'm only Phase 1. He's so quiet to me and still I know it would be overwhelming. Especially if I could feel him so close all of a sudden.

She looks at me then. 'I can't hear him clearly. But still I *feel* him. He wants to find me so bad. Bad enough to kill my parents, Pat. He'll hurt someone else, I know he will.' Her black eyes are welling over and a couple of tears fall out. 'I can't escape him. I should just let him find me.'

'No, Gabby.' Without thinking, my hand reaches for hers. She jerks away so suddenly she practically jumps off the bed.

I pull my hand back. 'Sorry, I didn't mean to—'

She shakes her head, holding her hand close to her chest. 'No, I'm sorry. I'm just—' Her skin has gone all red and blotchy and she stares at the mattress. 'I don't know what I am.'

'Gabby?' I say, trying to get her to look up. She doesn't. 'Gabby, Roth's not going to find you. We're out of here tomorrow. He won't have any idea where you've gone.'

She glances at me then – the Mover girl I've sat beside every day at school. The Mover girl that everyone loved to tease but never bothered to get to know. The Mover girl with secrets. Dark ones. Whom no one ever bothered to help.

'I won't let him find you,' I promise.

Her eyes drop back down. 'I don't want you to get hurt too.'

'Gabby, I'm serious,' I tell her. 'He's not gonna find you cos you're coming with us, whether you want to or not. I won't let him find you.'

She doesn't say anything, but there's the tiniest of smiles on her lips. And I suddenly feel a little lighter knowing Gabby believes me.

TWENTY-ONE

Avin's heart is Fellows Junction. Standing in line for the TLJ, waiting to go through security, every person in the city must be milling in and around the station. Underground commuters in business suits and carrying briefcases, families dressed for vacation struggling with luggage, university students with backpacks. I've only been to Fellows once before. Mom took me on the underground to go to the Avin Turbine. I'd been so excited, I guess I didn't pay much attention to what was going on around me. Now, standing in among the crowds, I'm sweating. It will only take one of them to recognise us. I feel my sunglasses in my hoodie pocket. I want to put them on, to hide my face, but Rani said I looked ridiculous with sunglasses and a hood. She said the same thing about Gabby's blue ninja scarf.

'The trick to hiding,' she said, 'is blending in. These get-ups scream, "Please don't look at me."'

So she shaved my head. With a little pink laser that's supposed to be for shaving ladies' legs. We Are Now was pretty considerate of its safe house tenants' hygiene. I rub the feathery stubble and see my face reflected in the shiny white tiled wall of Fellows Junction. My head's a weird shape. I miss my hair already. But Rani was right. I don't look like myself.

Gabby watches me rub my hair and her eyes dart to the shiny wall. She inspects her freshly bleached locks, neatly braided down her back by Rani. Just one bottle of bleach and Gabby looks like a completely different person. Her usual dark curls have gone platinum blonde. Her lips look pinker as she presses them together and I can tell she's not as unhappy about her makeover as I am about mine.

Maggie stands ahead of us in line, between Rani and Leonard, as we wait to pass through the security scanners. She managed to escape Rani's makeover. I guess she looks enough like a normal little boy with her hair under my hat that there wasn't much more Rani needed to do.

My eyes drift up towards the glass ceiling, metal beams criss-crossing to make Fellows look like a crystal dome. Not far away is Beauty, who's managed to find herself a nice perch among the pigeons. I wasn't happy about her following us, but she's kept her distance. It's like she knows she could give us away. Or maybe she's just taken the hint after Maggie spent all morning swatting at her.

The line begins to move and I feel a flutter in my stomach. We only budge two steps, but that's two steps closer to using my new FIILES. I reach into my pocket and feel the new droidlet's smooth surface. In moments, the security officer will pull up my bogus identity – Max Carver

– and scan the tickets Leonard loaded to the droidlet. I pull out the little grey sphere and swipe the surface so the holographic screen blooms to life. I pull up the TLJ ticket.

3 March 2083

From: Fellows Junction, Avin City

To: Pondu Terminal, Killberry Beach.

Killberry Beach. I swallow. Leonard chose Killberry Beach because it's still in the country. Me, Gabby and Maggie are minors. Can't leave the country without a parent or guardian with us. Leonard and Rani aren't coming with us. Rani's carrying Leonard's carefully packed duffle bag. They're off to some sunny island country somewhere. And Mom's not coming with us. My throat feels dry. Killberry Beach is on the other side of the country. I've never been more than a few blocks away from my mother. And as we shift closer to the security scanners, I realise I've never been away from my mother this long before. If we go to Killberry Beach, how long before I see her again?

'You remember what I said?' says Leonard, noticing me looking through the droidlet. His eyes glance around nervously, afraid someone is listening. 'The thing I told you about, uh, about your allowance?'

I nod. He's talking about the money. He set up bank accounts to our droidlets, one for me and Maggie, and one for Gabby. When we want to pay for something, his program reaches into other people's accounts all across the country – three cents here, a dollar there – giving us what we need without anybody noticing.

'That'll help you get by for two days,' he warned us back at the safe house. 'After that the program shuts down and you're going to have to figure out some other way to get money.'

'Why does it shut down?' I asked him.

'Cos it usually takes the bank forty-eight hours to notice a hack like that. If you don't want them to know you've been stealing people's money, I suggest you figure out a job as soon as you get to Killberry Beach.'

Stealing. It's only a little bit. But still. I feel like Mom wouldn't be OK with stealing. Then again, Mom's had Leonard set up FIILES for Movers before. I wonder if he set up the same kind of program for them.

'You two.'

I look up from my droidlet and see a sour-looking security guard wave Leonard and Maggie forward to the first scanner. The scanners are lined up – six silver doors in a white tiled wall. Maggie looks back at me nervously, and I nod to let her know it's OK. But I don't know it's OK. I hold in a deep breath. Now we find out how good a programmer Leonard is.

'You,' says the sour-faced guard, beckoning Rani forward. She directs her to the scanner at the far end, then points at Gabby. Gabby's scratching at her finger and I can see the security guard notice. My heart rate is supersonic, and there's a tingling in my skull as my Shadow reaches out for me.

'This one, please,' the guard says, motioning Gabby to one of the scanners in the middle.

Gabby shuffles forward and I follow on her heels, but the guard reaches out a hand to stop me. 'Wait your turn, sir.'

'Uh, yeah,' I stutter, stepping back. 'Sorry . . . s-sorry.'

I stand there awkwardly, trying not to fidget, though my nerves feel electric as I watch Gabby step into the scanner. I look across to where Leonard and Maggie have stepped into their scanner. I can't see them on the other side, but I don't hear any sirens or anything. So that's a good sign.

The guard points to the far scanner where she sent Rani. 'Over there, sir.'

''K, thanks.' I hurry over as Rani disappears inside the silver door. There's a sign above it. *Wait for green light.*

The light above the door blinks red.

Beside the door is a little stand with a small hole in the top. *Please deposit droidlet.*

My fist is sweaty, closed around the little sphere that holds my phony FIILES. *Leonard does this all the time,* I remind myself. *Mom was going to do this exact same thing. Mom knew this would work. This will work.*

The light still blinks red. What's taking so long?

This will work. Mom knew it would work.

And then the light turns green.

With my Shadow nervously pinging through my head, I step up to the door and hold my droidlet over the hole. My hand shakes. We're here now. We've come this far. And there's no way to go back.

Here goes.

The little grey sphere disappears into the hole and the scanner door slides open with a hiss. Knees shaking, I step into the black chamber. It's almost like being back in the closet at home. The door hisses closed behind me. There's a tick. Then another. And another. And then the ticks all run together in rapid succession as something grinds and purrs in the walls. There's a flash of light. Then two more.

And I'm left in quiet darkness.

I've never actually been in a security scanner before. As I stand there in the dark, counting the seconds passing, I wonder how long is too long. Is this normal? My blood feels icy and my brain starts to tingle as my Shadow senses my panic. He's pushing me, wanting me to stop it, but I don't. I can't. Because I *am* panicking. Because I've been waiting too long. Something's wrong. The realisation drops into my gut like a rock and my mind reaches out for my Shadow. I can feel him reaching back. And I cling to him, like a baby holding his mother's hand.

I'm nearly blinded by light as the sliding door in front of me hisses open and a guard blocks my way. He's got my droidlet in his hand, swiping through my FIILES.

'Sir, would you step over here, please?'

'I – uh – is something wrong?' I ask.

'Over here, please.'

I do as I'm told and he directs me over to the side, away from the turnstile that leads to the gates. Rani stands just inside, concern weighing down her brow.

'What's the problem here?' she demands. And the guard doesn't seem to care for her tone.

'Do you know this boy, ma'am?'

Rani's frown disappears instantly, looking less like the fierce forebrawler she is and more like a cornered rat. She struggles to come up with an answer and I realise she's wishing she hadn't opened her mouth.

The guard beckons to two more security officers, who come over and stand on either side of Rani. 'Step to the side, ma'am.'

Her head swivels from one guard to the other as they grab hold of her arms. 'What is this?'

'Your droidlet, ma'am.'

Rani ignores him, trying to pull her arms free. The guard on her left grabs the droidlet out of her hand and gives it to my guard. He drops the little sphere into what looks like a metal box, his eyes on a monitor that I can't get a look at.

'Amelia Walcott?' he says, with a raised eyebrow.

The fear in Rani's eyes gives way to something else – something determined. 'Yes, that's me,' she says, as cool as anything.

The guard looks back at his screen, his eyes moving quickly as they read whatever the scanner is showing him. What can he see there? He let Rani through already. What's there now that wasn't before?

Through the uniformed security officers surrounding us I see Leonard on the other side of the turnstile, his hands gripping tight to Maggie's shoulders as they watch us with gaping mouths. They made it through security. The guards aren't even looking at them.

'Mr Carver?'

Gabby stands beside Leonard and her dark eyes meet mine. She takes a step, like she's going to come back through the turnstile for me, but Leonard pulls her back.

'Mr Carver!' snaps the guard.

Oh right.

I'm Max Carver.

I look up at the guard, whose nose is crinkled like he can smell exactly what's wrong with the situation. 'Would you come with me, please?'

It's not a request. It's an order. He takes a firm hold of my elbow, the two of us following Rani and the security officers who are still holding her by each arm.

'Where are we going?'

The guard doesn't answer me. And it doesn't take me long to find out anyway. Because at the end of the line of scanners, there's a heavy grey door, a small sign that reads SECURITY PERSONNEL smack dab in the middle of it. Rani's escorts tap in a code and push her inside.

'Please wait in here,' says my guard, 'Mr Carver.'

The way he says it leaves no doubt. He knows it's not my name.

The room is small and white, with an old grey carpet and a bench against the far wall that Rani plonks herself onto. My hands shake as I take a seat beside her.

The door slams shut with a bang, and the two of us are left alone in the quiet.

My chest feels tight and it's hard for me to breathe. He knows I'm not Max Carver. He knows I'm not who my FIILES say I am.

And the question that's strangling my breath loops through my head again and again, my Shadow struggling to understand.

Do they know who I really am?

'Don't speak,' says Rani suddenly.

'What?'

She's not looking at me; she's watching the door. Her jaw is tight and I see the cords of her neck pulse as she swallows. 'When they get here, don't say anything at all.'

'When who gets here?' I shift nervously in my seat. Because I know who.

She looks at me then, her eyes cold and hard, like the forebrawler she is. 'BMAC.'

TWENTY-TWO

I've been staring at the door for ever. An hour? Two hours? Maybe three, who knows? Rani and I haven't said a word to each other, both of us quietly sweating as we wait for someone to come back for us.

I rub my face, trying not to think about Maggie, about Gabby. They got through security. The guards didn't notice anything wrong with their FIILES. But still I'm worried. After they shut me and Rani away, did security go back for my sister? For Gabby? They still had to get to their gates. What if the guards stopped them before they could board the TLJ to Killberry Beach? I chew the nail on my middle finger. What if they did get the TLJ? What if Maggie and Gabby have gone to Killberry Beach without me? How will I find them again?

The door flies open with a bang and I sit up. Rani was right. Two BMAC officers, stun staffs displayed prominently from their belts, stand either side of the door, letting two very serious-looking women enter the room. They're not wearing the usual grey uniform of BMAC officers. They're just in normal-looking grown-up clothes. But they aren't normal. They're BMAC for sure. I recognise the second woman, her hands clasped neatly behind her back. She was on *Avin News*, after Gabby's house.

I glance down at the badge dangling at her hip. It has the BMAC emblem emblazoned on it. There's a picture of her smiling, bleached teeth glowing next to her orangey-leather skin, her sandy-coloured hair tied in the same sloppy ponytail she's wearing now. *Special Agent Beadie Hartman, Investigations Division.*

The feathery wings in my stomach multiply so it feels like there's a whole flock losing their minds in there. Agents are serious. So very serious.

The security guard who stopped me enters behind them. He's sweating a lot more than when I saw him last. He's holding Rani's duffle bag, which he hands to Hartman's colleague. He hugs the wall as he slides in behind the agents, practically cowering as the women look at him like he's gum they found stuck to their shoe.

'Where's the girl?' snaps Hartman.

The security guard trembles as he looks at Rani, opening his mouth to say something, but the other agent cuts him off. 'You only apprehended these two?'

'That's right ma'am.'

Hartman tilts her head in my direction. 'The boy's been travelling with his little sister and Vargas.'

Maggie. Gabby.

'The girls have to be here somewhere. What were you doing when you flagged the boy? You just let passengers pass through like it's no big deal? What kind of opera-tion—'

The other agent holds up a hand to stop Hartman's rant before it can really get going, and Hartman breathes in, one noisy breath through flared nostrils.

'W-we didn't have reason to believe the boy was travel-ling with anyone but this woman,' stutters the guard.

'Have you reviewed the security footage?' asks the other agent. 'I want everything from the entrances to the food courts to the security gates, before and after these two passed through the scanners.'

'Yes, ma'am,' says the guard, heading for the door.

'I'm afraid to ask.' Hartman's eyes are closed tight, as if her head is hurting. 'Tell me you've suspended all TLJs out of the city.'

The guard stops, looks back, the beads of sweat drenching his sideburns. 'We didn't realise that would be necessary. We—'

'It is necessary,' says the other agent. 'No jets leave this station until I say so. I want every guard you've got at every gate looking for Vargas. She's in this station, and she needs to be found now.'

'What's the point?!' Hartman explodes. Her voice is shrill, frantic, but still she keeps her hands clasped behind her back. 'They've got a two-hour head start on us. I wouldn't be surprised if Vargas's halfway to China by now!'

My eyes shift to Rani – could they be gone? Could they have left Avin?

Rani doesn't notice. She's too busy watching the agent who has her bag, her mouth in a thin tight line. The agent waves the guard away, and he's all too happy to run out the door. She pats Hartman calmly on the shoulder and the agitated agent rolls her neck, trying to get a hold of herself.

'Rani Nair,' says the calm agent, zipping open the duffle bag. 'Caused the Movement activity seen over Holland's Street, 2078. This is you, yes?'

The agent digs through the contents of the bag, pulling up what looks like a lot of worthless junk. When she pulls out the pungit ray, I sense Rani freeze. The agent doesn't notice, inspecting the odd-looking flashlight. She clicks the on button, but when nothing happens she tosses it back in the bag like she did with all the rest of the garbage. She hands the bag to one of the other BMAC officers and starts scrolling through a shiny black droidlet.

She projects an image onto the wall between Rani's head and mine. It's an image of a girl, a little older than me, frowning for her school picture. Her angry eyes are still the same. The picture is Rani.

Rani crosses one leg over the other.

'BMAC's been looking for you for a long time, Ms Nair.'

Rani raises her chin just a bit, and Hartman scoffs.

The other agent smiles an unamused smile. 'I'm Special Agent Frost. I will be escorting you to BMAC's offices this afternoon. My associate Special Agent Hartman will accompany us and your young friend here.'

'I don't know the boy,' says Rani.

Frost looks back at Hartman, who shakes her head. 'She's not important to me,' says Hartman. 'She's all yours. I only want to speak with Mr Mermick.'

When she says my name, I feel as if I've been kicked in the stomach, my breath gone from my lungs. She knows me. I knew she did as soon as she walked in here, but hearing her say my name makes it even more real.

'Do you know why you were stopped, Mr Mermick?' says Hartman. Her eyes are an icy blue, with heavy eyelids and puffy bags underneath them like she hasn't slept in days. Her pupils are so small she looks crazy.

She holds up my droidlet.

I drop my gaze to my lap and don't say anything, just like Rani told me.

'Of course, you're only a boy, so I don't expect you'd know.' She pulls up a screen that is entirely code, a bunch of numbers and symbols that don't mean anything as far as I can tell. 'You see this? This is your SIT – secure identity tag. A string of sixty-four characters generated by the government to uniquely identify each individual person in the country.'

I keep staring at my lap. I don't understand what that means.

'Do you know how many combinations a string of sixty-four randomly generated characters allows for?'

No.

'Neither do I. The number would be so large I'm not even sure we have a word for it.'

'Infinite, I'd say,' says Frost.

'Not quite,' says Hartman. 'But still, enough that I'm sure you or whoever created this SIT for you knew the chances of repeating an existing number were next to impossible.'

When I glance back up, I wish I hadn't. Her crazy eyes are dagger focused at me under obnoxiously high arching eyebrows. '*Next* to,' she repeats. 'Unfortunately for you, this SIT number already belongs to a citizen of this country.' She projects an image from her own white droidlet onto the wall where Rani's picture had been. An old woman, shrivelled and bespectacled, smiles toothlessly back at us. 'One Mrs Addison Granger. Resident of Acra county. Ninety-two years of age. Quite the gardener, so I understand it from her profile.'

'When your SIT was flagged at security,' says Frost, 'they sent your image to BMAC.'

'I've had my officers running around the entire city looking for you for two days, Mr Mermick.' She bends down, her face uncomfortably close to mine. 'You and Gabriela Vargas.'

'I haven't seen her,' I croak.

Hartman's nostrils flare just a bit, and her crazy eyes go just a little wider. It's like there's a caged animal behind that fancy suit of hers, and for a second I'm afraid she's going to let it loose on me. Her voice is quiet when she speaks. 'We will get along much better, you and me, if you tell me the truth.'

'I am telling the truth.'

'Have it your way, Mr Mermick.' She takes a step back and nods at the BMAC officers standing beside the door.

I shrink back against the wall when I see them, the glowing, crackling electric blue in the officers' hands – current bindings. Like the kind they put on Dad.

Rani and I are hauled to our feet, and a hot burning

surrounds my wrists as the BMAC officer roughly binds my hands together.

Hartman looks down her nose at me, a filthy slug she can't get rid of soon enough. 'Load 'em up,' she orders.

TWENTY-THREE

My knees knock together as I sit across from Rani, our legs nearly touching in the back of the truck. The hum of our bindings fills the silence between us, my wrists itching from the heat as we speed off to BMAC Headquarters. Or worse.

'Will they find them?' I say, almost asking the universe rather than Rani.

She keeps her head resting on the wall of the truck, staring up at the ceiling, 'What?'

'BMAC. Will they find the girls?'

Rani sighs and lets her elbows rest on her knees. We both stare at the menacing electric glow of the bindings dancing around her wrists. After what feels like forever, she shakes her head. 'Leonard is with them. He won't risk getting on a TLJ now. Not with security on high alert. He'll find somewhere for them to hide. They'll be OK.'

I hope Rani is right.

But what about me? My eyes begin to sting.

'They're gonna Shelve us, aren't they?'

Rani keeps her head hanging, rubbing her wrists where the cuffs are starting to burn.

Yeah. They're gonna Shelve us.

I'm hot all over, my pits pouring sweat. It must hurt, the needle to the head. And how long will it take before the drug makes its way to my brain? And when it does, will I still think? Will I dream? Will I know I can't wake up? Or will I not dream at all? Will it just be nothingness?

My hands start to tremble and Rani sees it. 'Take a breath,' she orders, and I try but it hurts in my chest. 'Breathe even, breathe slow.'

I do what she tells me, shakily pulling the air into my lungs, then pushing it out.

'Pat, listen to me,' she says.

I take another breath, the effort causing me pain, and watch as Rani's eyes stare into mine. 'Don't show them you're afraid,' she says. 'We are what we are, and we're not sorry for it.'

Her throat throbs as she swallows and I can see even with her hard-set jaw that she's terrified. It's in there, hiding behind all the stone she's built up on the outside, but it's there, and suddenly I feel more nauseous. Rani is right. I'm gonna be Shelved, and I can't be scared.

'I'm sorry,' I tell her, my voice catching. 'I'm sorry I got you involved in this.'

Rani rubs at the skin beneath the binds. If she heard me, she's choosing to ignore it.

There's a change in the rumble of the engine and it's enough to tell me we've slowed down. My breath comes back in tight, quick gulps and I can't help it, the panic is drowning me as I wait for the truck to stop.

'Be calm, Patrick,' says Rani, my full name comforting in her smooth and steady voice.

My Shadow's reaching for me now, his worried presence trying to get a feel for what's got me so unravelled, and as the truck finally stops with a squeal of the brake I find myself reaching out to him, frantically trying to grab onto him like I did in the security scanner.

There are voices just outside the doors and a heavy clicking sound of locks being undone.

'Don't show them,' Rani warns.

My Shadow's there; I'm holding onto him so tightly and I'm relieved he's holding me back. What I've put out to the future has scared him, and he's not going to leave me to face it alone. I *feel* the air in my lungs, charged with terror, and I release it, blowing it out through puffed cheeks. I'm not alone in this. I can't be afraid.

The light bursts in as the door flies open and two BMAC officers reach for us. 'Let's go,' grumbles the heavy one, and he grabs me by the arm, hauling me out. Waiting patiently by the kerb is Hartman, her hands still held behind her back. She looks at me smugly, almost triumphant, before she turns her attention to Rani.

'Take her around the back. Special Agent Frost is expecting her in prep,' she says, and Rani's nostrils flare just a little. I can hear her breath waver, but Hartman takes no notice. 'The boy comes with me.'

Hartman turns her back to us and marches towards the giant building. I've never seen it from this side, but I know those obnoxiously shiny gold windows. BMAC Headquarters. I look over at Rani, who I can tell is trying her best not to tremble. Take her around the back? We both know what that means. The Movers' Prison is at the back. The Shelves.

The officer holding tight to Rani drags her back to the van while mine grabs me by the shoulder and pushes me forward. I crane my neck, wanting to call out for Rani, but they've already locked her back inside the truck.

I stumble a bit and the officer takes hold of my other arm. 'Keep moving,' he huffs.

I feel a gush of sweat in my armpits and my head feels dizzy the closer I get to the big gold building. When I was younger I saw it up close from the front once. Mom came to talk to someone at BMAC about Dad. I hated the look of it even then. The front entrance had a big overhanging triangle thing, that made it look like some kind of palace from outer space, with palm trees and hibiscus plants decorating the gardens even though this is a pine trees and birches part of the world. It had frightened me then. But from here, the side of it – one simple door that looks like a fire exit, no plants, no signs – I'm even more afraid. This is the Movers' entrance.

Hartman holds the door open for me. 'Just through here, Mr Mermick.'

As if I have any control over where I go now.

The inside is less expensive-looking than I imagined. I don't know what I thought I'd see. Marble hallways that echo as you walk maybe. But no. The floor is dingy salmon-coloured tile, and the walls are a chipped, cracked mess of faded yellow. You'd never know from the fancy shine of the outside just how sad the inside really is.

We load into a tiny elevator, barely big enough for the three of us, and the woman punches the button for floor 15, *Criminal Movement Investigations Department*. There's another surge of acid in my stomach. *Criminal*.

With a ding the doors open up onto another unremarkable hallway. There are carts with boxes and filing parked crookedly outside rows of office doors, and as we round the first corner, a lot of cubicles with fat BMAC agents yakking to each other or yelling into phones. It smells of old greasy food and bleach.

They all stop what they're doing when they see us coming, a lot of them clapping and congratulating Special Agent Hartman. She smiles at the applause and leads me deeper into BMAC, slamming through a set of double doors that open into a white hallway with green floors. It's quiet in here. Clean too. Not like the outer part. Doors line the walls, each one labelled *Room A*, or *B*, or *C*. Not enough to give me any clue of what the rooms are used for.

Hartman stops at the door marked *Room F* and finally turns to face me, her hands clasped behind her back. 'This would be you, Mr Mermick,' she says, as the fat officer roughly brings me to a stop. She gives him a nod and he removes my bindings. The skin is bright red, and it stings, blisters forming on the inside of my wrists. 'I'm not going to lie to you, son – you're facing quite a lot of trouble.' Her voice is stern but measured, like she's trying to reason with me over clearing the table after dinner. 'We're well aware that you've been helping the Vargas girl evade justice, and

I don't need to remind you that what she's done is a terrible crime. It would serve you well to know that I am here to help you out of this situation.'

She waits for me to say something, the corners of her mouth turning downwards with every second I don't respond.

'But I can't help you,' she speaks slowly, making sure I understand each word, 'if you don't co-operate with me.'

I keep my eyes on the green tile.

'Do you know where I can find Gabriela Vargas?'

There are flecks of white and blue in each tile. How long would it take me to count them?

'Mr Mermick,' says Hartman, raising her voice just a little, 'do you know the girl's whereabouts?'

I don't, not really. I don't know if they got the TLJ, or if Leonard took them somewhere to hide. And even if they got to Pondu Terminal, Killberry Beach, where they'd go when they reached there is anyone's guess. I suddenly realise I'm glad I know so little. Whatever this woman does to me, at least I know I can't give her what she wants.

'You've had a big day,' she says finally, turning to the blinking scanner mounted just beside the door. 'I'll give you the night to rest and think over what I've just said.' She places her index finger on the green grid and the red light blinks white, there's a click, and I'm shoved inside. The door slams shut behind me.

It's a white, windowless room. A plastic chair and a long black desk sit in the middle.

'Pat?'

In the corner on the floor, a beautiful lady dressed in

white, her brown hair in wild knots, sits up, her eyes wet as she reaches out for me. My heart swells at the sight of her. My knees feel weak and I burst into tears so suddenly that I collapse into her arms.

Mom.

TWENTY-FOUR

Mom's hair smells like her raspberry shampoo, and she rocks me back and forth as I breathe her in. I have to hold on so tight to make sure she doesn't go away again. She pulls me back from her, her hands on either side of my face, and wipes my tears away.

'Where's Maggie?' she says. 'Do they have your sister? Pat, you have to tell me, honey, did they bring her here?'

I shake my head. 'She's with Leonard.'

Mom looks as if she's going to faint at the sound of his name coming out of my mouth.

'He told me, Mom,' I say. 'He told me what you and Dad did for Maggie.'

She waits, and I know she can see it on my face. There's no disguising how mad I am.

'Why didn't you tell me, Mom?'

She starts to say something but it's like her voice gets caught somewhere in her throat cos nothing comes out. She runs her hand over my buzzed head and just looks at me, searching my face the way she does whenever I'm upset, as if the right thing to say will be sitting on my cheeks. This time she can't find it, cos this time is bigger than anything before it.

'I thought—' she starts – 'I thought I was protecting you. Both of you.'

And I knew that, before she said it, I knew that's what she'd tell me. But it didn't protect us, did it? Because I'm sitting here. And Maggie's out there somewhere, and so is Gabby. And what happens if BMAC finds them?

Or worse . . .

Roth.

'I hoped,' she says, shaking her head, 'your father and I both did, that we could protect you from all this. I hoped we could outrun it all. I was wrong.'

And it's not good enough. Her reason isn't good enough for me and she knows it, I see it in the tears on her cheeks. But it's all she's got. So she pulls me tightly to her and the two of us hang on to each other as we rock back and forth.

'How did you . . .?' she starts, but her voice is barely a whisper, trying not to cry. 'How did you even get here?'

I sit there, with my face pressed into her shoulder, and fill my lungs with the smell of raspberry. There's so much that's happened, so much that's changed since I saw her only just two days ago that I don't know if I have the strength to tell her everything. But she needs to know. She'll know what we do now.

'They stopped me at security at Fellows Junction. I figured out what you were gonna do, so I got Leonard to—' Mom clamps her hand over my mouth. She holds her finger to her ear, then points at the ceiling. BMAC's listening. That's why Hartman brought me here – to let me confide in Mom and use whatever I say to find Gabby and my sister.

I nod and lower my voice, resolved not to talk about Maggie. It's too dangerous here. So I tell her what BMAC already knows.

I tell her what happened at school.

I tell her about Gabby. And how our faces have been all over the news.

I tell her about how BMAC came to the apartment. About Hexall Hall. And the BMAC raid. About how Rani saved us.

And when I come to the end of it, I already feel a thousand times lighter, a thousand times safer. 'When they stopped me at security, they saw something wrong with my SIT number thing. So they called BMAC.'

Mom's eyes are welling up again as she looks at me, but her lips are pressed together like she's fighting a smile. 'My brave boy,' she says. She kisses my wrists where the blisters are turning white, then my head, my cheeks, over and over. 'You're such a brave, brave boy.'

But even as she holds me, I feel the dread churning in my stomach. I haven't told her the worst part. The part about Roth. I haven't told her that Maggie's Moved again.

'There's more,' I whisper. And I try to think of how to tell her without getting BMAC suspicious. 'Roth's here,' I say.

I feel Mom's muscles go rigid. 'Maggie?' she mouths silently.

I nod.

She doesn't say anything for the longest time, and I want to tell her more. I want to tell her that Gabby is Roth's

Mover. That he's looking for Gabby, and Maggie's with her. What happens if he finds them? What will he do to them?

'Pat,' Mom says quietly, 'is Maggie safe?'

'I don't know,' I say, and the tears start to flow, because I don't know. I don't know if they made it to their TLJ. I don't know if BMAC's found them. I don't know if Leonard is still with them. I don't know anything. 'I tried, Mom. I really tried.'

'Patrick,' she says more sternly. 'Patrick, you don't say anything, you understand me?'

I nod, but part of me starts to wonder if keeping quiet is the best idea. Would it be so bad if I talked? What if BMAC knew about Roth, if I just told them? Maybe they could find him, stop him. They could keep Gabby safe, keep all of us safe from Roth. I force the idea out of my head. No. If I did that then I'd have to tell them about Maggie. Maggie let Roth in. Maggie opened a door. *Twice*. That's all BMAC would care about. I can't put Maggie in that kind of danger.

So I hug my mother. I let myself believe she'll keep me safe, at least until BMAC comes for me. And when they do, I won't tell them anything, just like she said. I squeeze my mom a little tighter. My dad did it for Maggie. I can do it too.

I wake up with my arms still wrapped around my mom. She's rubbing my back and staring at the door. It's morning. I hear footsteps in the hall and I sit bolt upright. BMAC's coming.

The footsteps stop and we can see the shadows of their feet underneath the door.

'Whatever you do, Pat, don't say a word.' Mom stands and holds her hand out to stop me from getting up. 'Let me handle this.'

I pull my knees up to my chest. She can't handle this for me. BMAC won't let her.

The door clanks open and in walk two BMAC goons, followed by Hartman, hands still clasped behind her back. I wonder if she sleeps like that. She's not smiling but she isn't frowning either.

'Mrs Mermick,' she says pleasantly to my mother, but Mom's not having it.

'I don't know what you think you're doing, Beadie,' Mom says, 'but if I don't get to speak to my lawyer today – and I mean right now – you can bet that I'll have you thrown out of BMAC so fast, you won't even get a job as subway patrol in this city.'

Special Agent Hartman leans back with a smirk. 'My, don't we have a temper this morning.' Her friends standing either side of the door smile and I see Mom's hands flexing at her sides, trying to keep calm. 'I assure you, Mrs Mermick, that today will be the day I do my utmost to get you a phone so you can do that very thing—'

'Bullshit!' Mom spits.

Hartman holds out her hand to me. 'But for now your son and I have more pressing matters to discuss.'

Mom puts herself between me and Hartman. 'The hell you do. He's not talking to you about anything. I won't allow it. Not until I have the chance to speak with my attorney.'

'Fortunately, Mrs Mermick, I don't need your permission.'

Mom takes a step towards Special Agent Hartman and I watch the other two BMAC officers reach for their stun staffs. 'If you think for one second that I'm just going to let you take my son—'

'I don't think, Mrs Mermick,' says Hartman, her face still pleasant in spite of the poison in Mom's stare. 'I know.'

'You listen to me,' says Mom, and she closes the distance between them and pokes Hartman in the chest. The two officers move in, but Hartman holds her hand up to stop them, suppressing a grin as Mom starts up a sermon. 'Let's say I ignore the fact that BMAC regulations say a civilian, a Non-Mover like myself, should be taken to county lock-up if you have anything you wanted to arrest me for. You don't. But let's put that aside. You cannot take my child, a minor, for questioning without me present. So you won't. Come back with a phone.'

'Yes, well, if your child was not a Mover, that would be the case,' says Hartman. Her smile is gone and she glares at Mom with the same ferocity. 'But he is. And section 12 of the Registered Movers Act holds that any Mover under criminal investigation, including a minor, is exempt from the rights afforded regular citizens and is subject to evaluation by the Bureau of Movement Activity Control.'

Mom doesn't move, but I can see her hand has stopped flexing at her side. She's not saying anything and I think she's starting to figure out she can't save me.

'Now, Mr Mermick,' says Hartman, never looking away from Mom, 'I have some questions I'd like to ask you. Shall we?'

Mom's finger points at me. 'Pat, you stay right there.'

'Mrs Mermick, I really don't have time to go through this with you.'

'You're not taking my son.'

'I am,' says Hartman, signalling to her agent friends. With three heavy steps they're on top of my mom, seizing her by each arm. She swears at them both, not caring at all that they're twice her size, and tries to rip her arms free as they wrestle to hold her still.

'Stop!' I shout. 'I'll go. Just don't touch her.'

'Pat, honey—' Mom tries, as the officers keep their hands on her arms, but at least she's stopped fighting them.

'It's fine, Mom,' I say, and move in beside Hartman.

'There's a sport,' says Hartman, clapping me hard on the back. She leaves her hand at the base of my neck, holding on more firmly than I'd like, and guides me out the door. One of her goons follows while the other stays with Mom.

'He doesn't need to stay with her,' I say to Hartman once we're in the hallway.

Hartman lets go of my neck. 'Mr Mermick, I want to talk to you about your friend Gabriela.'

I look down and watch the specks in the green tile pass beneath my feet as we walk. She can talk all she wants. I don't have to.

'What your mother did – encouraging your little sister to flee from her phase tests – was foolish. And she will be punished for it of course. But one little girl and her phase upgrade doesn't matter much to me.'

217

It should. That one little girl started this whole mess.

'Do you see this badge?' she says, removing it from her hip. She stops and hands it to me. '*Criminal Investigations*. What your sister did was wrong, but she's by no means a criminal. I'm not interested in her.'

'Then why are you keeping my mom here?'

She smiles. 'I'm not keeping her here, Patrick. You are. Since we discovered your part in the Movement at Romsey, it seemed prudent that she be kept in our custody. Now that we've got you, your mother can go home right this minute if you tell me what I want to know.'

I glare at her but she just goes on smiling and points back at the badge, her finger tapping the word *criminal*. 'Now your friend Gabriela, she *is* a criminal, Mr Mermick.'

I roll my eyes and hand the badge back. If Maggie's not a criminal, then Gabby's practically a saint. Hartman reaches for the badge, but squeezes my hand in hers, staring at me. 'I'm sorry,' she says. 'Does the death of four people bore you?'

I stiffen.

'Vargas's own parents, not to mention two BMAC agents whom I knew personally.'

'Gabby didn't kill them,' I say.

'If you are trying to place the onus on Ms Vargas's Shadow—'

'Go look for him!' I shout. 'He's the one who killed them! Not Gabby! Why aren't you out looking for him?'

'We are looking for him, Mr Mermick,' she says calmly. 'But seeing as Miss Vargas's Shadow is not from this time, we don't have any information on him, do we? We have only a description to go on, and believe me when I tell you we are working hard with what little we have to bring this renegade Shadow to justice.'

I shift on my feet, uncomfortable with how hard she's squeezing my hand. After what feels like forever, she releases me and keeps walking.

'But still these four deaths are on your friend's hands. She let in her Shadow, who has proven himself to be uncommonly dangerous. Are you telling me she didn't know her Shadow's nature before she Moved him here?'

I don't answer that. Gabby knew. That's why she never wanted to Move him.

'It's her fault these people are dead,' says Hartman. 'As sure as if she held a gun to their heads.'

There's a stabbing in my heart at hearing Gabby's words echoed by this Hartman woman. *It's my fault they're dead.* But it isn't her fault. None of it. All she did was try and get Roth out of her head. And she'll be smart enough to make it happen! But still he found his way back here.

'How do you know she did it?' I say. 'How do you know Gabby made the Move at Romsey?'

Hartman huffs, amused. 'Did she tell you she didn't?'

I don't say anything, but Hartman takes that as a yes and stops in front of a pair of black doors. 'That doesn't surprise me. No one who knowingly breaks the rules wants to face the consequences of their actions. What else could she be expected to tell you? It's not your fault either, Mr Mermick. I know she's your friend.'

I wish she'd be meaner to me. I wish she'd come at me with whatever horrible thing she's hiding in her head. This friendly thing she's doing, this you-can-trust-me-little-boy act is only making me more angry. She thinks I'm an idiot.

She places her finger on another scanner and the red light blinks white, opening the door to a glass hallway. There's natural light here; I can see the sky above us and I realise it's a covered bridge.

'We want to help our friends. It's the nice thing to do.'

I feel like I'm in kindergarten.

'But, Mr Mermick,' she goes on, 'the nice thing to do isn't always the right thing to do.'

'She didn't do it,' I say impatiently. This lecture is a waste of both of our time.

'She did, son,' says Hartman as we come to the door at the end of the bridge and she scans her finger again. 'I'm a criminal investigations officer. It's my job to look at all the facts, all of the information, so we can know who is responsible for breaking the rules. I'm very good at my job, Mr Mermick. And I have no doubt in my mind that Gabriela Vargas is the Mover behind the recent activity above the Romsey Institute for Academics.'

You're not that good at it.

The door clicks and there's a hiss as Hartman shoves through the double doors. It's dark on the other side. Blue lights line the hallway and the temperature drops a solid ten degrees. The wall on my right has a large '15' on it in black, but I already know we're not on the fifteenth floor of BMAC any more. We're in the Movers' Prison.

I can feel Hartman watching me and I do my best to follow what Rani said before they took her away. *Don't let them see you're afraid.* I take a deep breath and force myself to be calm. There's a tingle in the base of my neck. My Shadow's with me. I'm not alone.

'Such a Move as the one your friend achieved over Romsey has never been seen before,' says Hartman. 'The scale, the power. There is much BMAC needs to learn from Gabriela Vargas so we can avoid that kind of destruction to our city again. You must understand how important it is that we find her?'

I look her dead in the eye and keep my voice as steady as I can. 'I don't know where she is.'

Hartman nods. 'All right. Maybe we can help you brainstorm where she might be.'

She leads me deeper into the Movers' Prison, and all there is to see are blue lights and close black walls. I feel ice creeping over my neck, reminding me that somewhere behind them is my dad.

We walk into what looks like a large dark theatre. Fold-down seats, just like at the movies, encircle a giant convex window. We're looking down on what looks like an operating room, a cold steel bed with restraints and all kinds of monitors and instruments that don't look friendly.

'Have a seat, Mr Mermick,' says Hartman, who's already sitting, facing the window. Her back is ramrod straight, and her hands are finally in front of her, folded in her lap like she's waiting for high tea.

I sit down slowly, like somehow the chair will come loose and fall through the window, delivering me to the operating room below.

As soon as I do, the lights in the operating room turn on, so bright I have to squint. When my eyes adjust I can see a little man in a lab coat working near the table. He turns and he's carrying a tray of syringes. Three syringes. My hands grip tight to my armrests, and I feel my forehead getting damp even though I've started to shiver.

Then the doors open and I have to stand up when I see who it is. Rani, her arms bound, followed by Special Agent Frost.

I look to Hartman. 'What is this?'

She casually scratches an itch on her nose and watches as the BMAC agents point to the operating table. 'Prep.'

Rani scans the room, her eyes lingering on the window above. My cheeks feel as if they're on fire and I can tell she can't see me. She knows someone is watching though; why else would there be a window?

The man in the lab coat fills the first syringe and orders Rani to lie down. She stares at the needle in his hand and I wait for the blow, for her forebrawler instincts to lash out and shatter the hideous thing. She doesn't. Instead, she obeys, carefully lifting herself onto the steel table and lying down, without her mouth so much as twitching.

I can't remember how to breathe. My brain won't work, can't think what to do, won't process what's about to happen.

Special Agent Frost straps down her arms and her legs and waist and that's when I notice Rani's chest, rising and falling as quickly as my own.

'She doesn't know anything,' I tell Hartman. 'She has nothing to do with anything!'

Hartman is redoing her ponytail. 'Rani Nair is a wanted Mover, Mr Mermick. She broke the rules.'

'You want Gabby!' I say. 'Rani didn't do anything!'

'Rani Nair moved her Shadow and has evaded justice for five years.'

My arm goes numb as the doctor injects something into Rani's bicep.

'What is that?'

'Just an atropine. Such a shame. Had she come to us when she was still a minor, Shelving wouldn't be necessary.'

'What?'

'Well, she's an adult now, Mr Mermick. If she'd turned herself in when she was sixteen, this could have been avoided.'

The doctor injects something else into her arm and I don't ask. I don't want to know.

'When a minor is guilty of Movement—' satisfied that her ponytail is secure, Hartman rests her chin in her hand – 'the punishment is far less severe. They're only children after all.'

I can barely hear her over the pulse pounding in my ears, but I know I don't believe her for a second. If she Shelved me now, who would stop her? Mom's locked up in a cell. And if she Shelved Gabby, who would know? Gabby's parents are gone. *The power*, Hartman said. *The scale*. How hard would it be to convince Nowbies that Gabby was too dangerous not to send to sleep?

Rani keeps focused on the light above her so that her eyes sparkle with that forebrawler fire while the doctor flicks a big syringe filled with a liquid the colour of blue-raspberry punch. I see spots and I feel so dizzy I have to lean on the seat in front of me. This is the last needle.

Rani doesn't take her eyes off the light and all I want to do is rush down there, break the window and tell her to run.

'It was like a thousand years ago!' I shout. 'She didn't hurt anyone!'

'She's hurting everyone,' says Hartman, the same way Mom talks to Maggie when she's having a temper tantrum. 'This world is for the people who live here now, not the ones who don't like the time they come from. When Rani Nair let someone come back here who wasn't supposed to be here – every time her Shadow eats, every time he drinks, every time he finds a corner of the planet to call his home – her Shadow takes something away from the rest of us. She did this to herself, Mr Mermick.'

'No, you're doing this. You're doing this to her!'

The doctor brushes wisps of Rani's dark hair aside, and I can't even feel my own body any more but that doesn't stop me. I have to get to her. I clamber over the row of chairs in front of me, then the next, and the next, until I'm pressed against the window and banging as hard as I can. 'Stop it!' I scream. 'Let her go!'

'Step away from the window, Mr Mermick,' orders Hartman.

I don't. 'Run,' I beg Rani, even though I know she can't hear me. 'Please, run.'

Her face hardens as if she's telling me to keep quiet. I can't stop this; she knows I can't. And then she looks back at the bright light above her as the doctor pushes the needle into her temple.

Rani closes her eyes and so do I, my heart stinging in my chest like it's barely holding together. Rani is sleeping. Sleeping because of me.

TWENTY-FIVE

I'm sitting by myself in the theatre. Hartman left me alone, but not before posting two officers at each exit. She wanted me to think about what just happened. The operating table is empty now. They took Rani to the Shelves, leaving me with the memory blistered into my brain.

My temples feel warm, my Shadow quietly trying to get my attention. *I'm fine*, I lie. What's the point of telling him the truth? Cos the truth is I'm not fine. Rani has been Shelved and it's all cos of me. I brought this trouble on her. I brought Maggie and Gabby and BMAC into her life, and she tried to help me. She didn't have to, she didn't even know me, but she did. And now she's sleeping. Special Agent Hartman didn't do this. I did.

My eyes are puffy and stinging from all the tears. Who else will sleep cos of me? Special Agent Hartman will do anything to get her hands on Gabby. She's proven that.

But I don't know where Gabby is. I breathe in the cold air and lean back in my seat, grateful that we got separated when we did. Even if Hartman manages to convince me to help her find Gabby, there's no way I can. I don't have the first clue where Leonard's taken her. So what happens to me when Hartman figures that out?

I start to shake, trying not to think about that blue syringe coming for my head.

There's a bang as Hartman bursts back into the amphitheatre and slams the door behind her. Her heels click on the tile as she strides confidently to where I'm sitting and she collapses in the seat beside me, her arm draped over the back of mine as if we're old friends.

'Well,' she says, 'that wasn't much fun, was it?'

I keep my eyes on the empty silver table.

'How about it, Mr Mermick?' she says. 'How about you tell me what it is I need to know, and we get you and your mom home? Get your sister home too. Wouldn't that be good?'

I study her face, not sure if she means it or if I just want her to. 'You'd let my mom go?'

'If you tell me where to find the girl, sure.'

The girl. The unlucky Mover who got stuck with a nasty Shadow. 'Gabby didn't do anything wrong.'

Hartman sighs and takes her arm back. 'She did, son. And you know she did. The point is, I need to find her, and you know where she is. So all this back and forth, who did what is irrelevant.'

'I don't know where she is,' I tell her.

'Don't test me, boy,' she says, and the friendly veil all at once disappears. 'I'm a pretty patient person, but I have my limits.'

Patient? What patience? Was that patience when she told her officers to take Rani right to the Movers' Prison? Every second I don't respond makes the creases in her forehead get a little deeper, and I want to do everything I can to make those creases worse.

'So what?' I say, glad to see I've pissed her off. 'You can't do anything to me.'

'You're wrong about that,' she says, and I know from the hoarseness of her voice that she means it. 'Where. Is. Gabriela. Vargas?'

'I have no idea.'

'This is the last time I ask nicely, son,' she says. 'Where is the Vargas girl?'

Her nose is practically touching mine and it's right there in the downturned corners of her mouth that she's not going to let me, or Mom, or anybody involved in this out of here so easily. And I hate her for it. Now I want to make her hate me as much as I hate her, and I know exactly how to do it.

I take my fist and bump my forehead.

Hartman's skin drains of colour and she gets to her feet. 'Get up,' she says. 'Get up, right now.'

I don't really have a choice and she makes me follow her out of the amphitheatre, up a tight, winding metal staircase, stopping at a small door that looks more like a hatch on a submarine. Another finger scanner here, and Hartman gives it a quick swipe, the hatch hissing open. An icy wind whooshes in, freezing the sweat on my forehead, and she climbs through the door.

'Let's go,' she snaps.

I duck through the hatch and my feet make a clanging

sound as we step out onto a grated pathway. It's freezing in here, like a giant refrigerator.

'Look around you,' she says, but I'm ahead of her. There are feet, everywhere, lined up around the circular walls, rising up level upon level all the way to the top of the chamber. It's like a giant silo of human feet, resting on what can only be described as shelves. The Shelves. Every pair of feet is attached to a sleeping Mover. My stomach lights up like a furnace and I feel as if I'm going to throw up over the guardrail. Below are more shelves, more feet than I can count, all of them sleeping.

'This way,' she says, but I can barely move. This is just one chamber. I know from the pictures that the Movers' Prison is made of six different silos. And there are more being built. Does each one house this many Movers?

Hartman grabs me by the scruff of the neck and shoves me forward, climbing the gangway, more metal stairs that shake and clang as we stomp along. I feel as if I'm disturbing them, as if the noise will interrupt their slumber, and suddenly I'm stomping harder, hoping to wake them all up. After what must be the fifth staircase, she marches me to the end of another grated pathway and stops in front of a pair of big pale feet. They're veiny and knobby, the skin so white it's nearly see-through. Every pair seems to have a glowing plate beneath it and this one is just the same. I squint to read it.

M. Mermick.

Dad.

Suddenly I can't remember how to do anything. How to stand. How to breathe. He's here, right in front of me. All I can think is that he's in there, that face I haven't seen for six years, sleeping.

'There's plenty of room,' says Hartman behind me. My fingers reach out and trace the digital letters, making sure I'm reading it right. 'Lots of spots in Silo 3 that would fit you perfectly.'

His blood pressure reads 90/50. Is that good? Is he healthy?

'Shelving one more Mermick is no skin off my nose.'

O_2 Sats: 100%. Metabolic Ratio Rate, 2:1. What does this mean? Is he all right in there? My hand hovers just above the nameplate and part of me wants to touch his frozen-looking toe. Does he know I'm here? Can he feel me, sort of like I feel my Shadow?

Hartman leans in, her warm breath on my ear. 'Or three.'

Mom. Maggie.

My hand drops and my heart seizes up. Hartman doesn't miss it.

'You can't Shelve us,' I whisper, forcing myself to believe it, but she can hear the tremble of doubt in my voice.

'Try me.'

My heartbeat kicks alive again, thudding like a thousand terrified crows, and I don't know what to do. Part of me wants to tell her something – Pondu Terminal at Killberry Beach, anything – just give her Gabby so she'll leave Mom and Maggie alone. But I can't do that. I don't want to do that. I don't want to see Gabby on that table.

'I don't know where she is,' I say, the tremor in my body so bad I'm worried I'll fall over.

'Have it your way then,' says Hartman, and she pulls out her droidlet. 'Call control.'

There's a click and a beep from the droidlet's centre.

A man's voice. 'This is control.'

'I want Dr Elgin back in prep,' she barks. 'And get me two officers to Silo 3.' Her foot taps on the metal as she walks away from me, still giving orders, and each clang is like a hammer inside my head, visions of everyone I love blasting across my mind as they lie on that table, waiting for the needle. She can't hurt them. I can't let her hurt them.

But I don't know how. The only thing she wants from me is Gabby, and I won't give her that. I struggle to think. There has to be something else – anything else – that will convince her to let us go.

An idea shoots through the terrifying visions and I latch onto the lie before I even have the chance to really think it through.

'Wait!'

Hartman stops her conversation as my voice echoes through the silo. My heart is pounding so hard that the thump of my blood is getting in the way of whatever my Shadow's sending. I push him back from me, as if somehow Hartman could get to him too if I let him get too close.

Hartman faces me, her arms held patiently behind her back, waiting for me to speak. I have to speak.

'I know the cure for Movers.'

She scoffs at me and turns on her heel.

'It's true!' I shout after her. 'I know lots of things you don't about Movers.'

230

'I doubt that,' she calls over her shoulder.

'Pungits!'

She stops and turns back to face me. 'What's that?'

'I think you know.'

She puts her hands on her hips. 'What have you heard?'

'I've seen them,' I say.

'How?'

'Get me Rani's duffle bag and I'll show you.' Leonard's pungit ray is in there. 'And then I'll tell you the cure.'

TWENTY-SIX

Hartman's eyebrows dip low as the black specks dance around my head in the beam of Leonard's pungit ray. I'm surrounded by a bunch of BMAC agents, standing on crusty pink carpet between rows of cluttered cubicles.

'Would you look at that?' says a young guy who looks more like a wrestler than a BMAC officer. He's squinting at the pungit ray in my hand. 'You made that?'

'Yes,' I say, ignoring the sweat in my palms.

He laughs. 'Well, that's a lot easier than the massive machine we have. Stupid thing takes up an entire room.'

'Who taught you how to make that?' says Hartman.

I have no interest in telling her that. She's never mentioned Leonard, so I won't be giving her any reason to look for him. 'A friend.'

'A Shadow?' she says, raising an eyebrow.

'A fugitive!' barks a fat guy.

'He's from the 2300s, and they know lots about Movers there,' I say defensively, wondering if somewhere Leonard's cursing my name. I feel guilty, but I'm running out of cards to play – and I haven't mentioned his name.

What Leonard told me races through my head, again and again and again. About how BMAC wants as much information about the future as they can get. I swallow. I start to wonder if I've made the wrong decision. Because showing BMAC the pungit ray changes history, doesn't it? How it will do that, I can't know. But I know I've started something. I've kicked off a whole new timeline or parallel universe or something and I brace myself for the world to implode.

It doesn't.

But it's enough to make the sweat in my palms run hot like lava.

'And you can make them go away?' asks Hartman.

I look at the pungit ray in my hands, trying to make it look like I'm struggling to decide whether telling her the cure for Movers is something I really want to do.

'Yes,' I say quietly.

'How?'

I lift my eyes to Hartman's. This is the most important part, the whole reason for the lie. 'My mother.'

'What about her?'

'She goes free. Then I tell you how.'

Hartman shakes her head. 'How about you just tell me?'

'No.' If I can't save myself, at least this way I can save her.

Hartman stares at me a long time and I stare right back, letting her know how serious I am about this part of the deal. The officers sitting around us are guffawing and murmuring to each other, half of them of the opinion I'm

233

asking too much, the other half discussing the ray and how if someone's shared enough knowledge about the science of pungits with me to make a machine that small, who's to say I don't know how to manipulate pungits somehow?

Hartman's eyes dart around the room, from conversation to conversation, and I can tell by her scowl that she doesn't like hearing her fellow officers' views. She likes it even less that I wasn't lying about knowing things she didn't about Movers. The little pungit ray has taken her by complete surprise, and she's mad at me for it.

'Come with me,' she says, grabbing me by the arm.

She takes me out into the hall and throws me in Room B. 'Sit down,' she orders, slamming the door shut behind her.

I do. 'I'm not telling you anything else until my mother is released.'

Hartman chews her bottom lip, hating this change in dynamic, hating that she's given me enough of an edge to make demands. But she's convinced I have something she wants, something all of BMAC wants. 'Fine,' she says quickly. 'It's done.'

Lies.

I shake my head, 'Now. Release her now.'

'It's already noon,' says Hartman. 'It's too late to do it today. She'll have to wait until tomorrow.'

I shrug. 'Then I guess you'll have to wait until tomorrow.'

Hartman slams her hand onto the table and glares at me, and I glare right back. If I don't do this right, me, my family, Gabby – we're all Shelf-Meat.

'Fine,' says Hartman. 'I'll release her tonight.'

I lean back in the chair and cross my arms.

'What are you doing?' she says, a wild glint in her eye, and I try my best to keep confident, like Mom.

'Waiting,' I tell her. 'Waiting until you let her go.'

She shoves the table away from me with an angry grunt and storms back to the door.

'And I want to see it,' I say as she opens it to leave. 'I want to see my mother released and I want a car waiting to take her home when she is.'

She slams the door shut again. 'I don't have the authority to make that happen.'

Her colour has changed from the orangey fake tan to red and her forehead is glistening with tiny beads of sweat. She wants this information. They all do. They'll do whatever it takes in order to get it. And I need to know my mom is safe before they find out I'm lying about a cure. 'Then you'd better find someone who does.'

Hartman stands there, out of excuses or ideas, and the frustration twisting her face into a million lines is almost funny. Finally she flings open the door to leave.

'And a meatball sub,' I say. 'For me. No onion.'

She doesn't turn back to me, but her shoulders tense up to her ears. She wrenches the door shut behind her, the deafening bang quickly swallowed up by the silence of my little cell. There's nothing more I can do now but wait.

And wait.

And wait.

Finally, after what must be hours, I'm woken up by a bit of commotion outside the door and I lift my head off the desk, waiting for Hartman to enter. But she doesn't. When the door opens, there are two uniformed BMAC officers, stun staffs brandished across their chests. I shrink back a bit in my chair. They look so stern that I wonder if maybe Hartman's superiors have called my bluff. The uniformed officers stand on either side of the door as four men walk in, wearing well-fitted suits and silver haircuts, their eyes laser-focused on me. Behind them I get a glimpse into the hallway as the door shuts. There are two more uniformed officers posted outside. I'm in trouble.

'Mr Mermick,' says one of the men. His black suit is the slickest-looking of the four, and his thick-rimmed glasses make him look like some sort of rocket scientist, with a round, bulbous nose for sniffing out liars. 'I hear you have some information you are willing to share with us.'

I swallow, trying to get some moisture into my suddenly dry throat.

'I'm Bureau Minister Vaughan. Special Agent Hartman has been telling me that you are aware of the existence of pungits. Is that right?'

I nod, my fingers fidgeting nervously on the table. *Bureau Minister.*

'And that you have a special contraption that enables you to see them? One you can hold in your hand?'

'It's not possible!' grumbles one of the men at his side. 'The X-magnets alone don't allow for anything smaller than the DEM we currently have.'

'Yes, Mandel,' says Vaughan, an annoyed edge to his voice, 'you've voiced your protests already, thank you. Unfortunately the Direct Energy Machine currently in use by the Bureau is neither cost-efficient nor practical for use in incorporating pungits with the phase-testing program.

So an opportunity to explore an alternative technology is more than welcome, wouldn't you agree?'

Mandel throws up his arms but doesn't argue any more.

'Now, Mr Mermick,' says Vaughan, 'you demonstrated one such technology for Special Agent Hartman this afternoon, is that correct?'

I nod again.

'Could you repeat the demonstration for us, please?' Vaughan turns to one of his associates, who places the pungit ray on the table.

I look at it, not sure my plan was a good one after all. Something about the officialness of these guys. Bureau Ministers are all the way from the top floors. I reach out for the pungit ray slowly, a cold dread that I've started something too big to control seeping into my bones.

My fingers are trembling so badly it's hard to align the delicate wires in the same way I'd seen Leonard do at the safe house. When the wires are in place, I click the on button and there's a quiet hum, letting me know it's working. I turn the ray machine round and point it into my own face.

I don't know what I'm waiting for. Stunned *oohs* and *ahhs*, or maybe even cursing, but there's no sound. Nothing. And I feel like crawling under the table to stop them all from looking at me so hard. All of their faces are blank, staring at the space above my head. All except Mandel, whose mouth hangs open dumbly.

'May I?' asks Vaughan, reaching for the pungit ray.

Unsure, I place it in his hand and he steps away from me.

'Thank you, Mr Mermick,' he says, waving his other hand at his colleagues, who file out without a word. 'Sit tight, son,' is all he says to me, and he follows the rest of them out, still holding the pungit ray, leaving the men with stun staffs posted on either side of the door.

I try not to look at them, though their being here is making me feel more than a bit uneasy. I wonder if the two officers outside the door are still standing there. If they are, this is a lot of security. Does that mean they believe me? About the cure? And now they have the pungit ray. What will that do to the future? Have I just changed everything?

Once again, all I can do is wait.

And wait.

And wait.

And the waiting is made all the more uncomfortable by the two uniforms watching me all the time. Or not watching. Every so often I glance at their expressionless faces and see them staring blankly at the wall ahead. They catch me staring, and I clear my throat, turning my head to try to find something else to stare at while I wait.

Finally a knock sounds at the door, and the guards let in an officer holding a brown paper bag. He plops it on the table in front of me. 'Your sub.'

I can smell it already, and instantly my stomach is roaring so loud, demanding I stuff the whole thing into my mouth at once. I tear open the bag and unwrap the tin-foiled bundle of melty warmness. The golden crusty bread is still hot, the sides oozing tomato sauce and cheese. I rip into it with the biggest bite I can manage, savouring the cheesy tomatoey meaty goodness. And when I've managed to gobble the whole thing down, my stomach swollen with sub, I'm again back with nothing to do but wait.

And wait.

And wait.

And then there are voices outside and the door clicks open. Another uniformed officer enters, carrying a small computer. He sets it down in front of me and signals to the officers standing outside. They flick off the lights as the officer does some typing on the little computer. There's a *bloomp!* sound, and a beam of light springs out of it, projecting a blank white rectangle on the wall.

'So you can see the release, Mr Mermick,' says the officer, and leaves me alone in the room with my two guards. The release? Are they really going to let my mother go?

The white screen dissolves away and a picture of the front entrance to the BMAC building replaces it. It's just like I remember, the ugly triangle entranceway, the hibiscus and palms. And there's a big black private car sitting right outside the doors. They must have shelled out big for a car like that.

I sit up a little straighter, my bum barely on the chair, and my leg shakes anxiously. I'm almost believing that this lie of mine might work. There's movement at the front doors, and they open to reveal several uniformed officers, who march their way towards the car. Behind them is Hartman, scowling more than ever, and she's got her hand firmly clenched around my mother's arm.

Mom.

She's fighting Hartman, probably refusing to leave without me, but Hartman doesn't slow down, practically dragging her to where one of the officers is holding the door to the car open. Behind them I can see Vaughan and the other high-ups standing officially, and I know Mom must be having some kind of heart attack.

I watch as she pulls herself free from Hartman's grasp, and I see her shaking her head, gesturing wildly, demanding I be allowed to come with her. Hartman's shouting right back, and several of the uniformed officers step into the mix.

'Just go, Mom,' I whisper to myself. 'Get out of here!'

It takes three of the officers and Hartman, but they manage to force her into the car and shut the door in her face. I take a deep breath, proud that I've done it. She's safe. Maybe now she can find Maggie. I imagine Maggie crying, so happy to be scooped up into Mom's arms, and Mom thanking Leonard for taking care of her. And Gabby – maybe Mom can help her. But there's a painful swelling in my throat, and I can't help being aware of how alone I feel. Mom's safe, but she's gone.

TWENTY-SEVEN

The swelling in my throat extends to the rest of my body and all of me feels sore, heavy, like the full force of the giant shit-storm that's about to come my way is pushing against every part of me. When they find out I lied – I grab my hair in my fists and rest my elbows on the table – Vaughan could have me Shelved for a thousand years.

It won't be long before they come for me. Vaughan, his minister buddies in their fancy suits, Hartman, an army of uniformed officers – all of them will stand here, waiting for me to tell them the big cure. What am I going to say? I have to tell them something, if only to buy enough time for Mom to go find Maggie. It's not like I can just say, 'I lied.' I bite my lip. Hartman would strangle me on the spot. Before I get a chance to wonder if any of the nearby uniformed officers would bother trying to pull her off me – probably not – there's a thumping sound out in the hall. I look over at the officers standing beside the door, but they're looking at each other, just as startled. Another thump.

Thump-thump.

BAM!

The three of us are silent, looking at each other nervously, waiting for Vaughan or Hartman to open the door. Nothing. Just quiet. The guard on the left nods to the one on the right, and he knocks on the door three times.

Silence.

He knocks again.

Nothing.

The hairs on the back of my neck stand on end and I guess the guards are just as uneasy cos they let their stun staffs drop from across their chests into their hands. The one on the right twists his wrist, bringing the electric current to life. Before the one on the left can do the same, the locks click and the door opens.

There's no one there.

And then I see the boots. I shove myself back from the table at the sight of the lifeless legs and arms of the guard outside, now lying just beyond the door. There's something above them, like a ripple in the fabric of the air. I blink. The guard on the right doesn't wait to find out what it is, stepping into the hall with his staff at the ready.

But he doesn't get to use it. There's a blast of white-hot blue, a ribbon of lightning that harpoons him in the gut, and he suddenly goes rigid, as the other guard rushes to help him.

'Wait!' I shout, but I'm too late, and another flash catches him in the head. They both crumple, like coats falling off hangers, into a pile in the doorway. I stumble back, pressing myself into the corner as if somehow that will hide me.

The lightning leaves no doubt.

Roth is coming.

And then he's there, standing in the doorway. His face is all heavy, sharp angles, with a razor nose, like a perfect L, and brow ridges that cast a shadow over his dark eyes. His mouth is set in a fine line, expressionless, as his gaze falls on me.

All I can do is stay there, hunched in my corner, staring at him, waiting for the lightning. I can see the strange contraption strapped to his open left palm, buzzing with the angry current that took out the guards. The Punch.

He just watches me, like he's in absolutely no rush, and I don't know if he's waiting for me to try to run or to say something. His left hand twitches, and the middle finger jerks, barely at all, but when it does, the current disappears and the buzzing goes away.

'Get up,' he says, his voice grinding like truck tyres on gravel.

I don't. I don't want to. I want sounds, any sound other than my own panicked breath – the pounding of BMAC feet thundering down the hall, an emergency alarm, anything.

'Get up,' he says again.

Where's Hartman? Or Vaughan? Or the army of BMAC agents that should be coming to save me? My brain clings to the hope that they're on their way, but Roth's cool, detached expression tells me that's not going to happen.

He's here for Gabby.

His head tilts to the side, hair buzzed down so fine that the shape is like a square, and he seems to be waiting for me to do something. His left hand starts twitching again, and the circle in his palm buzzes to life. He lifts his palm towards me and I see a ripple of heat in the air around it. I curl up against the blast, and a piece of the wall beside me splinters as the lightning slams into it.

'Get up!' he growls.

My face is buried in my arms and I listen to myself breathe. My Shadow tugs at my brain and I reach for him, sending out every bit of how scared I am. He receives it all, absorbs it until I feel just the smallest bit of courage to move.

Slowly I slide myself up the wall until I'm standing, and Roth's chest rises, a satisfied breath whistling through his large nostrils.

'I don't know where she is,' I blurt out.

He answers with another blast from his palm, sending a chunk of wall exploding beside my head and I cower. The corner of Roth's mouth twitches the slightest bit, as if his lips have forgotten how to smile.

'Doesn't matter,' he says. 'She'll come to us.'

'BMAC's looking for her. She can't just waltz in here and expect them not to—'

'That's why we won't make her come here.' He readjusts the weapon strapped to his palm, not so much as blinking at what I said. 'She will come where I call.'

Where he calls? 'She can't hear you,' I tell him. 'She told me – the connection is a jumbled mess. She can't understand you.'

'Maybe not on her own,' he says. 'But with your sister's help . . .'

Maggie.

244

'. . . she'll be a good girl.' When he's satisfied the weapon's secure, he turns to the doorway. 'Wait here.'

He steps into the hall and I watch the empty doorway. The boots of one of the fallen guards are shaking as Roth works just out of sight, and then there's a quiet snap that turns my stomach.

'Shall we, Pat?' he says, standing in the doorway with a pocket knife in one hand and a severed finger grasped loosely in the other.

I want to puke. I want all the heaving juices in my stomach to spew out of me. I want to squeeze my eyes shut and the gruesome scene to go away.

'Pat,' he says again, 'shall we?'

Pat. The way he says my name, familiar, sets my neck hairs on end, and I listen one last time in desperate hope that Hartman might be on her way. There's only silence. I can't do anything but obey.

We step out into the hall and there's nothing but us and the crumpled guards. I look back towards the room with the cubicles, and through the windows in the doors I can see several other agents collapsed across their desks.

'Are they dead?'

'Unconscious,' he says, shoving me in the other direction. 'The Punch is designed for Movers, but it still has its uses with Norms.'

Punch. It's too small a word for that thing in his palm. A weapon designed for Movers. 'Does it kill Movers?' I say, nearly choking on the words.

He shakes his head, but I don't feel any kind of relief. If it doesn't kill them, what *does* it do? Why would the

Commander of the Shadow and Mover army need a weapon against Movers?

He shoves me around corners and down hallways until we're standing in front of the doors to the covered bridge. He wants to go to the Movers' Prison. When Hartman took me there, there was no one around but us and the sleeping Movers.

My Shadow is quiet inside my head, like smoke seeping through the crack at the bottom of a door. I can feel him prodding around in my brain, softly trying to get a handle on what's happening. He doesn't bother me directly. I need all my wits about me now, and somehow he can sense that. He's just watching, like a fly on the wall of my mind.

'What does it do?' I blurt out, wanting to give my Shadow what he's looking for.

Roth looks down at me with a blank stare. There's nothing I can read in that face. 'Reverses the pungits,' he grumbles.

My breath comes in quick little bursts as he lifts the guard's finger to the lockpad. Reverses the pungits? I remember what Leonard said, about Roth going back. Something to do with the Punch. Is he going to reverse someone's pungits to Move him and Gabby back to the future?

Gabby.

'She won't come,' I tell him. Not if it means facing her Shadow. Not if it means letting him control her. 'She's too smart for that.'

He grabs me by the arm and shoves me onto the covered bridge, his stony expression demanding I move forward. I do, but not before I make sure he sees the fury on my face.

'She will,' he says to my back. 'I know she will.'

I hate the calm confidence in his voice and want more than anything to shake it. 'How?'

His head cocks to the side again, and this time there's the faintest hint of a grin. 'I'm her Shadow, Pat,' he says, pointing to his head. 'I've lived there. And I've seen how she feels about you.'

This hits me like a blow to the gut. No – deeper than that, like a stab, like he's shot his Punch right into my belly, grabbed my stomach and squeezed. Gabby doesn't feel anything about me, she can't. We barely ever talked before the Move.

His faint grin oozes into a wide, toothy smile. 'Trust me. For you, she'll come.'

TWENTY-EIGHT

Roth's pace speeds up as we clang our way across the grated gangway of the Movers' Prison. I barely notice the cold as I hurry by pair after pair of marbled white feet. Each belongs to a stranger, but a part of me feels like I know them. I guess I do. Their story is my story. The story of Movers.

Somewhere in his brain Roth must be thinking along the same lines, cos he's practically running now, hating being near these feet as much as I do. Does his stomach clench with the fear of being Shelved? Does he worry his Move for Gabby will get him sentenced to sleep?

My heart pounds faster as I'm forced to keep up with Roth, each beat hurting as I tell myself not to think of her. He's wrong about her. He has to be, and that's it. Even if – my face feels hot against the ice in the air – even if some dark, selfish part of me hopes Roth is right, hopes she could care about me enough to come save me, I need him to be wrong. I promised her I wouldn't let him find her. I promised.

Roth stops abruptly and I slam into his back, squishing my nose against his hard shoulder blade. The sting of it radiates into my eyes and Roth grabs hold of me, pulling me in beside him. There's murmuring below us, and through the grate beneath our feet I can see a couple of what I guess are the prison guards, laughing about some dancing dog video they're watching on one guy's droidlet.

There's a faint sound beside me, like a high-pitched surge, and I see the blue glow of the current in Roth's hand. Without thinking, I grab his wrist to stop him and he cuts me a hard glare as he shoves me to the ground, rearing his arm back for the strike.

'Look out!' I shout, as the ripple in the world pulses out from Roth's hand and the two guards look up.

They pull their rifles, but not in time, and the lightning lashes out at them, striking one in the face while the other manages to duck and roll.

Roth is on top of me, his giant fingers digging into my arm as he drags me along, barrelling towards one of the hatches I climbed through with Hartman.

And then the bang. That loud, sickening pop I heard back at school. It's behind me now, and there's a ping, and more pops, as the guard fires everything he has at me and Roth.

'Open it,' orders Roth, slapping the severed finger onto my chest. He shoves me at the hatch and turns back to fire on the guard.

Terrified of getting shot, I grab the index finger, so cold and obviously dead that I have to force myself to not drop it. The red light blinks white, and I let the hideous thing fall out of my hands, grasping hold of the wheel on the hatch and spinning it as hard as I can. It screeches as it turns, and there are more pops and shouts from below us. The guard has company now.

Roth lets loose another bolt, and the shouts are louder as the door finally gives and I dive through.

This is it.

Run.

Roth glances back at me, crouched inside the hatch. *Run!*

I snatch the severed finger from the ground and reach out to slam the door shut on Roth, but he's too fast, sticking his foot in before I can close it. He shoves me back, hard, bruising my chest, and kicks the door closed behind us.

He grabs me by the neck again, forcing me down the winding stairs, pushing me faster than my feet can go and I nearly wipe out, but Roth stops my fall.

'Hold it!' Three BMAC agents appear on the stairs below us, their guns pointed right in my face. I fall back into Roth, squeezing my eyes tight, waiting for the bullets, but he blows them back with a blast from his Punch.

'Move,' he orders, and shoves me so suddenly that I'm forced to step on one of the unconscious agents, nearly rolling my ankle as I try to manoeuvre over him and continue on our way down the stairs.

I know we're at the ground level now, cos there are two doors here. One on the right that leads back into the Movers' Prison, and one on the left with a glowing red sign above it: *EXIT*.

Roth slams me against the wall beside the exit door.

'Stay there,' he says, and I'm not about to go anywhere. I can barely get a handle on my own breathing. More agents could come running down the stairs at any second, others flooding in through the doors. I have no idea where to go, what to do.

Roth's brain seems to be working better than mine, cos he's planted himself square against the exit door and is fiddling with the Punch in his hand. He's flipped it open somehow, revealing a mess of little lights, all blue, blinking and pulsing.

My Shadow carefully seeps his way into my brain, flooding it with this warmth that makes my breath come back to me. And there's a red ball, tied to a sort of paddle thing – a game. I close my eyes to better hold the image, and the memories with it – happy, safe. I love that game.

My eyes shoot open, suddenly confused and frightened. The memory isn't mine. It's his. My Shadow's. He's never put an image in my head before. Never could.

Roth slams the Punch shut and I see his middle finger twitch. He opens the exit door just enough to fit his hand through, and I can hear the sirens and the voices outside. BMAC is waiting.

There's a blast from the Punch, and it's bigger than any before it. I feel the rumble in the ground and Roth has to steady his arm with the other hand, gritting his teeth against the kick of it. There are screams and booms just outside, and the wall vibrates against my back from whatever Roth has done.

I don't have to wait long to find out, cos he pulls me to my feet by my collar and holds me in front of him just before he kicks open the door. The parking lot is a mess of overturned BMAC vehicles and scrambling officers. There must be fifty out here waiting for us, but with one blast Roth has managed to devastate half of them; the other half are pointing their weapons right at us. Roth locks one arm around my neck and uses the other to blast the remaining officers. The Punch erupts with another bolt, and the kickback nearly takes Roth down, me with him. But he manages to stay on his feet and I watch the lightning connect with one of the BMAC vehicles, blowing it back so that it rolls over several more cars, officers running and ducking for cover.

'Go!' shouts Roth, shoving me out the door. We run together, his massive hand squeezing my neck, for the nearest BMAC vehicle that he hasn't completely destroyed.

A few brave officers manage to recover themselves enough to try and stop us. They're firing their guns, and all the muscles in my back and stomach have clenched up, curling in as if my body is trying to shrink too small to be hit. Roth lets loose another blast, but still the officers fire, and all my limbs feel electric, waiting for the bite of one of those bullets to catch me somewhere.

Finally the car is close enough that I can touch it if I reach out, and I throw myself to the ground, hiding behind the front wheel as Roth fires another bolt.

He opens the front door and practically lifts me inside, shoving me into the passenger seat as I try to keep below the windows. Roth starts up the nav computer, then presses the severed finger against a button near the steering wheel. There's a tremendous roar from somewhere in the machine's mighty chest and I can feel it humming through the seat.

'Destination?' the calm electronic voice purrs through the chaos.

'Override,' growls Roth, gripping the steering wheel. 'User drive.'

The computer barely finishes saying, 'User drive engaged,' before the tyres screech as Roth speeds us out of the Movers' Prison parking lot.

I let myself peek over my shoulder at the destruction we've left behind us, black smoke rising into the sky, and my stomach feels like it's on fire, everything in me buzzing with fear and adrenaline. And then it's there again, that wonderful red ball and paddle, and I take a slow breath through my nose as if I can smell the rubber and tin they're made of, and the buzzing takes over my body again.

No. I shove the image back at my Shadow. *How are you doing that? You can't do that. I'm Phase 1. We're Phase 1!*

My Shadow retreats from me, taking the image with him as Roth speeds through the downtown core. Between the streets walled by skyscrapers I can see it directly ahead of us, piercing the clouds like the blue syringe that put Rani to sleep.

The Avin Turbine.

TWENTY-NINE

The Avin Turbine has stood on the waterfront, rising above the cityscape, my entire life. It's been there, visible from the roof yard of my school, for as long as I can remember. I've probably looked at it a million times in my life, but never really thought about it.

From the looks of it, no one else thinks much about the Avin Turbine either. The only people here are the two teens manning the ticket booth and an old guy who works the elevator. All three of them run as soon as they see us, and Roth figures out how to work the elevator himself.

We're side by side, watching the city shrink below us in the floor-to-ceiling window as the elevator climbs to the observation deck. Every ten feet the shaking in my legs gets worse, and I'm not sure how much longer I can stand. If Gabby doesn't come for me – no, *when* Gabby doesn't come for me – Roth is going to lose his mind. And I'll be in his crosshairs. I glance sideways, watching his broad chest rise and fall as he stares grimly out the window. He'll kill me, but what has me most afraid is all the ways he could do it. I close my eyes, not wanting to imagine myself falling from this height if he decides to chuck me out of a window.

A robotic voice chimes as the elevator comes to a stop: 'Observation deck.'

The doors slide open and there's a family wearing Avin Turbine T-shirts staring at us blankly. Their little boy raises his droidlet and snaps our picture.

'Get outta here,' grumbles Roth.

The family just stands there, the parents exchanging nervous glances.

'Now!' shouts Roth, blasting the wall with a shot from his Punch, and they practically knock each other over in their scramble for the elevator.

And then we're alone.

The windows on the observation deck run all the way around, allowing for a 360-degree view of the city. The inside wall shows the different stages of the city being built through time. I watch as the little neighbourhoods morph into apartment buildings, and the apartment buildings give way to skyscrapers, bigger and bigger as the years roll by.

Roth doesn't care. He's watching a television monitor mounted by the elevator. *Avin News.* The TVs flash with the image of the chaos outside BMAC. Hartman rushes by a crowd of reporters, refusing to comment. Her face is furious.

'I'm not going to hurt you, so you can calm down,' Roth says, still facing the monitor. 'I wouldn't hurt one of my own. We're the same.'

'No, we're not.'

His focus is on the news and I can feel my pulse throbbing in my neck.

'You killed people,' I say. He went to Gabby's house. Her home. He had no right to go there. He's got no right to be *here*! When Roth Moved, it was supposed to be up to Gabby.

He glances at me briefly before turning back to the monitor. 'She's better off with me than with them.'

With him. I hate the sound of it. I hate the idea of it. I hate that he thinks she belongs to him, and even more that he thinks he belongs to her somehow. She was *stuck* with him. She never wanted to be with him. Why can't he just accept that? Why can't he just let her be free?

'Hello?!' I scream. 'She cures herself to get rid of you! She doesn't want to be around you. You terrify her!'

There's a crease between his eyebrows and I can't tell if I've just pissed him off or confused him.

'I'll make it up to her.'

'You can't,' I tell him. 'And you won't, because all you care about is your war in the future.'

'When I take her back with me,' he says, 'she'll see why I've done what I've done. When she sees what they've done to us.'

'You can't take her back. She doesn't belong in the future; she belongs here.'

'She's left me no choice,' he says simply. 'I can't risk her cutting herself off from me again.'

'What are you so mad about, huh?' I shout. 'What's so terrible about Nowbies that you can't stand to be one of them?'

The crease between his brows smoothes out and his face is back to that unreadable, emotionless expression. 'They turned us out of the cities,' he says. He walks over to the window, looking out over Avin. 'The Norms left us to live in the filth and garbage and decay on the outside.' He watches the world below us, his arms folded across his chest. 'They Shelved my mother, because she gave birth to three Shadow children. They Shelved my father, because he spoke out against it.'

I look down at my feet, wishing he hadn't told me that. Hating myself for feeling the briefest moment of sympathy for him.

'This time is so much brighter,' he says, 'with all the lights. Like little stars climbing out of the earth. Land stars.' He nods to himself, liking the sound of it. 'The fighting hasn't started yet here. Once it does, it will turn out all the lights.'

The picture he's painting of the time he came from is taking shape in my head. I look out at the lights below us, imagining them all flicking off.

'What about you?' he says, looking back over his shoulder. 'You lost your father to BMAC, didn't you?'

I swallow as goosebumps race up my neck. 'How do you know that?'

He taps his head. 'Because she knew. She's had a special interest in you, Pat. Ever since the first day of school, when you let her take the empty seat beside you.'

It was so long ago, but the faintest memory of Gabby, younger than my sister, standing shyly outside the circle of kids. 'No one's sitting here,' I told her.

She surprised me in my apartment, when she knew

about Dad. Special interest. Did she read up on my dad because she liked me?

'She's watched you, even when you didn't care to look at her,' he says. 'And because of that, so have I.'

I can't help wondering what else her mind showed him about me.

'I know you know better than most the cruelty of the Norms,' he says. 'When Gabby and I go back, they won't be able to hurt us again. When we go back, I will end the war for good.'

'But you're here now,' I snap. 'How do you think you're going to get the two of you back there?'

He smiles to himself, then looks at me. 'That's where you come in.'

'What?'

'What do you know about your Shadow, Patrick?'

'Shut up,' I say. No one's ever talked about my Shadow. He doesn't know about my Shadow. I don't want him to know about my Shadow. My Shadow is *mine*.

'You have your sister's eyes, don't you?' he says. 'The same wavy brown hair. Well—' he motions to my shaved head – 'you used to. It's a beautiful thing, how alike two siblings can be.'

'I said *SHUT UP!*' Because I don't know what he's getting at. I don't understand him. But he's scaring me.

'Once I was connected to your sister and learned she had a brother,' he says, 'I knew his pungits would be similar to hers. I read any BMAC record I could find of you, and found out my suspicions were correct. Your Shadow resides around 2340, much like Oscar Joji – your sister's – did. *My* time, Pat. You Shadow is a man in the slums. No allegiance to anyone but himself, the coward. But still, he'll do the job.'

I lunge for my Shadow. I grab him and hold him to me as if Roth is about to steal him.

'Your pungits will be very useful to me, Patrick.' Roth points at the Punch in his palm. 'Just have to change the direction.'

My mind holds so tight to my Shadow I can feel him squirming from the force of it. But I need to know he's there. I need to know he's mine. *Don't let him steal you, don't let him.*

My Shadow envelopes my mind, trying to soothe me. *I won't.*

'You can't steal my pungits,' I say, trembling.

He smiles to himself. 'Well, you're certainly not as smart as she gives you credit for.'

I hear a bang.

Somewhere on the observation deck, a door has slammed shut.

THIRTY

'Roth!' shouts a deep voice. A voice I know.

My blood drains into my feet. *Don't be here, Gabby. Don't be here.*

Roth turns round, smiling now; everything he came for is on its way down the observation deck towards us.

Don't be here, don't be here.

Leonard rounds the corner, a giant gun held at the ready. His face is withered and hollow, like he hasn't slept. He knows exactly what he lost to BMAC. *Rani.* All that's left is rage, and it's laser-focused on Roth.

Following behind Leonard is Gabby. She came. How could she be so stupid? Why would she come here?

My stomach drops into my feet. Because holding Gabby's hand is my little sister, Beauty riding on her shoulder.

Maggie. How could they bring Maggie?

'What are you doing here?!' I blurt out, horrified and ecstatic to see them both.

Gabby takes a step towards me, and at once I know

Roth was right. This was her idea. She came here for me. Leonard puts out his arm to stop her.

'Leonard,' says Roth. 'What a pleasant reunion.'

'You just shut your mouth, you hear me?' says Leonard, his voice low and dangerous. 'You back up against that wall. We're taking the boy and we're leaving. You're not gonna destroy the lives of these kids like you destroyed mine.'

'He's yours,' Roth says with a shrug. 'Just leave me the girl.'

It's a trick. I know it is. He needs my pungits. He won't let either of us get away from this so easily. 'No!' I shout. 'He's lying!'

'Pat,' says Leonard, 'get over here, beside me, now.'

Roth holds out his palm towards me, the Punch buzzing.

'Pat!' screams Maggie, and Gabby hides my little sister behind her as Beauty lets out a screech.

'Don't move, Pat,' says Roth. He holds out his other hand to Gabby. 'Come to me, and he lives.'

'Don't be stupid, girly,' says Leonard, his grip on the gun tightening.

Gabby looks to me and I shake my head. There's sadness all over her face and I shake my head again, but her expression doesn't change. She takes a step towards Roth.

'Gabby, don't!' I shout.

She takes another step.

'Vargas,' snaps Leonard, 'you do this and he'll get exactly what he wants, then kill the rest of us anyway.'

There's a rattle from Roth's throat and I shiver when I realise it's his laugh. 'I should have started with you instead of the woman, Leonard,' he says. 'If I'd known you'd turn out to be this big of a headache to me, I would have killed you first.'

'Save it, Commander,' says Leonard. 'The only reason you didn't kill me is because an angel saved my life before you could.'

Gabby stands frozen between Leonard and Roth. Not for me. She can't do this cos of me.

'Ah, yes, your Mover,' says Roth, and I can see the veins in Leonard's temple as he scowls . 'She's Shelf-Meat now, isn't she?'

Leonard's scowl falters for just a moment. His eyes go big and round, soaked with tears for the woman who saved his life. And as quickly as the scowl broke, it's back, sharper and harder than before and . . . *BAM!*

He pulls the trigger, knocking Roth back to the floor. It's so fast, he's down so quick.

And then there's a groan.

Roth's alive.

He reaches up from his spot on the floor, the Punch aimed forward.

'Run!' I shriek, and lunge for Gabby's hand as Roth fires the punch at Leonard, who dives to the side as windows shatter behind him.

My hand clamped on Gabby's, I make a break for my little sister. 'Maggie!' – and she runs into my arms as another gunshot explodes.

The three of us run, hand in hand, Beauty screeching overhead. Everything in my body feels like it's going to explode from too much fear, too much adrenaline, too much blood, but each blast from Roth's and Leonard's weapons makes me beg myself to hold together, to hide Maggie, to hide Gabby, to keep them safe.

I notice two grand steel doors on the right and I shove one open. 'In here!' I tell them.

Beauty's the first in, circling the room like she can't decide if it's safe enough to land.

There are tables with pink linens and carnations and wine glasses on them. We're in the restaurant.

'Pat,' Gabby whispers, squeezing my hand, 'I don't hear anything.'

She's right. The blasts of the shoot-out have stopped. There's only quiet.

'Hide,' I say.

Maggie doesn't need to be told twice, and she makes a sprint for the table furthest from the door, Beauty swooping after her. Gabby and I follow, all three of us huddling together beneath the tablecloth.

'What the hell are you doing here?!' I hiss at Gabby. 'Why would you come? Why would you bring Maggie?!'

'I wanted to save you!' says Maggie, but both of us ignore her.

'What did you want me to do?' says Gabby. 'Roth told her he'd hurt you! Roth told her how to find you. Were we supposed to just ignore it? Leave you on your own?'

'It's better than Roth getting hold of her.'

'He doesn't want her,' says Gabby, the venom in her voice shutting me up. Roth doesn't want Maggie. He wants Gabby. She knew that when she came here.

For me.

'You shouldn't have come,' is all I manage to say, but Gabby's not listening to me at all. She's holding her breath, listening to the world beyond the tablecloth, her hand still tightly clasped to mine.

There's a squeal as the big steel door pulls open.

'Leonard?' whispers Maggie, shaking as Beauty nuzzles her arm.

I hear the sound of heavy-booted feet, and every second Leonard doesn't call out to us, I know with more certainty that Roth won the shoot-out.

Maggie starts to cry and grabs Gabby's other hand. 'He'll find us!' she squeaks.

From my toes to my hair, I'm frozen, like death is reaching out its fingers and taunting me as Roth moves quietly through the room. And my Shadow can feel every bit of it. He feels it himself. Like he's right here with me.

'Gabby!' shouts Roth. 'Come out now, and your friends go free.'

And my Shadow's there, at the front of my mind, seeing the colour of the linens all around me, feeling the sweat of Gabby and Maggie's hands in mine. I can see it all through eyes that aren't mine, evaluate it all with a wisdom that took decades of fight-or-flight to build up. My Shadow's wisdom.

Gabby's grip on my hand loosens and she moves to lift the tablecloth. I pull her back saying, 'He's lying.' Only I don't know if it was me who said it.

I must have, cos she answers me. 'There's nothing else we can do.'

There has to be. My mind races, searching for something, anything, that will keep her from Roth.

There's a loud crash as Roth flips over one of the tables. 'Gabby!' he roars.

And words, like flames, shoot into the front of my mind in such thick black angry smoke that it's hard to know what they are until they fall out of my mouth. 'Rip him apart,' I hiss.

Gabby and Maggie look at me, surprised, and my heart pounds as I realise the words don't belong to me. The idea isn't mine. It's my Shadow's.

'Rip him apart!' I say again, understanding what my Shadow means.

The girls wince beside me as another table crashes.

'Gabby,' I say quickly, 'you're connected to him again, right? And Maggie too?'

They both nod slightly.

'Move him,' I say, shifting onto my knees and holding their hands tighter. 'At the same time, you have to Move him.'

'What?' says Gabby. 'Pat, he's here.'

'But you're still connected! If you're connected, you can Move him.'

'To where?!'

'To you! And Maggie will too. If you each grab onto him—' I let go of their hands and lock my fingers together in front of me to show them what I mean, 'and Move him to where *you* are.' I tear my hands apart and Maggie gasps.

'I—' Gabby stammers. 'I don't know. I'm only Phase 2.'

'You have Maggie,' I say. 'She's strong, she'll help you. Just concentrate.'

'I don't know if it works like that.'

I don't either. But the certainty is there, inside my head.

It's coming from my Shadow. My Shadow knows this will work.

'Just try!' I beg her. 'Feel it, feel that nagging part of you that can do it, the part that wants to Move.'

Gabby swallows because she knows exactly what I'm talking about – that twitching, instinctual feeling in the deepest part of every Mover's gut, that itch we all have from birth, the one we're taught over and over to ignore. The itch we're told to pretend isn't there.

Her mouth sets in a determined line. She nods. No more pretending now.

There's a blast from the Punch and I hear glass shatter. He's taken out some windows now.

Maggie's sniffling behind Gabby. 'No, Pat,' she says. 'I don't know how to do that.'

'Yes, you do, Mags,' I say, grabbing her face in my hands. 'Look at me. Yes, you do.'

'No, I was scared last time! It was an accident!'

'Are you scared now?'

She nods.

'Then you're good to go,' I tell her, my heart bursting at the idea that this might work.

Maggie takes a deep breath, her cheeks puffed out as she tries to calm down. Finally she lets it go and wipes her eyes. When she's done, she looks at me and forces herself to smile.

I look at Beauty, hiding in my sister's arms. 'She's got a part in this too.'

She pulls the bird close and for a second I don't think she'll let her go, but when her eyes meet mine she nods and hands me Beauty who, by some miracle, keeps her beak shut. It's like she already knows what she needs to do.

I tuck her under my arm and lift the corner of the tablecloth.

'Where are you going?' whispers Gabby.

'When I say . . .' I tell her.

'Pat!' she squeaks, and I spin back on my knees to face her. 'Thank you,' she says.

'Don't thank me yet.'

'No, not for this,' she says.

'For what?'

She shrugs, her chin quivering. 'For being my friend.'

She keeps her eyes on the floor and I want to tell her to take it back, tell her not to thank me for being what she should have had all along. I want to tell her I'm sorry, for not being there for her until now, for everyone who was ever mean to her, for leaving her alone in her mind with Roth. But I don't. There isn't time.

'OK, when I say,' I tell her. 'It's gonna work.'

Gabby nods.

I keep low, crawling on my elbows with Beauty cradled to my chest, moving as close to Roth as I dare. I stop and I can see him, only a few steps away, throwing chairs and turning over tables. He's getting closer to where the girls are hiding and I know we're running out of time.

I whisper to Beauty, 'For Maggie,' and the bird makes a little cluck. 'Don't get shot.'

I give her tail a little tug and the bird explodes from my hands with a shriek that makes Roth turn away from the girls' table. He fires the Punch wildly and Beauty keeps flying, screeching and ducking each blast.

In the chaos I take my chance and hurry under the next table. I pause, trying to spot Roth's feet from under the cloth, but I've lost sight of him. I'll have to risk it again. Beauty's stopped screeching. I peek my head out but there's no sign of the bird, or Roth, and the carpet here is covered in shattered glass. I snake my way along and duck under the tablecloth of the next one.

I can't hear anything.

Just wind.

And then there's a roar and everything goes bright as the table is thrust onto its side and I'm face to face with a furious, psycho-smile Roth. He holds out his hand, the Punch in my face.

'Now, Gabby! Now!' I scream, just before I see the ripple in the air, and the light in the centre of the Punch explodes.

And its fire, shooting through my veins. My limbs lock up and my muscles clench and it feels as if the meat on my bones is being cooked from the inside. I try to scream but I'm paralysed, my brain swelling like a balloon ready to burst. And there's a spot, right in the deepest meat of my brain, where a hole is burning through. And I know it's the pungits. I can feel them grinding to a halt and piling up against this one spot in my brain before they swell out, reversing direction. It's sharp and it's hot and I want to scream so loud and I can't.

And then it's over. I drop to the ground and I can feel my limbs again. My lungs gasp in air and my eyes blink back stars. My head feels like mush, as if whatever the lightning did cooked my brains.

And my Shadow's in my head – just as confused, just as cooked. But he's there. He's with me.

Roth takes hold of my shirt, hauling me to my feet. He's breathing heavily, and a single laugh escapes him as he gets a firm grip on my neck.

'Time to play your part, Patrick,' he says, and from his hip he pulls out what looks like a crown – just like the one Leonard said Roth used on his friend, Misha – and puts it on my head. 'Time to give up your pungits.'

The wind in the room whips my hair into my eyes. It's cold and strong – it's the Eventualies, the Movers' wind – and all I want to do is breathe it in, but Roth's grip on my neck won't let me. His veiny eyes, wild and crazy, bore into mine as he holds the glowing Punch to the crown. I feel the crown heating up, and feel that hole in my mind opening up again. And my Shadow's screaming somewhere on the other side, screaming at me to stop it, to hang on. But I can't hang on. All I can feel is the burning, the horrible hideous burning.

Roth smiles a big toothy grin, crooked and hideous as he watches the crown glow a brilliant electric blue.

This is my chance.

I swing up my knee as hard as I can, connecting with his crotch, and he releases me with a grunt.

I drop to the floor, gasping in the frigid air before I scramble away. Out of the corner of my eye I catch a flicker of black outside the window – Beauty riding on the churning wind. When I whirl round, I see them, Gabby and Maggie, holding hands and staring down Roth who's watching them dumbfounded, the hair whipping around their faces like the wind belongs to them.

It does.

This is their Move.

Roth starts to scream, gripping onto his head as the girls pull his pungits in two different directions, his voice like an animal's as he pushes on both sides of his skull, desperate to make it stop. But they don't stop. Both of them are concentrating so hard, their faces blank and their eyes unfocused as if they can't even hear what agony they're causing him.

Roth falls to his knees, and the tower shudders so violently that I let out a scream. I can see the lightning outside, shooting in blinding streaks towards the ground. And then Roth is glowing, his head haloed with white, crackling sparks. The sparks lash out in bolts of their own, and Roth rears back. I watch, knowing this is it, knowing the Move is happening. But then he's reaching, reaching his arm out towards Gabby and Maggie, and I remember he's got the Punch.

I scramble to my feet and launch myself on top of him, wrestling his arm to point in any other direction. He bucks beneath me, but I hang on as the lightning coming from inside him burns my eyes and my chest, and my Shadow's in my head, panic clouding whatever he's trying to say.

'Pat!' shrieks Gabby, and I look up to see her face, her hair loose and flowing as tears streak down her cheeks.

There's a roar from Roth and then a snap.

And everything goes quiet.

THIRTY-ONE

A snap.

Or a wink.

On, then off.

And it's quiet.

Quiet and dark.

I'm on my back, greedily breathing in the air but it tastes different now. It's heavy and damp, and there's a smell like mould.

Roth is gone.

I don't hear Gabby, or Maggie.

I'm dead.

I try to lift myself onto my elbows but a pain so intense shoots up from my gut and rips through my head that I collapse again with a groan. I pant from the effort, and I grab my head, relieved to feel my fuzzy hair, the sweat on my forehead. I'm alive. I'm pretty sure I'm alive.

There's a shuffling noise to my left.

As my eyes adjust to the dark I see there's a figure,

hunched over, scuttling amongst some containers, and I want to call out for Gabby. I want her to answer me. But my throat hurts so much when I try that all that escapes me is a rasp.

The hunched figure freezes and turns towards me.

I tell my body to move, to run, but there's so much pain that I groan again and stay where I am as the figure hurries to my side. It drops to its knees and shines a light into my eyes, dazzling me a moment before it places the light by its side.

And then a face comes into view, staring nervously at me. A wrinkled face, worry lines etched into its forehead, scowling down. A man. A man with patchy black stubble and black hair that's receding ever so slightly. Eyes the colour of smoke.

I know him.

He grumbles something to me that I can't understand. He doesn't speak my language.

But I know him.

He holds some water to my lips and lifts my head to help me drink.

The water runs down my aching throat and soothes my frightened heart.

He speaks again, and while I don't know the words, I can tell he's asking if I'm OK.

And then he hands me a red ball and wooden paddle. The one I saw inside my head when Roth was taking me from the Movers' Prison. My Shadow showed it to me, to calm me down.

My brain doesn't understand what I'm seeing.

His face is the face of my Shadow.

SENTENCING OF MINORS WITH MOVEMENT ABILITIES TO CHANGE IN WAKE OF VARGAS TRIAL

16 APRIL 2083

The trial of 14-year-old Gabriela Vargas came to an end last Thursday after a speedy investigation following the Movement incident at the Avin Turbine. Vargas pleaded guilty to Moving the Shadow responsible for the attack on BMAC last month and, most shockingly, the murder of classmate and fellow Mover Patrick Mermick.

While the severity of Vargas's crimes cannot be overstated, the country was nevertheless stunned when she was sentenced to BMAC's high-security Movers' Prison rather than a juvenile facility.

The decision, according to jury member Michael Winston, was made as a result of the extreme nature of Vargas's crimes. As witness for the prosecution and best friend to the deceased Ollie Larkin put it to the press, 'Movers are different from us. Pat taught me that.'

But should their differences as Movers make their age irrelevant? Not according to the victim's mother, Isabelle Randle-Mermick, who despite having lost her son has publically expressed her disapproval of the controversial sentence. The blame, she suggests, should fall to BMAC, who kept her separate from her son just before he was kidnapped from their facilities by Vargas's Shadow.

Responding to Mrs Randle-Mermick's comments, Criminal Investigations Special Agent Beadie Hartman told *The Hourly Times*: 'The only person to blame in this situation is Gabriela Vargas. Her actions put a great many people in danger and resulted in the deaths of Mr Mermick and several BMAC officers. But while Miss Vargas has taken from our community, Mr Mermick was able to give, providing BMAC with crucial insight into the Mover affliction. I believe his contribution to society will be remembered in times to come.' When asked what information Patrick Mermick was providing, BMAC responded only that it would be the force behind significant changes in phase status testing.

In the meantime, history has certainly been made by Gabriela Vargas, the youngest Mover to ever serve time in BMAC's Movers' Prison. Right or wrong, the message is clear – Movers in Avin City, beware.

A MESSAGE FROM TOMORROW

My name is Pat Mermick. I was Moved to the year 2383 by my Shadow, after Commander Bram Roth reversed my pungits. And it's nothing like Leonard said it would be. There's no war. Just fear. Movers and Shadows living in secret, in hiding, from a BMAC that's trying to 'cure' them all. To wipe Movement from existence.

Because Roth never came back. After what Maggie and Gabby did to him, there was no coming back for Roth.

The Shade Unit has been defeated.

Movers and Shadows are on their own.

I don't belong here.

I have to go back.

Go back to save my family.

And to save my family, I have to save her.

The girl that started this whole mess. Everything, all of

it. My dad, my sister, Rani and Leonard. Pungits. All of it goes away if I can just save her.

I've been looking for her. I've scoured every archive and census and library, doing anything to get my hands on information that can tell me what happened to her after my Move. It's taken me months, but what I've discovered, I wish I hadn't.

When my Shadow Moved me, I just disappeared. Everyone thought I died.

And she blamed herself.

She thought she killed me, and she let them punish her for it.

Because she always let them punish her – BMAC, her parents, her Shadow.

But I can change that.

If I can go back to the start of all of it, I can save her.

And then I'll save us all.

ACKNOWLEDGEMENTS

There are three people who helped me wrestle this book to the ground when it nearly got away from me.

First – my amazing, brutal and brilliant editor, Charlie. You've made me better. I owe you.

Second – my best cheerleader and super-agent, Ali. Your readiness for pints and problem solving saved Pat and Gabby on more than one occasion.

And finally – my husband, Ian. You lived with this book as long as I did, and always, always listened. Thank you.

Phew. Time travel. What a beast.